Chapter One

Jenna strained her ears for the echo of footsteps in her wake. The drizzling rain muted sounds and turned the blue-white light from the halogen streetlights to a sickly gray.

She felt eyes boring into her back. Fear, like skeletal fingers, touched the nape of her neck and sent tremors down her spine. She rubbed at the goose bumps on her arms and hurried her steps.

Jenna had thought she'd be free of fear once she was released from prison, but it had followed her home like a stray dog, begging for morsels of her sanity. It wasn't fair. She'd paid the price. Now, she just wanted to be left alone.

She felt anger slowly replace the fear. She felt cheated. This wasn't the way it was supposed to be. She didn't want her freedom tainted.

She stopped and slowly turned to face her pursuer. The street was empty except for a yellow cab that drove too close to the curb and sprayed her with dirty brown water.

She peered through the darkness, looking for a telltale movement to betray her pursuer's hiding place.

A glint of light had her head snapping around to a doorway across the street, but nothing moved except a loose pane rattling in the door.

"Ollie, Ollie oxen free. Come out, come out wherever you are." She singsonged the words to the childhood game while her eyes continued their vigilant sweep of the deserted street.

"Show yourself, you coward!" she yelled with courage she didn't feel. "This is your last chance. After this, I'll be looking for *you*!"

The street remained silent.

An old woman stared at Jenna through the window of an all-night laundromat. Her expression said she thought the younger woman was an escapee from a mental institution.

Jenna pulled her coat collar close to her ears and turned away. She screamed when her face hit a hard chest and strong hands grabbed her arms.

She stared up into a stranger's face.

"You should watch where you're going, lady," grumbled the tall man as he set her away from him.

"S…sorry," she stuttered, but he had already strode away.

The fear had returned.

She turned and ran toward the debatable safety of her small, dismal apartment.

Secret Obsession

By Ruth Kohut

PublishAmerica
Baltimore

© 2005 by Ruth Kohut.
All rights reserved. No part of this book may be reproduced, stored in a retrieval system or transmitted in any form or by any means without the prior written permission of the publishers, except by a reviewer who may quote brief passages in a review to be printed in a newspaper, magazine or journal.

First printing

At the specific preference of the author, PublishAmerica allowed this work to remain exactly as the author intended, verbatim, without editorial input.

All characters appearing in this work are fictitious. Any resemblance to real persons, living or dead, is purely coincidental.

ISBN: 1-4137-2114-1
PUBLISHED BY PUBLISHAMERICA, LLLP
www.publishamerica.com
Baltimore

Printed in the United States of America

This book is dedicated to the memory of my father,
Robert James Stacey,
and my brother, Allan James Stacey.
Forever in my heart.

My most sincere love and thanks to my family and friends
who have been so supportive of my writing efforts,
and especially to my husband, Carey,
for always being there for me.

Chapter Two

Jenna watched Butch's spit sizzle on the grill, then saw him place three pieces of bacon and two eggs on the tested spot. Revolted, she turned back to the sink full of dishes. She'd be thrilled to get away from this diner. 'The Greasy Spoon' was more aptly named than its patrons realized. She'd only been here for two weeks, but if she had to watch Butch cook for much longer, she'd be turned off food forever.

Jenna sighed and plunged her hands into the hot, soapy water, gasping at the swift burning sensation that quickly subsided as her hands became acclimated.

Butch grunted. "I tole ya to wear rubber gloves."

Jenna shook her head. "Do you know how long it's been?" she asked.

"Yeah, yeah." He flipped two perfect sunny side up eggs onto a chipped plate alongside bacon and hash browns. "Number six, up!" he bellowed, and plunked the plate on the stainless steel ledge of the pass-through dividing the kitchen from the diner. "Eight years. Eight years without a sink full of soapy water; eight years without smellin' cut grass; eight years without seein' the stars. Gimme a break. Who'd wanna smell grass anyway? Makes me sneeze." He wiped his nose on the back of his hand, then scraped a spatula over the grill and broke more eggs on its surface.

"Hey, Princess, somebody to see you."

Jenna cringed as Rosie's strident voice pierced her eardrum like a toothpick. The first time the woman had called her Princess, Jenna's hackles had gone up. In prison, any character slur had to be dealt with immediately, or risk the label of an easy mark. When confronted, Rosie explained the odd nickname. "No offense, but you don't belong here. You look like you should be in some snooty neighborhood with three cars and a gardener." Jenna understood that Rosie tossed out the salutation not as an insult, but as an endearment, one that now brought a smile and a warmth of belonging to Jenna's otherwise cold, barren life.

"Hey," yelled Butch. "Don't be long. I'm not paying you to talk all day. You got work to do."

Jenna nodded, squared her shoulders and took a deep breath.

"Who is it?" she asked, but the older woman sped off with plates full of Butch's special of the day balancing on her forearms. Who knew she was here?

Jenna wiped her hands on her apron, then untied it and slipped it over her head.

She stepped through the door and almost knocked over the reed thin woman waiting on the other side.

"Irene? Thank God you found me! Is Chase all right? I've been trying to reach you for weeks, ever since I got out." Jenna's breath came in fast gulps. A mixture of fear and joy squeezed her heart, its long fingers tearing into her. She clasped her sister-in-law by the arm.

"Shut up, for God's sake," whispered Irene, her voice coated in gravel from a surfeit of cigarettes. "I knew where you were all along." She jerked her arm out of Jenna's grasp. "Of course Chase is okay. I know how to protect my nephew." Her tone made it clear that Jenna couldn't say the same.

"Did you bring him with you?" Jenna looked over Irene's shoulder toward the diner window, trying to get a glimpse of her son.

"Of course not. As far as I'm concerned he'd be better off thinking you were dead."

Jenna gasped. "Irene, he has to get to know me before he moves back home."

"Chase is home," Irene hissed. "He's not going anywhere."

"What are you talking about? I'm his mother. You know you can't keep him."

Irene's smile curled Jenna's stomach. "That's where you're wrong.

You won't ever get him back, because you'll never be out of this hellhole. You'll never be able to prove to Social Services that you can support him. Look around you, Jenna." Irene spread her arms wide to encompass the grungy room and its less than reputable occupants. "This is your life."

Jenna refused to take her eyes off Irene. This was not her life. With any luck she would be out of here as soon as possible. Not that she was on good terms with Lady Luck, but things had to change eventually. Didn't they? Jenna thought of the many resumes she had delivered to local businesses over the past two weeks and the absence of any responses. She ground her teeth.

"Where have you taken him? Everett says you haven't been home for two weeks."

"Oh, yes, Everett, your trained dog. I allowed him to play go-between for you and Chase while you were in jail, but that's as close as you'll get for a long time."

"No," Jenna moaned. "You have to let me see him."

Irene pushed her face close to Jenna's and said in a low voice, "Now you know what it's like to lose someone you love. Now you may have some inkling of how I felt when you murdered my brother. The only reason I'm here is to tell you to stop calling my office. You'll be sorry if you make me lose my job." She turned toward the door. "Hope your life is hell, Jenna. You deserve it." She walked out before Jenna could recover from the attack.

"I'll call the police," she whispered, knowing she wouldn't. "I'll get my son back."

Jenna jumped when she heard Butch behind her.

"Jesus Christ, I'm not paying you to stand around talking to customers. Get back to work," he growled, and smacked her buttocks with one beefy hand.

She rounded on him, all her pent up frustration curling into a hard ball of resentment. "Don't touch me! Keep your filthy hands to yourself or I'll call the police."

Butch raised his hands. "Whoa, whoa. Chill out, baby. Sheesh, you on the rag, or what?"

Jenna squeezed her eyes shut in disgust. She couldn't afford to lose this job, or she'd never get Chase back. She turned and walked into the kitchen, repeating her mantra from prison. "I will get out of here. I will get out of here."

After a hellish day in the kitchen with Butch, Jenna slid through the back door into the alleyway that ran behind the diner and screamed as a hand fell on her shoulder. She whirled around to face the shadowy figure that stood behind her.

"Oh, it's you," she breathed, hand to her chest. "You scared me."

"Sorry, Jenna," said Everett, pushing his John Lennon spectacles up with an index finger. He flicked a mud brown ponytail off his shoulder.

Jenna chuckled at the thought of being frightened by her one and only friend. The beat of her heart slowly returned to normal.

"I'll take you home."

"You don't have to do that, Everett. I'm only a few blocks away from my apartment."

"I don't like you out by yourself." He slipped his arm through hers and led her to the late-model LTD he affectionately called 'Big Bertha.'

"You worry too much," said Jenna, patting his arm. In truth she looked forward to the short walk home each evening, reveling in the joy of freedom and the feel of a gentle breeze brushing her face.

With a shrug, she smiled and allowed herself to be pulled toward the car. Everett had done so much for her over the past eight years she couldn't bear to disappoint him now.

She shook her head as she slipped into the passenger side and craned her neck to see the road. It was Everett's habit to store the detritus of his life between the dashboard and windshield. Papers, maps, parking tickets and movie stubs piled up until his vision was impaired enough that a police officer would finally pull him over and demand its removal. The pile would go under the seat and a new treasure trove would begin.

"What's this?" she asked, as he handed her a brown wrapped package.

"A gift." At her raised eyebrow, he added, "For getting out. It's nothing big. I wanted to commemorate your release in some way and since you won't let me take you out to dinner…"

"...And I still think that's best. I need to focus on rebuilding my life with Chase. I'm grateful for your friendship, but it can't be anything more than that."

"You say that now, but..."

"I don't want to lose you as a friend, Everett. Let's just leave it at that. Okay?"

Everett shrugged. "Sure, Jenna. Whatever you want." He tapped the package in her hands. "But you have to accept your gift. In friendship."

Jenna smiled like a small girl at Christmastime. "I love presents," she admitted and ripped into it.

She sighed wistfully when she saw what was hidden under the last piece of wrapping. She opened the slim book of nineteenth century poetry and ran a thumb over the thin pages. "Wordsworth, Coleridge, both Brownings, oh, I love poetry." She hugged the book to her chest. "How did you know?"

"You always seemed interested when Angus helped me prepare lessons for our poetry classes." He reached for the book, flipped a few pages, and passed it back to her. "'The Lady of Shalott' is a favorite, I believe."

Jenna nodded. "Did you ever hear Angus read this?" she asked, her mind going back to a university classroom, Angus dominating the front of the room, reading the poem with such emotion it brought tears to the eyes of every female student. "'God in his mercy lend her grace, the Lady of Shalott.' I love that line." She gazed at the words on the page, thinking of another time and place when her life was simple.

"Hello, is anybody in there?" Everett's voice intruded on her thoughts.

Jenna shook her head slightly and a corner of her mouth turned up apologetically. "See what poetry does to me? I can drown myself in it for hours. Thanks so much, Everett. I love it. Really."

He put the car in gear and drove the few short blocks to her temporary domicile. She refused to call it a home, because she didn't intend to stay there long. She told him about Irene's visit and her despicable conditions for seeing Chase.

Everett patted her hand. "Don't worry, I'll talk to her. We'll get Chase back with you in no time."

"Oh, Everett, you've been so wonderful through this whole nightmare. How will I ever repay you?"

Everett smiled, his small teeth showing between his lips. "By having me to dinner when you and Chase get that house in the 'burbs."

Jenna laughed. "It's a deal." It also seemed a long way off.

Everett dropped her at her front door after eliciting a promise that she'd call him if she needed anything.

Jenna sat on the front stoop of her apartment building for an hour after Everett left, sipping tea, unwilling to return to her dingy one-room apartment. It would do for now, but she couldn't—wouldn't—bring Chase here. Earlier she had watched a centipede as long as her foot scurry across the floor. She almost threw her new poetry volume at it, but stopped herself when she realized she had only one book to her name and plenty of centipedes. She shuddered and let the insect live.

Jenna inhaled, taking in the smells of the city. She loved to watch the Detroit traffic as it sped or sauntered past her porch view. Women who must have been sweltering in full-length mink coats on their way to the Fox Theater; bag ladies picking through trash cans searching for that one perfect morsel to add to their strange collections; teenage boys, nails polished in black, earrings gleaming, dodging traffic on their skateboards; huge pink Cadillacs ambling after women in short leather skirts and knee-high boots.

She treasured them all. The pure jumble of citizens fed her imagination, replacing the hard gray walls and the hard gray people of prison.

Reluctantly, she stood and returned to her deprivation tank apartment. She climbed into bed, checking first for insect stowaways, and nodded off thinking about the bright future she was determined to have with her son.

At two in the morning, Jenna woke to shouting and thumping from the apartment above her. It didn't last long, but memories of her marriage to Angus swarmed in like flies on road-kill. She closed her eyes and tried to sleep, but jerked awake several times just as his fist was about to make contact. She groaned and rolled over, finally falling asleep just before her alarm screamed its wake-up call.

She jolted to a sitting position and panicked when she found the sheets wrapped around her, binding her arms to her sides. Frantically, she tugged them free and sat still, breathing hard, a nightmare fresh in her mind.

Jenna rubbed her hand over her eyes. She had never dreamed of the night Angus was murdered before. Was it a dream? Or a memory? She didn't know. Couldn't tell. Either way it was terrifying.

In the dream-memory, Angus had called home in a terrible mood, livid over an imagined slight from the Dean. Worried, she had put Chase to bed early, hoping he wouldn't have to witness another scene that would upset him. She heard Angus drop his keys at the door and his bellow of rage turned into the shriek of her alarm.

Jenna wrapped her arms around her waist and rocked back and forth on the narrow bed. She didn't know if it was better to remember that night, or to leave it buried deep within her.

Chapter Three

The door opened and closed. Feral eyes trained on the far wall and a chuckle ricocheted off the walnut paneling. Like a hunter's trophy, Jenna's head was mounted on the far wall surrounded by a red cherry frame. Her celluloid likeness stared back, a Mona Lisa smile touching her lips. The other photos, all candid, surrounded the framed focal point of the room. A single pot light in the ceiling cast a soft glow over the gallery. The weapon of choice, a 35mm Pentax equipped with a telephoto lens, lay on the corner table. Its ammunition, rolls of unprocessed film, stood like soldiers awaiting their call to duty.

Several of the recent photos were taken through the diner window, Jenna clearing someone else's dirty dishes, Jenna sweeping the floor, and laughing with the gray-haired hag waitress.

Karma's head tilted and the eyes focused on the outdoor pictures. An uninformed viewer would think them odd. Jenna's face was always turned to the sky. She was so enthralled with the dips and dives of swallows she never noticed anyone was watching her. The observer observed. You'd think she would have learned something from those eight years in prison, but no, she was the same naive Jenna who married a man and believed she'd live happily ever after. Hah! Only three people knew she was innocent of her husband's murder, and one of them was dead. She'd pretended she was shocked by the whole incident and what followed, but relief must have mingled with her emotions. After all, she wouldn't have to explain away the black eyes or the sprained wrists anymore.

The whisper of stockinged feet led to the large recessed window sill on which sat a miscellany of items that once belonged to Jenna. Blue satin hair ribbons, a sea-colored silk scarf, and two small ceramic figurines vied for space with cheap jewelry and old postcards from her classmates. Nothing of value was ever taken; nothing that would be missed right away.

A light touch to each item brought a satisfying vision of the day Jenna's corporeal form would be added to the collection. An expectant smile curved Karma's lips. Methodically, with pleasure in each movement, the objects were rearranged.

Slowly, quietly, the footsteps were retraced to the door. A padlock snicked into place, Jenna's cache safe for another day.

Chapter Four

"Hey, Princess, you're getting popular. Somebody else here to see you."

Rosie's voice snapped Jenna out of her reverie. She had been thinking about Chase and how their first visit since the guilty verdict would be incredibly bittersweet. The intervening years had been stolen from them, and now Irene had stolen one more week. They'd have to make up for lost time. Soon, they'd be able to go to the park and throw a football around, or go rollerblading together, or anything else he wanted to do. Jenna ran a hand over her misty eyes. First, she'd have to find him.

Rosie stuck her head around the swinging door. "He's kinda cute, nice pecs, so you might want to hurry."

Jenna smiled at the incongruity of this grandmotherly figure lauding the merits of a young man, but her next thought erased any trace of humor. Who would be asking to see her? Irene wouldn't be back any time soon. Jenna had only been out of prison for two weeks and had kept pretty much to herself, other than her twelve-hour days at the diner and her weekly visits to her parole officer. She groaned. Surely he wouldn't show up here. No, he could never be called cute, and Jenna was sure no one had seen a pec on his Yoda-like physique for decades.

Only one way to find out who her mystery visitor was. She pushed on the grimy door and stepped into the diner, surveying the tables for a familiar face. She caught Rosie's eye and shrugged. The other woman pointed a gnarled finger to the corner table by the window and winked.

Jenna examined the back of the man's head for some clue to his identity. Finding none in the dark wavy hair and long lean back, she stepped toward him. As if aware of her presence, the man swiveled his head and caught her in the beams of his intense green gaze. Like a stage-struck actor, Jenna stopped, unsure if she should move forward or retrace her steps to the safety of the kitchen. A premonition of impending change washed over her.

Jenna shrugged. What was one more change when she was starting a new life? She'd had many changes to contend with over the past two weeks. Her release from prison, finding a job and a place to live, reacquainting herself to life on the 'outside,' and trying to locate a son she hadn't seen in eight years. She welcomed almost every one of these changes with a joy so intense she thought her heart would burst. Most people undervalued their freedom.

She stepped toward his table, ignoring the quizzical stares from the three grizzled counter patrons who were permanent fixtures in the diner.

"I'm Jenna McDougall," she said to the young man at the table. "You asked to see me?" She searched her memory for some clue to his identity. She thought she had seen him somewhere before. But where?

He waved a long-fingered hand at the chair opposite him and she sat down, placing her hands quietly in her lap.

He didn't say anything at first, then, "You don't remember me, do you?"

His voice triggered her memory. A voice created for storytelling, each word produced a vibration in her soul, like the deep thrum of a double bass.

Jenna smiled, pleased to prove him wrong. "Yes, I do, actually. You work at the Detroit Computer Training Academy. I gave you my resume last week and you said I wouldn't want to work there because the owners are 'little Hitlers.'"

He chuckled, the sound rumbling in his chest. "That's right, but that's not what I'm referring to."

Jenna's eyebrows drew together. "Do I know you from somewhere else?"

"Do you remember Catherine Sawyer from Tecumseh High?"

"Yes, of course. She was in my senior year homeroom. I tutored her in Math."

"That's right. She had a younger brother."

Jenna grinned. "A long string bean of a boy, if I remember correctly."

"That's me, Finn Sawyer."

Jenna's eyes widened and she let them travel over the wide shoulders, down to the well-developed 'pecs,' as Rosie called them, and follow the tapering line to a small waist. "You've filled out nicely," she said with a smile.

The corners of his full lips curved up. "You haven't turned out so badly yourself."

Jenna glanced down at the stained bib-apron she had neglected to remove and put her hand to the riotous auburn curls she had tried to tame into a ponytail. No make-up enhanced her face. With a mental shrug, she decided it didn't matter. She was free and she would soon see her son, or die trying. Everything else would come in time.

"I have to get back to work," she said. "Is there something you wanted?"

"Yes. I wanted to offer you a job."

"I thought you said the owners were dictators?" Not that that would bother her. She'd worked—hell, she'd lived—with worse.

"They are, but it's not for them." Finn leaned forward, his excitement evident in the sparkle in his eyes. "I'm starting my own computer training company and I want you on my team."

Jenna sat back, speechless.

"I want to provide quality training for companies in the Detroit area. There's an excellent market. We can offer group training or one-on-one, but it should all be hands-on. Eventually, we'll need a computer lab, but at first we can rent one or reduce our fees for companies who have their own labs."

Jenna sat motionless. Finn was describing her dream. In prison, she had planned out a strategy for her future, taken correspondence courses, and practiced teaching basic computer skills to the other inmates. She knew it would take years to realize her plan, but the wait would be worth it. She'd be able to provide a good life for her son while working at a job she loved.

"What about manuals?"

Finn's eyes lit up at her apparent interest. "That would be your job at first, plus answering phones, booking training sessions, and helping me set up and establish the business. Eventually, you'd be a trainer, too."

Jenna's heart thumped to the rhythm of bongo drums as she listened to plans so similar to her own.

"You'll need at least one computer to start out with," she said. "Two would be better, plus a color printer for printing our own brochures and flyers, a photocopier for the manuals. We might be able to get some cheap office equipment if we go to some of the big companies like Edison, Lear, Visteon, or GM. With all of the downsizing, there should be extra desks around. I've seen some ads in the paper."

Jenna stopped, sucked air into her lungs, and tried to calm her rapidly beating heart. She realized she was pressing forward into the table and that Finn was trying, unsuccessfully, to suppress a huge grin.

"Gee, Jenna, it's too bad you're not more excited about this."

She sat back with an embarrassed smile. "Sorry, I get carried away sometimes."

"Don't be sorry. I'm thrilled that someone else shares my vision. You've obviously thought about this a lot."

"I've had eight years to make plans. In prison." Jenna waited for a reaction, but Finn sat silently. She cleared her throat, hating the thought of losing this chance, but wanting no confusion that could wreak havoc with her life later on. "Which makes me wonder why you'd want me on your team. You know where I've been. It's on my resume. *Work experience: Tutoring fellow-inmates at Wayne County Correctional Facility.* I didn't want there to be any surprises."

Finn's eyes remained on hers for several long seconds. He pulled his left ear lobe and leaned toward her. "Catherine described you as studious, intelligent and kind. That's who I want on my staff." He sat back and crossed his arms. "I've followed your case from the start. You had no defense. You were there when your husband was shot, but you had no memory of what happened. Your record doesn't bother me, Jenna," Finn said, his eyes never leaving her face, "because I believe you're innocent."

Jenna made a sound that was half laughter, half sob. Unexpected tears filled her eyes. Few people believed in her innocence.

"Besides," he continued, "I spent enough time watching you in high school to have a pretty good idea of your character. I had a huge crush," he added by way of explanation, any sign of self-consciousness at his admission curiously absent. "You couldn't hurt another human being if your life depended on it."

But what if it was my son's life? Would I hurt someone then? The events of that night were still a black hole in Jenna's mind. How could she protest her innocence when she didn't know? After scrutinizing every possibility for eight years, the only reason she could imagine killing another human being was to protect her son. Is that what happened? Her mind reeled at the possibility. She might never know.

"Hey, Princess." Jenna jumped as the sound of Rosie's voice intruded on her thoughts. "Butch said to get back to work. The dishes are piling up."

Jenna stood. "I have to go."

"You haven't given me an answer."

Jenna stared at him, her mind whirling.

"Think about it and I'll call you tomorrow."

"I don't have a phone. At least not one you should call. I share a phone with seven other tenants in my building and I don't always get my messages."

"Then I'll come back here."

Jenna nodded and hurried back to her sink full of soapy water.

After work she made her way through the crowded streets until she reached a decrepit yellow brick building huddled between two mirrored skyscrapers. Jenna climbed to the top floor and tapped on the open door of her parole officer's cluttered office. He dropped the phone into its cradle and waved a huge arm for her to enter.

She had never seen a human shaped like a pyramid before she met Yuri. Great slabs of fat like melted wax seemed to drip from his body and his face looked like someone had pressed a cookie cutter into dough.

Jenna stood in front of his desk feeling like a child called to the

Principal's office. Yuri Dmytrazcko, better known as Yoda, looked at her over the square eyeglasses perched on his nose. They pressed against his fat cheeks changing the ruddy skin beneath to an unnatural white. A trickle of sweat meandered down his left temple.

"Want one?" he asked, pointing to the open box of double-chocolate cream cookies on his desk. He looked relieved when she declined.

"Still got your job at the…diner, wasn't it?"

Jenna nodded.

"Missed any days?"

"No."

"In by 8:30 every night?"

"Yes."

"Good." He sat back and tried to cross his arms over his huge stomach, then gave up and rested his wrists on the desk. "So, what's up?"

"What do you mean?" She fidgeted as his ice-blue eyes speared her to the floor.

"You don't look so good. What's wrong?"

Jenna shrugged, which didn't seem to satisfy him. He waited silently. Finally, she heaved a sigh and looked at the floor.

"I haven't seen my son yet. My sister-in-law, his guardian while I was in prison, won't let me see him. She says no one will force her to give him back to me until I can prove that I can support him."

"She's right." As Jenna started to protest, he flapped his hand at her. "Okay, okay, sit down for a minute, will you?"

Jenna perched on the edge of the plastic chair across from his desk. She fidgeted with the fabric of her cotton slacks.

Yoda tugged at his collar and folded pudgy hands on the desk. "Legally, you should get him back, but no one is out there worrying about the rights of convicted murderers. Well, there are a few," he amended, "but they don't count."

"But that's not right!" Jenna burst out. "He's my son and I want him back with me."

"Fine. Then, what are you doing about it? Get off your ass and get a better job."

She was about to offer a sarcastic retort about *his* ass when she noticed the grin all but lost in the folds of fat.

"As a matter of fact, I've been offered a job in a new computer training company," she said proudly.

Yoda lifted his chin and looked at a file card through the bottom half of his bifocals. "It says here that's right up your alley."

"Yes, I can't believe my luck."

"Yeah," he said dryly. "The harder you work, the luckier you get. Didn't you put out about sixty resumes?"

"Yes, but it turned out to be a guy I knew in high school. At least, he knew me. I went to school with his sister."

Yoda lowered his eyebrows. "And this guy just happened to have a job opening?"

"No, that's the great part. He's starting his own training company and he wants me."

"Have you checked this guy out? Maybe he's someone who makes big promises, but doesn't follow through."

Jenna laughed. "In other words, don't quit your day job. Okay, I won't, but I know he's for real. I'll keep you posted."

"Damn right, you will. Okay, get out of here."

Jenna rose and headed for the door, suddenly feeling better about her future. "See you next week."

She walked through the streets of Detroit enjoying the constant activity and myriad colors of the city. Jenna let her mind wander to the rainbow-hued future she was planning for her and Chase. They'd live on a quiet street lined with majestic oaks, where neighbors gathered and shared recipes over coffee.

Lost in her dreams, she nearly missed the dismal entranceway to her apartment building. Graffiti marred the red brickwork and iron bars covered the lower windows. That and the disgusting creatures who cohabited with her helped make up her mind about Finn's job offer. Not that she needed any encouragement. She was desperate for Chase to move in with her so they could begin their new life together. That couldn't happen until she got a better paying job and a decent home. This job offer was her salvation.

It's too good to be true, a little voice whispered into her ear. Good things do not come to those who wait in prison for eight years.

She tossed her head. But what did she have to lose? A first-rate job as a dishwasher? A cell-sized apartment full of roaches, beetles, centipedes and nauseating dinner smells?

She was being offered a second chance. The first time around, she'd given up her education and future career to have a family with Angus. Then, throughout her short, abusive marriage she gave up little pieces of her self-esteem, personality, interests, career, self-confidence, self-worth and all of her friends, until she was left with nothing. Her life centered on her son and avoiding her husband's unpredictable fists. By the time she entered the prison she didn't know who she was or of what she was capable.

This was her new life and she was going to grab it with both hands. She'd reach Finn tomorrow and tell him she'd accept the job. Then, somehow she'd get a message to Irene and insist on seeing her son. After all, the law was on her side—this time. Excitement bubbled in her chest and she ignored the few passersby who looked suspiciously at her smile.

Chapter Five

Jenna arrived at the diner at six AM to help Butch prepare for the day. She pulled an apron over her best jeans and a new pink t-shirt she had purchased with the two hundred dollar going-away gift the state bestowed on its guests. A narrow pink hair ribbon completed her ensemble. She felt hopeful for the first time in years.

She busied herself with cleaning up after Butch, but every time the diner door opened she peeked through the opening over the grill to see if Finn had arrived. By eight o'clock she had chewed off all her lipstick. By ten her fingernails were gone, and by eleven o'clock she was ready to jump out of her skin every time Butch rapped the spatula on the grill.

Still no Finn.

Now that her mind was made up to accept Finn's job offer, Jenna was afraid something would happen to make the deal fall through. After all, what did she really know about him? Not much. She was so desperate to believe him, she hadn't asked for any references or proof of sanity.

Jenna groaned inwardly at her stupidity and scrubbed harder at the greasy pan.

"That's clean enough," said Butch. "Try this one." He dropped another frying pan into the sink of soapy water, causing a minor tidal wave. Jenna jumped back, but not quickly enough. Greasy water flecked with black spilled over the edge of the sink, thoroughly soaking her apron and seeping into her t-shirt and jeans.

She clenched her teeth and looked down at her ruined clothes. Her closet was far from full and she couldn't afford to replace anything without a lot of soul searching.

"I will get out of here," she muttered. "I will."

At twelve-fifteen, Jenna heard a deep rumbly voice and rushed to look out the swinging door to the diner. In her haste, the glass she was holding slammed against the side of the sink and shattered. She looked down as crimson drops of blood splashed onto the stainless steel counter. Tears of self-pity filled her eyes, not from the pain, but at the thought of her dream taking flight.

"That's it!" Butch's shout made Jenna jump. "What the hell's wrong with you today? You've been stretching your neck every time a customer walks in and driving Rosie nuts with that same question: Is anyone asking for me?" He mimicked a squeaky high voice that had no resemblance to hers, then pointed to her hand. "I'm taking that glass out of your wages. Now, get back to work and pay attention to what you're doing or you'll be looking for a new job." He slammed a pot on the stove.

Anger at this lack of compassion dried her tears. She'd look for a new job, anyway. Anything to get away from his tyranny.

Jenna wrapped her hand deftly, cleaned up the glass and blood and tried to put Finn Sawyer out of her mind. It didn't work, but she stopped listening for his voice and refrained from scanning the faces of the diners every five minutes.

At three o'clock Jenna swept the floor with long, uninspired strokes and tried to think positive thoughts. It didn't work. Depression draped itself around her like a dark cloak and she held out little hope for Finn's arrival.

"Jenna, come here, will you?" yelled Rosie.

Jenna dropped the broom and raced for the door. She emerged into the diner breathless, eyes alight with expectancy.

"I need tables three and four cleared," said Rosie. She looked twice at Jenna's face and patted her on the back. "Sorry, honey, I know you're waiting for someone, but he hasn't shown."

Jenna cleared the tables, then filled her remaining hours with constant movement, anything to get her through the day.

She checked the clock. Six o'clock. Shift over. No Finn.

How could she have been so wrong about a person?

She knocked her knuckles against the side of her head. What made her think anything had changed? She had married Angus, hadn't she, thinking he could dull the cold ache left by the sudden deaths of her parents. After the first few months, he hadn't even pretended he cared anymore.

Jenna gathered her belongings, stepped out the back door and started down the alley. She unleashed her riotous curls from the pink ribbon she had tied on with such optimism that morning. As she was about to turn the corner, she heard Rosie's shout.

"Hey Jenna, hold on a minute. Your boyfriend's here to see you."

Jenna's heart leaped into her throat. She rushed back inside, stopped at the swinging door long enough to smooth down her unconfined hair, and pushed through to see Finn waiting for her. Her breath stuck in her throat. The sudden onslaught of hope made her dizzy.

Finn reached for her hands. "Jenna, I'm so sorry. I got sent to Marysville today, and my bosses didn't even give me a warning. I had to train some business people on their new e-mail package. They knew so little I was busy the whole time. I couldn't even break away to make a phone call. Please forgive me for being so late."

"Don't worry about it. I knew you'd come."

Rosie, walking by, rolled her eyes at Jenna's words.

"Well, what's your answer?"

Jenna pointed to a table in the far corner. "Let's sit down first." Before they were fully in their seats, Jenna blurted, "Yes, I accept."

"Woo hoo! We'll be such a great team, I know it."

Jenna breathed deeply. When she exhaled, she envisioned all of the negativity from the past leaving her body in a steady dark stream. Only good things would be allowed into her life from now on. She smiled at her new boss.

"Okay, what do we do first?" she asked.

They spent the next two hours poring over the real estate ads, circling potential locations for their new business. Jenna hadn't felt as much hope and excitement in years. It was clear that Finn wanted a business partner, not just an employee.

By the end of the session they had an appointment with a real estate woman for Monday morning, Jenna's only day off. Their newspaper search had found eight possibilities in regular office buildings and one prospect in a house in Mount Clemens, a community just outside of Detroit.

Finn insisted they at least look at the Mount Clemens property. "I know you don't think the house will be suitable, but it won't hurt to look."

"For that price, you know it'll be a money pit," Jenna groaned. "There's definitely something wrong with it. We'll just be wasting our time. Besides, city people don't think life exists outside of the city limits. We'll never get our customers to come to us."

"That's the beauty of it. We don't need them to come to us. Getting our own lab will be out of the question for the first year or two, so we'll go to them."

"So, we move back into the city in a year or two?"

"Maybe, or we make them need us so much that they're even willing to travel outside the city." Finn's grin and mischievous eyes resembled those of a little boy who's come up with a brilliant idea.

She smiled. "Well, I admire your optimism."

Jenna floated home on a magic carpet of hope and dreams, ignoring the inner city smells of diesel fumes and cooking oil. She and Finn planned to meet for dinner later to go over the details of the new business.

She pinched herself to make sure she wasn't dreaming and laughed out loud at the sharp pain. "It's real. I can finally begin my life."

"Talking to yourself? You've been alone too long."

Jenna drifted down to earth long enough to notice Everett, arms draped over his raised knees, sitting on her front steps.

She laughed up at him. "You are so right and I intend to do something about that right away."

"Really?" Everett smiled, showing teeth too small for a man's face. He was the only person Jenna had ever seen who looked better without a smile. "You're ready to let me move in?"

"Don't be silly, Everett." Jenna laughed. "I'm ready for Chase to move in." She clapped her hands, needing to express her exhilaration in some physical way. She'd skip if she didn't think little men in white jackets would come and cart her away.

"Well, go ahead, tell me what you're so happy about. But be quick about it, because I have good news for you, too."

Jenna stopped and reached for Everett's hand. "Chase? Can I see him?"

He nodded and she squealed.

"Irene's a tough cookie, but she finally agreed to let you see him on Saturday at three o'clock. There's only one catch."

Jenna held her breath.

"She doesn't want you in her house. She says you have to wait on the corner of Colonel Talbot Way and Thomas Street. She'll send Chase out to see you."

She shook her head at Irene's petty control games. Her sister-in-law was more like Angus than she realized.

"So she's still in the red brick bungalow on Thomas Street?"

"Yes."

Jenna nodded and looked up to find the last piece of sunset slivered between the grimy buildings. She pictured her first visit with Chase, near strangers whose lives were inextricably entwined. A mixture of fear and anticipation clutched at her throat and she swallowed hard. Jenna desperately wanted to see her son and hoped he felt the same.

She gazed at her friend, her eyes stinging. "Thank you, Everett. You're a blessing. I don't know how I'd get through this without you."

"I'll always be here for you, Jenna. Don't ever doubt it."

She patted his arm. "I know, Everett. You're the best friend a woman could ask for."

Everett stood, but stayed on the bottom step which made him a few inches taller than Jenna. "How about we get some take-out Chinese to celebrate?"

"I'd love to, but I'm going out tonight." Jenna grinned.

He went very still. "A date?"

"No, silly. Who would I have a date with?" A light wind blew her hair into her face and she brushed it back with both hands, wondering what she'd done with her hair ribbon. "I didn't tell you my news. I've been offered a wonderful job, and I'm meeting my boss tonight to go over some plans for it."

Everett nodded. "What kind of job?"

Jenna tilted her head and eyed him. "You don't look surprised."

He looked down at his shoes, then pushed his glasses up the bridge of his nose. "I knew it wouldn't take you long to get another job. My offer still stands, you know. You could work for me."

"You know you can't afford to hire me, and the university would never approve." She didn't want to remind him that his own job as Teaching Assistant wasn't that secure. He had been passed over for several promotions. "Anyway, this job is exactly what I've been looking for. It's a new computer training company."

Everett's brow furrowed. "What do you know about this guy? He doesn't seem very stable."

Jenna's eyes jerked to his and she stepped back. "When did you see him? Have you been spying on me?"

He reached for her arm. "Now, don't get like that. I didn't see him. I just mean that if it's a new business, it doesn't *sound* very stable."

She relaxed and laughed ruefully at her suspicious nature. Nothing was as it seemed in prison. Now that she was out, she'd have to retrain herself to trust people.

She told him everything she knew about Finn and his company, which, she had to admit, wasn't much.

"I have to go, Everett." She placed a hand on his scrawny arm and felt it quiver. "Thanks so much for setting up my meeting with Chase. I'll let you know how things work out."

She sprinted up the stairs to get ready for her evening and ran smack into the well-muscled chest of Billy Channing, a second-floor tenant in her building. Immediately she was engulfed in a cloud of cheap cologne.

"Whoa, there, little chickie. Where are you going in such a hurry?" He placed his thick-fingered hands on her arms and pulled her into a hug.

"Let go of me!" said Jenna, furiously pushing away from him. She stepped to the left and he moved to block her way. She moved to the right. He moved with her.

"Hey, look, we're dancing," said Billy, laughing and showing yellow teeth. A wave of whiskey-laced breath washed over her. She winced and stepped back.

"Let me by," said Jenna in a low voice. She glanced behind her and saw Everett by the curb watching with narrowed eyes.

Billy crossed his massive arms over his chest. "Oh, that's right. You're too good to talk to me, aren't you?"

"I'm not allowed to talk to ex-cons and neither are you, so it's best you just leave me alone."

Billy's dark bushy brows lowered. "Who said I was an ex-con?"

Jenna looked pointedly at his brand new cowboy boots, new jeans, the tendrils of a homemade tattoo creeping down his forearm and encircling his wrist, and his muscled body. She didn't need a release form to tell her he was a recent parolee.

She knew she shouldn't answer, shouldn't spend an extra second in his company, but anger at his cocky attitude replaced common sense. "Are you going to tell me you're not?" she asked, lifting an eyebrow and looking him in the eye for the first time. Red tendrils crept across his eyes like cracked egg shells.

"What's it matter to you?"

"It matters because it violates my parole, and it violates yours, too."

Billy shook his head. "Not me. I did my full time. Those ass wipes on the parole board didn't want to see big bad Billy out on the street any sooner than possible. Now, they'll find out how right they were." He threw his head back and guffawed loudly at his own private joke.

Jenna took that moment to dart around him and run for her door. She slammed it as he came pounding down the hall yelling, "You can run, but you can't hide, Princess. I know where you live, remember? And me and Rosie at the diner are bosom buddies." He cackled loudly, obviously enjoying her unintentional cry of distress.

Jenna leaned a shoulder against her door and slammed all four deadbolts into place with shaking fingers. She wrapped her arms around herself and shivered. Billy had been making lewd comments whenever he saw her since he moved in two weeks before, but he'd never tried to strike up a conversation with her before. It would be difficult to avoid him, but she'd have to try until she could move out. That day couldn't come soon enough.

She didn't have to press her ear to the door to hear the angry male voices that filled the hall. She cringed when she recognized Everett's voice along with Billy's lower one. She put her hands to her cheeks as she thought of what Billy would do with her slightly-built friend. Everett was half the size of Billy and completely unfamiliar with street fighting.

A third voice joined the altercation and within seconds, the front door slammed. Jenna ran to the window in time to see Everett stalking to his car and the building manager standing on the steps shaking a fist at his retreating back. Jenna sighed in relief. Everett looked infuriated, but unharmed.

She shook off the dregs of apprehension from her encounter with Billy. She'd deal with that problem another day. Now it was time to get ready for her evening with Finn.

Forty-five minutes later, Jenna met Finn at a tiny Greek restaurant two blocks from her apartment. Between mouthfuls of lamb kabobs and rice pilaf, they discussed plans for the new business and compared ideas. It thrilled her to find they had many ideas in common.

Happy dreams of Chase, Finn, and her new life filled her sleep that night.

Jenna went into work early the next morning, hoping to put Butch in a good mood. She needed to ask for a few hours off on Saturday so she could meet Chase. She couldn't really afford to lose the four hours pay, but she didn't want to upset Irene by trying to change their plans, and she wouldn't miss this meeting for anything.

Jenna skirted the raggedy man sleeping in the alley and hurried her step toward the diner. She had promised Yoda she'd keep this job until the other one was a certainty. She also needed the money until she started receiving a paycheck from Finn. Butch could be a pain, but there was no reason he wouldn't let her go if she called the evening dishwasher in early. She had it all planned out and was rehearsing her spiel when she entered the back door of the diner for her early morning shift.

"Keep out of Butch's way today, Princess." Rosie pulled Jenna aside within seconds of entering the diner.

"What's going on?" asked Jenna, glancing around the dingy room.

"Someone's thrown paint on the front door, and he thinks it has something to do with him being Jewish," whispered Rosie. "He's some upset." She dragged Jenna over to the opening in the wall, which allowed them a view of the front door.

Jenna stared in horror at the blood red mess splattered on the glass door. "Why does he think that? I didn't even know he *was* Jewish."

"Because there's a huge J drawn into the paint. He's telling the cops it's a hate crime."

A frisson of apprehension skittered up Jenna's spine. She shook it off and crept into the diner, trying to avoid Butch's eye as she approached the door. She needn't have bothered. His angry eyes snapped between the officer and the door.

"They're after me, I tell ya," Butch whined. "This is just the beginning. Them gangs want me out of here."

The officer made calming noises and led Butch through the open door to stand on the sidewalk. They surveyed the damage, then peered closely at the ground as if looking for clues.

Jenna stared at the huge J centered in the frayed red oval. Dead fish flies stuck to the surface of the paint. She crept closer and noticed something tied to the door handle. A pink hair ribbon trembled in the light breeze. Jenna gasped. Her hand shot to the ponytail tied with a ribbon at her neck. She shivered and knew this had nothing to do with Butch.

Was this Irene's idea of a calling card, warning Jenna to stay away from Chase? Surely Irene wouldn't waste her time on such a useless act. Could it be a relative of someone in prison, jealous that Jenna was released on parole without serving her full sentence? Or was it Billy, giving her a warning?

"What's that?" Jenna jumped at the sound of Rosie's voice directly behind her.

She turned and looked into Rosie's perpetually flushed face. "It's my hair ribbon. The one I wore yesterday."

"What's it doing there?" Rosie reached out to snare the strip of satin. She gave a sharp tug when it stuck to the paint.

"I don't know, but it gives me the willies. Maybe the J is for Jenna."

Rosie hooted and rolled her eyes. "Paranoia strikes again. Between you and Butch we could start our own psycho ward. Really, Princess, I doubt if this ribbon has anything to do with that." She nodded at the door. "Anyone could have found the ribbon on the ground and hooked it on the door handle. It's just a coincidence that it happened the same night as the paint."

Rosie handed the ribbon to Jenna and walked away mumbling and chuckling to herself.

Jenna looked down at the strip and jerked back as if stung. The ribbon fluttered to the floor. Marks with an unnerving resemblance to blood stained one end of it.

She shook her head, impatient with her own thoughts. As Rosie said, the most logical explanation was that it had nothing to do with her. She snatched the ribbon off the floor and jammed it into her pocket.

"It's just a coincidence, that's all," she muttered. "Just a coincidence."

Chapter Six

A slammed door could not dissipate the scalding venom that poured through veins more used to ice. Rage intensified in the throbbing brain, reaching a crescendo once closed inside the room dedicated to Jenna's sanctum.

Red-stained fingers lit all nine candles on the altar, then traced along the lines of her face. The paint had long dried, so none bloodied the smiling portrait.

The paint episode had been a mistake, born of fury. Nothing could be achieved from a game curtailed by being caught. There was too much still to accomplish.

Wrath returned like a gust of foul air. Jenna had plans for the future. She mustn't be allowed to find the answers to her dreams so easily. Not yet.

She needed to be dependent, perhaps uncomfortable for a time, maybe even fearful. Yes, fear would bring her to the place she was supposed to be. It must be a slow process, incurring niggling doubts that would grow into wild accusations smacking of paranoia. A dry chuckle passed the rigid lips. The future looked golden.

A leather-bound diary held secrets of well-laid plans. In red ink the pen scratched across the page. *Next steps: watch, listen, collect, make contact, wait. Wait. Patience is a virtue I have cultivated. I can follow her anywhere, find out things about her she'd never dream of. She'll never be alone. She won't get away from me. I'll be watching. I'll be waiting. She's mine. In the end, she will follow my will. In the end.*

A tiny brass teddy bear, a recent acquisition, added to the collection. Place it with the windowsill collection or the corkboard? Finally, the bear was hung by its neck from a silken ribbon and tacked to the 'Jenna board.'

Chapter Seven

The next few days were a whirlwind for Jenna. She worked all day at the diner, then spent the evenings designing marketing brochures for TechnoTrain, the new business.

Saturday morning dawned bright and warm, perfect conditions to meet her son. She arrived at the designated corner twenty-five minutes early and spent the time chewing her nails and pacing in circles.

Throughout her years in prison she had kept up with Chase's life through Everett. Her friend would appear every Thursday with stories and photographs he'd collected from his Saturday visits with Chase, along with a cherished letter. She would devour the information, but, no matter how dog-eared the priceless mementoes became, it hurt her to see her baby grow up in pictures. She had missed his first day of school, his last eight birthdays, when he learned how to swim, and his first cruise on a two-wheeler. She'd missed coddling him when he had the chicken pox and wiping away his tears when he scraped a knee. Jenna's mouth set in a stubborn line as she resolved that they would start making real memories together from this moment on.

At two fifty-five, Jenna looked up and saw a boy walking toward her. Her heartbeat reverberated in her ears. Taking a calming breath, Jenna's eyes did a greedy inventory of her son. He was a little shorter than she imagined, but she'd only seen him in photos.

When he neared, she cleared her voice and whispered, "Hello."

The boy looked at her strangely, said "Hi," then looked both ways and crossed the street. Belatedly, she realized it wasn't Chase at all. Tears of anguish sprang to her eyes and she punched a fist on her thigh. What kind of mother didn't recognize her own son? Self-pity engulfed her until she noticed movement near Irene's front door.

She dried her eyes with the back of her hand. She didn't want Chase's first sight of his mother with tears streaking her face. Jenna gazed down the street, heart in her throat, as a long, lanky boy sauntered toward her. She looked him over carefully. He was about the right age, but his hair was long. In all of the school photos she'd seen he had short hair or was wearing a ball cap.

When he was about three yards away, she hesitantly said, "Chase?"

"Yeah." He stood with slumped shoulders, hands in the pockets of his low-slung corduroy pants.

Jenna felt like a steel band had been snapped from around her chest, allowing the first unrestrained breath in years. "I'm so glad you could meet me."

Chase remained silent.

She stared at her son with hungry eyes, searching for the toddler she'd left behind.

He gazed back at her with his father's ice-blue eyes, lightened considerably from the cornflower blue of babyhood. His nose had lengthened, but retained the slight lift at the end. It was in the fullness of his lips that she found her little boy. When he was a baby, he had the most kissable rosebud lips. He still did. His eyes roamed over her face, probably searching for some lost memory of the mother who had left him eight years ago.

"May I hug you?" she asked tentatively.

He shrugged and allowed her to press him to her. Tears filled her eyes and threatened to spill. Her heart felt like it might burst in her chest and her throat closed with emotion. She blinked rapidly and stepped away from him. She smiled through her tears and reached out to touch a strand of his hair.

"Long hair. I'm surprised Aunt Irene would allow you to grow your hair long."

Chase snorted. "It cost me."

"What do you mean?"

"We made a deal. I'd eat all of my broccoli without complaining and I could wear my hair anyway I wanted."

Jenna smiled. "Boy, you win both ways."

Chase's lowered brows reminded Jenna of her father.

"How do you get that?" he asked.

"Because broccoli will keep you healthy."

Chase rolled his eyes. "Oh, jeez, are you on a health kick, too?"

"No. I'm just a mother. Mothers do that."

He shifted his weight to his left foot and she realized they had been standing on the corner for several minutes.

"Did you want to go for a walk?" she asked.

He shrugged his left shoulder. "Sure."

He turned and fell into step beside her. She noticed that his right foot turned in ever-so-slightly, a replica of her own. Jenna smiled at this small proof of kinship. They walked in silence for a moment.

Jenna's mind whirred with questions. How are you doing in school? What's your favorite subject? Who's your best friend? How has your life been for the past eight years?

She rubbed her forehead. Where do you begin when you haven't seen your son for eight years?

Finally, his eyes slid up to hers. "Aunt Irene says you murdered my father."

Jenna inhaled sharply, but she knew he had every right to ask. "What else did she tell you?" she asked in a quiet voice.

"She said that you're a liar and that you betrayed him, that you betrayed all of us."

"Do you believe that?"

He shrugged his left shoulder again, a trademark move by now. "Uncle Everett says you're innocent and that you're a wonderful person." Thank goodness for Everett. "I don't know who I'm supposed to believe, so I thought you could tell me."

Jenna sighed. "Oh, Chase, I wish I could."

"You mean you won't?" He squinted his eyes at her accusingly.

"It's not that I won't. I can't. I don't remember what happened that night. I don't think I could deliberately hurt anyone, but I just don't know for sure."

He snorted. "I must get my bad memory from you. Aunt Irene gets mad all the time when I forget to make my bed."

Jenna smiled. "This is a little different, I think. I *want* to remember what happened."

"Then, why don't you?"

"The doctor said my mind is trying to protect me from a traumatic event." Jenna shrugged at his look of disbelief. "I don't understand it either, but she said it could come back at any time. Or not at all."

"Will you tell me when you remember?"

Jenna hesitated. What if she remembered that she pulled the trigger of the gun that killed his father? Could she tell him the truth? She watched a look of suspicion wrinkle his forehead. She inhaled slowly and nodded. "Yes, I promise I'll tell you the truth."

His face cleared and she exhaled in relief.

They wandered into the park at the end of the street and sat on a bench beside the duck pond. She looked at his face and knew her questions would have to wait.

"Is there anything else you'd like to ask me, Chase?"

He didn't say anything for a moment. "Why…why did you leave me?"

Jenna's eyes jerked to his. "I was sent to prison, Chase. I didn't have any choice."

"But you could have let me visit you."

She shook her head. "Prison is a horrid place. I didn't want my little boy to see his mother in surroundings like that. I thought I was doing what was best for you. It's all I ever wanted." She wasn't getting any warm fuzzies from him, but at least he was talking to her. In many ways, it was more than she deserved from him.

Chase seemed to digest her answer for a while, then asked, "Am I going to live with you?"

"Yes," said Jenna. "Very soon. As soon as I can find us a nice place to live, you can move in with me."

"Will I have to change schools?"

"Yes, you will, Chase, but probably not until the fall term. Will that be a problem?"

He shrugged. "No, it doesn't matter."

They spent the rest of their time together wandering around the park, talking about Chase. His likes and dislikes, his friends, his schoolwork, interests, anything and everything.

"In your last letter you mentioned you were trying out for the track team. How did that go?" asked Jenna.

Chase's eyes lit up. "Coach says I run like a deer and jump like a gazelle. I saw gazelles on a National Geographic special and they're great jumpers."

Jenna smiled. "You must be really good. I was on the track team in school, too."

"You were?" He looked at her with a skeptical eye.

She laughed and tugged a lock of his hair. "I wasn't always thirty-two, you know."

He looked at her more closely as if trying to visualize her at his age. Finally, he shrugged and they rounded the far end of the pond. He scooped up a handful of pebbles and the soft plop of them dropping into the water accented their conversation.

Jenna felt like she had grabbed a piece of heaven. From this moment on, she would always relate the smell of fresh cut grass and blooming lilacs with Chase.

Too soon their time was up.

Chase glanced at his watch. "I have to be back in five minutes."

She thought she heard a touch of regret in his voice, or maybe that was wishful thinking on her part.

"Yes, I promised Aunt Irene I'd have you back. Let's go."

She wanted to reach for his hand, but he still seemed skittish and she didn't want to scare him off.

At the corner, Jenna dug into her pocket, drew out two small pieces of paper, and handed him one. "Here's my number at work. If you ever need me for anything or if you just want to talk, call me there. Okay? I'll get a message to you this week to make arrangements for our next time together."

He shoved the paper into the front pocket of his jeans.

She handed him the other piece of paper, a photograph. "This is you with your father and me on your second birthday." She pointed to the happy figures in the picture, watching his eyes for any kind of reaction.

Chase glanced at the photograph, then slid it into his back pocket. "I have to go."

She reached over to kiss his cheek and whispered, "I love you, Chase, and I missed you. I'll see you next week."

He turned and walked away from her, never looking back. He hadn't called her 'Mom' even once and although she didn't expect him to so soon, it still left an ache in the region of her heart.

When he was almost to Irene's house, he slipped a hand into his back pocket and retrieved the photo. Jenna watched his back curve protectively over the treasure in his hands before sliding it back into his pocket, patting it once and opening the door to his aunt's home.

Over the next two days, Jenna replayed their visit several times. She remembered the feel of his wiry young body when she hugged him, the silky softness of his hair, and the boy-smell that lingered on his skin.

Monday arrived with a much needed distraction from her thoughts. Finn picked her up at eight o'clock and their search for a business location began.

Their first stop was at a shopping center in the east end of Detroit. The small office space which sat between a bicycle repair shop and a custom window-covering store was the first of many to be rejected. Too small, too big, too much this, not enough that. After several more stops, they drove out to the nearby community of Mount Clemens to see Finn's 'money pit,' as Jenna termed it.

Finn pulled up to the curb and cut the motor. The sudden silence after the deep rumble of his souped-up Barracuda was heaven to her ears. Jenna rubbed her foot one last time, then slipped her shoe back on.

"Mrs. Wheeler must be waiting for us inside. Her car's here." Finn pointed to the inferno-red Intrepid parked in the driveway.

Jenna nodded. They stood, shoulder to shoulder, at the foot of the sidewalk and surveyed the property. The large farmhouse stood in stately disrepair, like an aging matriarch trying to ignore the encroaching signs of age. A wraparound porch skirted the building and cried out for a fresh coat of paint. Three stories of windows reflected cumulus clouds and a pink-streaked sky.

"What do you think?" whispered Finn, as if the house would hear their discussion.

"I'm reserving judgment until I get a good look at it. First impressions have been beaten out of me by our first fifteen stops," she added dryly.

Mrs. Wheeler, the real estate agent, beckoned from the front door. Jenna and Finn approached, but tried to stand outside the plump woman's cloud of 'White Diamonds'.

"Well, this is it." Mrs. Wheeler sighed, an unmistakable note of disappointment in her voice. "It's obviously not what you were looking for since it's outside the city, but shall we go through it anyway?"

Jenna cast her eyes around the spacious foyer that gave way to generous alcoves on either side with a large room in the middle. Centered at the rear of the house was a wide staircase leading upstairs.

They followed the real estate agent as she pointed a pink fingernail at the chipped paint, the scuffed baseboards, and the huge lawn. "Much too much maintenance for a business," she opined. "Don't forget, we still have that lovely property in Bloomfield Hills we could go to. I'm sure we could come up with a suitable fee schedule. You get what you pay for." She nodded sagely.

Neither Jenna nor Finn said a word as they followed her through the huge main room. Jenna lifted a corner of the grimy once-plush carpet. After taking note of the floor, she dropped the carpet back in place and stood, wiping her hand on the leg of her jeans.

"Oh, I know, the carpet's filthy," said Mrs. Wheeler. She flapped her hands. "It would all have to be replaced. The owners have been renting this place out for the past two years. It's just a crime what renters will do to a place." Her chirpy voice faded as she walked down the hall toward a back room.

Jenna and Finn followed, silently pointing out the oak trim, the expanse of the living room, and the huge windows that allowed a golden light into every room in the house. They climbed the staircase side by side, their hands lingering on the curved lines as the shellacked wooden banister flared to both sides at the top of the stairs.

"There's one apartment on this floor with two bedrooms, and a smaller one-bedroom on the third floor. The one upstairs has an outside entrance, as well. Did you want to bother looking at them?" She glanced pointedly at her delicate watch and raised her eyebrows. "I'd really like you to see the other one today. I know it will be just perfect for you."

Jenna hid a smile. The property in Bloomfield Hills would be just perfect for Mrs. Wheeler's bank account and not so good for Finn's.

"Yes," said Jenna, looking at Finn. "Let's take a look at the apartments." He nodded and they waited patiently while Mrs. Wheeler fished a key out of her skirt pocket and unlocked the heavy oak door. Jenna pictured the plywood door of her apartment and almost laughed out loud.

They stepped into a large room. Jenna was instantly warmed by the same golden light as downstairs. She strode across the room and sat on the window seat overlooking the back yard. When she let her gaze travel outside, she gasped. A green expanse of overgrown grass and weeds filled the back yard and led down a small hill to a meandering creek.

Mrs. Wheeler hurried over. "Imagine having to cut that huge lawn." She shuddered theatrically. "And you'd have the neighbor kids catching minnows and frogs in the stream. My goodness, I don't know what got into my head to bring you here. This is not suitable for your business at all. It's much better suited for, well, I don't know who it would be suited to. It's just so…so…so unsuitable."

Jenna put a hand over her mouth to hide a smile.

"Mrs. Wheeler," said Finn, "would you excuse us for a moment?" He herded her to the door and closed it the second she stepped over the threshold. He turned to Jenna, hands on his hips. "What do you think?"

"I love it."

Finn grinned. "Me, too."

"The rooms to the left and right of the foyer could be our offices…," said Jenna, her voice laced with excitement.

"…and the center area could be our show room."

"The back room would be perfect for storing manuals and training materials."

"And there's a basement for a computer lab," added Finn.

"And hardwood floors hidden under that grungy carpet."

"And you could live in this apartment," they said in unison.

"Me?" said Jenna. She shook her head, stunned, and feeling once again like she was in some wonderful dream from which she would awaken any minute. "I can't live here."

"Why not?"

"Because it's too...beautiful and cozy and warm and perfect." She glanced out the window and pictured Chase running across the lawn toward the stream, fish net in hand. It grieved her to turn him down. She wanted so much to provide a lovely home for her son, but it was too much to ask of Finn to give it up. "Finn, thank you for thinking of me, but this should be your apartment."

"Just hear me out. I've been thinking of this ever since Mrs. Wheeler said it had two apartments. Here's the plan: I buy the place, renovate the main floor for the business, rent out this apartment to you, and live in the third floor apartment." When she tried to interrupt, Finn held up a hand and shushed her. "I don't need this much space. If I take the rent money directly out of your paycheck, it lowers my monthly business expenditures, plus I don't have to worry about finding a suitable tenant. An added benefit to you is that you'll pay less income tax."

He stopped, but when she didn't say anything he continued. "My final argument is that it looks like a great neighborhood to raise your son. It would be a favor to me if you'd accept. Oh, and I'll pay for any renovations needed to this apartment before you move in. As a landlord it's my duty to make it habitable."

Jenna laughed. "You're making it very difficult to refuse."

"Why would you want to?" asked Finn.

"I wouldn't. I'd love to live here. Let's do it." Jenna clasped her hands and didn't even try to suppress a whoop of excitement.

While Finn made the arrangements with Mrs. Wheeler, Jenna wandered around her new apartment visualizing new carpet, freshly painted walls, and Chase's shoes and book bag tossed at the door. She shook her head at the way Finn was changing her life. He was quickly becoming her fairy godfather. She wondered what would happen when midnight struck.

Chapter Eight

Jenna nibbled on the end of her pencil as she reviewed her list: meet with Yuri; pick up Chase; buy paint and wallpaper for his bedroom and for their apartment; meet Finn at house and begin renovations.

Every one of these tasks held something new and exciting for her, and represented a break with the past and a step toward the future. Even the Yoda-like Yuri held some appeal today since she'd be able to tell him that her diner days were almost over. One more week with Butch, then her new life would begin in earnest. She smiled and twiddled the pencil between her fingers.

Her head shot up at the faint rustling noise near the door. She drew her hand back, ready to fire her pencil at a foraging mouse, but she stopped it midair. A small cream-colored envelope lay just inside her doorway partially under the door.

By the time Jenna had hurried to the door, pulled back each deadbolt, opened it, and peered out, her delivery person had vanished. She slowly closed the door and reached for the envelope.

As she turned it over, a chill ran up her spine and settled in her neck. Her dead husband's name stared back at her in calligraphy. He had always maintained that a university professor should have his own stationery to demonstrate his place in life, and now someone wanted her to believe a message had arrived from beyond the grave.

Jenna's fingers trembled as she ripped it open and unfolded the single sheet of matching paper. *MOVING CAN BE DANGEROUS TO YOUR HEALTH.* She shivered and let the envelope drop to the floor.

Within seconds, anger had overridden the apprehension in one burning wave. Irene must be behind this. She had the most to lose because Chase would be moving in with Jenna, much to Irene's displeasure. Only last week Irene had threatened to take Jenna to court. She soon backed down when she realized she didn't have a case and that Yuri would support Jenna's claim. Irene had no further rights.

Jenna was confident she had found her culprit.

Who else would have access to Angus's stationery? Only Irene. And Chase. The last thought gave her stomach a sickening lurch. *Oh, please don't let it be Chase,* she prayed. She clenched her hands, crumpling the letter. No, it couldn't be Chase. They had spent many hours together over the past two weeks. She was beginning to get to know him again and she was sure he was looking forward to their new life together as much as she was.

Her mind reeled as she sought another explanation, any other explanation. She paced the tiny room, shredding the paper in her nervous fingers.

Suddenly, a far more sinister face swam before her mind's eye. Billy Channing. He'd been a constant irritant lately. He wouldn't want her to move because that would take her away from him, but how could he have gotten Angus's stationery? Could Billy and Irene have an alliance?

Jenna rubbed her forehead and dropped the letter into the wastepaper basket by the door. She scooped up the envelope and, with one last look at the return address, threw it away, too. She had too much to do today to waste any more time worrying about a childish intimidation attempt. In prison, threats were more plentiful than mirrors, and just as useless.

She grabbed her purse and ran out into the cloudless day, barely slowing down until she reached Yuri's office, where he wished her a gruff "Good luck." After a brief meeting, she hurried to the bus stop to meet Chase. He had insisted that he was old enough to ride a bus by himself, so she'd given in with some misgivings. She waited, biting her thumbnail, until his bus pulled to the curb with a soft whoosh and a wave of diesel fumes.

Jenna met him with a quick hug as he stepped down from the bus. His black Red Hot Chili Peppers tee shirt hung well past his hips. "How was the trip?" she asked.

"The trip?" Chase raised his eyebrows. "You mean all eight blocks of it? Well, let's see, I got mugged twice and one old lady tried to hit me with her cane, but I fought her off. Other than that, it was a pretty boring 'trip.'"

"Okay, okay, I get the hint. It's no big deal for you to ride a bus all by yourself. Point taken."

"I could have ridden my bike, you know."

"We'll save that for another day. I'm not up to it yet." She linked her arm through his and they sauntered down the street toward Bell's Paint and Wallpaper store.

"What about this border?" Jenna asked Chase for what seemed like the hundredth time. She held up a strip of paper.

"No, I'm not into baseball," he said and flipped open another sample book.

"I thought you said you liked to watch the Tigers."

"I do, but I don't want them all over my room."

Jenna sighed. Now she understood what her mother had gone through when she too was a child. She remembered going to the department store to buy doll clothes and looking over every item before finally making a decision on how to spend her five dollars.

Jenna opened a sample book and whooped in delight. "Oh, Chase, this is perfect! I've always wanted to do a child's room in this."

Jenna watched his face as he caught sight of the pink ballerina slippers and tutus that danced across the paper border. "Imagine this on pink walls," Jenna enthused, even while his eyes widened in horror and his mouth fell open.

"You're kidding, right?" he asked.

Jenna's mouth twitched as she tried to suppress her mirth. When she burst out laughing, he visibly relaxed.

"That was really funny, Mom. Ha, ha. Now, can we really look for some wallpaper?"

Jenna's laughter sputtered to a halt and tears filled her eyes. She hadn't expected him to call her 'Mom' quite so soon. She gave him a quick hug, then turned away and surreptitiously wiped her eyes and swallowed the lump in her throat.

An hour later, they were lugging their purchases up the front steps of the house in Mount Clemens. Jenna was thankful they only had to carry the bags from the bus stop on the corner. Any further and her arm would become dislocated.

The pungent tang of sawdust accosted them as they reached the open door. Finn appeared in the opening, a belt sander in one hand and his face covered with goggles and a surgical mask. A flour-like powder covered every available surface of the room including his dark hair. When he removed the goggles, Chase and Jenna laughed.

"You look like a raccoon," said Chase. "An old raccoon."

"Keep laughing, mister, and you'll get this horrendous job." Chase backed away in mock horror. "This is all your mother's fault, you know," Finn continued. "Why we couldn't install carpets like every other self-respecting business, I don't know, but, no, no, we have to have hardwood floors. Do you know the reason someone invented wall-to-wall carpeting, Chase? Because it was his job to sand and urethane the hardwood floors." Finn shook his head in pseudo disgust.

Jenna patted his shoulder. "Poor Finn. We'll get you a nice, cold lemonade and then *back to work*." She mimed cracking a whip and, chuckling, headed for the kitchen at the back of the house.

While Jenna added water to the frozen lemonade concentrate, Chase reached into cupboards for three tall glasses. The tart smell of lemons filled the room. They heard the whir of the belt sander start up again. Jenna glanced at Chase as she stirred.

"Chase, are you okay with moving in here with me?"

His hand stilled on the glass. "Why? Don't you want me to?" The look on his face told her he'd already thought of that possibility.

"Of course, I do," she hastened to reassure him. "More than anything in the world. I just want to make sure it's okay with you."

"Sure," he said. He placed the glasses on the counter in front of them, but didn't look up. "Aunt Irene says you'll only want me for a while, just until you find a boyfriend. Then, I'll cramp your style."

Jenna clenched her jaw. She reached for his chin and turned his head so he was looking her in the eye. "You know that's not true, right?"

He shrugged, but when she didn't let go, he said, "I guess so. Yeah."

"Good, because you'll never 'cramp my style.' I want you to move in with me more than anything. I've missed you so much."

She released him and he poured the lemonade into the glasses. In a low voice, he said, "Me, too."

Jenna's shoulders finally relaxed. She smiled and picked up two of the dewy glasses. "Come on. We'll show Finn our purchases."

It took another six days before the renovations were finished. Jenna and Finn worked tirelessly until every surface was painted, wallpapered, or urethaned.

Three weeks after finding the house, they stood on the sidewalk, shoulder to shoulder, unwittingly replicating their stance from the first day, and surveyed their handiwork.

"The flowers are blooming already," said Jenna, pointing to the kidney-shaped garden on their right. Her gaze brushed across the tasteful sign, posts rooted in the garden, that advertised their business with elegance.

Slowly, they walked toward the front door, Jenna's eyes skimming the freshly painted wraparound porch, the forest green trim that accented the windows and shutters, and the sparkling windows.

"Looks good so far," said Finn.

Jenna shot him a look. "It's perfect."

They climbed the stairs. Finn held the door open for her. Despite the open windows, a faint mixture of urethane and paint still hung in the air. She stood in the doorway and drank in the view. Reaching for the second floor, the gleaming stairway banisters promised thrilling rides for a daring child. The hardwood floor shone like liquid honey and spread into the sunlit alcoves on either side of the foyer.

Jenna strode into the chamber on the left and trailed her fingers along a walnut desk.

Suddenly, she whooped with joy and laughed when Finn jumped. "I can't believe it, Finn. This is really happening!"

He grinned and joined her in a silly, lurching polka. Their laughter echoed around the room.

"This is exactly what I was afraid of." The condescending rasp brought the pair to a stumbling halt.

"Irene! I didn't hear your car pull up." Jenna pulled away from Finn and straightened her sleeveless shirt.

"That is painfully obvious." Irene stood in the doorway, arms akimbo and mouth pulled into a grim line. "I can't believe I have to deliver that poor child into circumstances like this."

Jenna tossed her head. "Oh, for God's sake, Irene. Get over it." She brushed past the older woman and met Chase lugging an overstuffed duffle bag halfway up the sidewalk.

"Let me help you with that," she said, reaching for the bag. "Do you have more stuff in the car?"

"Nope. This is it." He tugged on the handle. "I can get it." Jenna looked down at the bag and wondered what kind of Spartan existence he had been living for the past eight years. How could his entire life fit into one bag?

She walked ahead and forced Irene to move out of the doorway. "I can't wait for you to see your room," she said to Chase. As he moved to climb the stairs, Jenna reached for his elbow. "Thank your aunt for bringing you. I'm sure she has to get back to work."

Irene snorted at Jenna's dismissal and bent to give Chase a stiff embrace. As she straightened, her eyes glistened with tears.

Jenna sighed, and cursed herself for being too soft. "Maybe you could show Aunt Irene the wolf cub border you picked out before she goes," she said softly, running a hand over his hair.

She watched them climb the stairs and felt a hand drop onto her shoulder. "After all she's done to you, you could have rubbed her nose in it," said Finn.

"I know, but I remember how it feels to hand him over to another woman. I doubt if she likes it anymore than I did."

"Knock, knock."

Jenna turned to see Everett standing in the open doorway. He tucked his hair behind his ears and looked around the room.

"Everett, how on earth did you ever find us out here? I haven't had time to call and let you know our new address."

He resettled his glasses on the bridge of his nose. "Oh, uh, Irene told me. I had to come to Mount Clemens to pick up a book anyway, so I thought I'd drop in. I hope it's not a bad time." He ducked his head and gave them an apologetic look.

"Actually, we're pretty busy getting settled right now," said Finn, reaching for the door. "Maybe you can come back another time, after you've called."

Jenna stepped in front of Finn and patted Everett's arm. "Actually, Everett, now's a great time for a visit. Why don't you go on up and see Chase and Irene. First door on your left."

She waited for him to reach the landing before turning on Finn. "How can you be so rude? Everett's been a wonderful friend to me. I don't know how I would have survived in prison without him visiting me every week and bringing me news of Chase. I owe him so much."

Finn crossed his arms over his chest. His lips drew a hard white line across his taut face. "I don't like him. And I don't think you should have anything to do with him."

"I beg your pardon?" Jenna stuck her chin out and put her hands on her hips. She could feel the heat rising in her face. "Who do you think you are? You have no right to tell me who I can see. We might live in the same house, but we are not family and you don't have any say in who may or may not visit me, or when."

Jenna felt like she was fighting for her life, for her independence. Angus' bid for control had begun much like this. After that, his control had accelerated into physical and emotional blows. The suddenness of both had left her reeling. She had thought at the time that there was no way to predict his sudden move to violence, but now she knew better. The signs had been there to see, but she had chosen to ignore them. At first, she had been flattered by Angus' overprotectiveness, until she realized it was a control issue with him. She wouldn't make that mistake again.

"You have overstepped the bounds of employer, and even friend. In the future, I'll thank you to remember that." She turned on her heel and stomped up the stairs.

Chapter Nine

The flames shot higher and reflected in the eyes of the wiccan revelers. Sparks floated into the night sky, short-lived fireflies. The witches swirling and dancing made the perfect cover for this clandestine operation.

Jenna and the boy appeared and sat on the window seat of their apartment. That provided an unobstructed view, a just reward for patience. Their heads tilted toward each other as if looking at some object between them. From time to time, one or the other would hold something up. They made a perfect picture, their heads silhouetted, haloed in soft light.

The Pentax was safely ensconced in an inner pocket of the voluminous cape, but it would be better left hidden for now. Too many witnesses tonight. Another opportunity would present itself. Patience was invariably rewarded. Rightly so.

Jenna peered out into the night and their eyes locked. She must surely feel the pull of their destiny, the same thrill through her body at the contact. Her lips moved, as if trying to convey some secret message. A plea? A wish? A prayer?

A sudden movement to the left. The grassy expanse between the house and the woods held dozens of dark-clad witches, but none that appeared too interested. On the roof of the head witch's house, however, a white-blonde huddled low to the shingles. The perfect oval of her face reflected the orange blaze seventy-five feet away. Her prying eyes didn't waver for long seconds. Finally, she stood, made her way to the left and dropped onto the roof of the attached garage. It took her several minutes to climb down the rose-blanketed trellis on the side of the garage.

Eventually, the woman stood in the center of the yard and craned her swan-like neck, searching, scanning. Keeping the crowd between them, circling in counter-balance to her moves was child's play. However, the original game must be abandoned. The enjoyment was destroyed with the presence of the meddlesome witch.

A last glance at Jenna's house, the empty window no more telling than a blank face. Its secrets were safe for the moment.

More opportunities would arise to watch the prey. The hunt could be a leisurely sport. The finale that much sweeter.

Chapter Ten

The second night in the house, Jenna brought out her 'treasure' box to show Chase the few things she had salvaged from her former life. The plain tin box that once held shortbread cookies now cradled her most cherished possessions. She had very few mementoes to remember her years before Angus' death. She didn't care that Irene had taken everything that had belonged to him. She caressed the box that held the precious gems that reminded her of Chase.

They sat cross-legged on the window seat facing each other, with the treasure box between them.

Chase dug his hand into the box and held up a tiny clear plastic bag. "What's this?" he asked.

Jenna reached for the bag. "That's a lock of hair from your first haircut. You cried because you thought it would hurt." She laughed and tugged his hair. "It must have had a psychological effect, because you still don't like haircuts."

Chase grinned and delved into the box again, pushing aside clumps of yellowing cotton. He came up with a photograph of a small child sitting on a huge toy truck. "Is this me?" he asked, peering at it closely.

Jenna nodded. "You loved your trucks. You even wanted to sleep with them, but there wasn't enough room in the bed." She tilted her head to the side. "Do you remember my nickname for you?"

Chase squinted his eyes as if unsure of the reliability of his own memories. "Tonka?"

"Yes." Her throat closed and she fought back tears. She hadn't dared to hope he would have any memories of their life together, but he had just proved her wrong.

The next item was a 'Baby's First Christmas' ornament in the shape of a gift-wrapped box with 'Chase' engraved on the back, then a necklace with Chase's birth stone in a single drop, three hand prints from the first years of his life, and his first finger painting masterpiece. Jenna related stories about each item, fingering them lovingly as she spoke.

As Chase explored the remaining items, Jenna glanced outside. A huge bonfire at the rear of the neighbor's yard flickered in the dusk. Dark-clad figures danced around it. Swords, points embedded in the ground, marked the boundaries of the circle. Many others milled around between the house and the fire.

"What's going on out there?" Jenna wondered out loud.

"Oh, Rhia's having a fire festival to celebrate the summer solstice," answered Chase without looking up.

"Who's Rhia?"

"She's our neighbor. I met her today. She's cool."

Jenna wondered what made her 'cool,' but she didn't ask. She squinted at the window. "Does that person on the edge of the yard look like he or she is looking at us?"

Chase turned to look out the window, but just as he did the figure turned away.

A glimmer of light glanced off something on the person's face. Glasses, perhaps? A flash of memory flickered in Jenna's mind, but it was gone before she could grasp it. That little glimmer of light meant something to her, but what was it? Jenna shook her head. It was gone.

Chase pressed his nose against the window. "Nope, I don't see anyone looking up here."

"Come on, kiddo, you're leaving nose prints on the window. Time for bed." She stood and offered him a hand, tugging him to his feet.

As Chase slumped off to get ready for bed, Jenna glanced out the window. Her eyes roamed the yard, but couldn't differentiate the caped figure from the other revelers. She shivered and moved away from the window. For the rest of the evening she tried to push the apprehension and the sense of *deja vu* from her mind.

The next day was Sunday and Chase's friend, Joel, arrived to spend the day with him. The boys played outside for most of the morning and rode their bikes around the new neighborhood. By the time they came in for lunch, both boys were sweaty and smelled like they'd been playing in the creek behind the house.

"Mom, Rhia wants to talk to you," yelled Chase from the bathroom. He came out drying his hands on a now-grubby towel.

Jenna frowned. "Did she say what she wanted?"

"Nope."

"She's a wiccan, you know," added Joel, green eyes alight with excitement.

Jenna looked at the skinny, tow-headed boy in surprise. "Pardon?"

"She likes to be called a witch, not a wiccan," corrected Chase.

Jenna's head swiveled between the two boys. "Hold on a moment. Rhia, our neighbor, is a witch and she wants to see me?"

"Yup," said Chase. He bit into a tuna sandwich and hummed in appreciation.

Jenna's apprehension from the night before returned tenfold. "Chase, I don't think it's a good idea for you to go over there anymore."

"Ah, Mom, Rhia's really cool and neat to talk to. She knows lots of stuff." His blue eyes beseeched her to change her mind.

"I don't know anything about her. How do you know if she's a good witch or not?" Images of boiling cauldrons and broomsticks flitted through Jenna's mind.

"She has to be good because of the Law of Three," said Joel between bites of his carrot stick. "'Any energy...' What is it?" He turned to Chase.

"'Any energy you send out will come back three-fold,'" quoted Chase. He drank some milk and ran his tongue over his milk mustache. "That means if she's mean to someone else it will come back to her three times as bad."

Jenna raised her eyebrows. "How much time have you been spending with her?"

"Mom, you should go over and talk to Rhia, then you'd see she's nice."

She nodded. "I think that's a good idea."

The phone rang and Chase bounded over to answer it. "Hello?" He waited, winding and unwinding the telephone cord around his arm. "Hello?" He dropped the handset back into its cradle and returned to the table.

"Who was that?" asked Jenna.

"No one. They hung up."

Jenna drew her eyebrows together. "Have you given our number to anyone, Chase?" she asked.

"Nope. Just Aunt Irene. And Joel."

Joel beamed.

Jenna nodded, sure Irene was behind the call. She hoped Irene would stop harassing her soon and get on with her own life.

"Don't give it to anyone else. Okay?"

"Sure."

Jenna watched the boys finish their lunch, then, after cleaning up their mess, walked over to the small brick bungalow next door. She knocked on the front door, but when no one answered, she followed the sidewalk to the back. Turning the corner, she stopped at the scene framed by the bay window.

A beautiful woman dressed in a skintight, black leotard sat on a small round Formica table surrounded by flickering votives. Her closed eyelids flickered and wisps of long black hair floated as if a light breeze blew through the kitchen. The woman's legs seemed to be tied into a pretzel position and her hands lay, palms to the ceiling, on her knees. Jenna stared and jumped when she realized a pair of almond-shaped eyes were staring back.

She hurried to the door, embarrassed at being caught peeping in a window, and knocked on the cedar-trimmed screen door.

"Come," called a mellifluous voice.

Jenna hesitated, then pushed the door open and entered the room. The scent of incense tickled her nose and she sneezed.

A musical laugh filled her ears. "A lot of people have that reaction."

The woman slid off the table with the grace of a jaguar.

Jenna stared into mahogany eyes and felt like she was looking at a wild animal. Not crazy wild, just unpredictable from a human perspective.

The woman held out a hand and said, "Hello, I'm Rhia, the good witch. You must be Jenna."

"Witch?" Jenna feigned a lack of knowledge. She didn't want the other woman to think she'd been discussing her.

The woman tilted her head forward slightly. "At your service."

Jenna hesitated, then clasped the other woman's long-fingered hand. Her caramel-colored skin felt like silk against Jenna's work-roughened hands.

"You need to know that you may be in danger," said Rhia.

Jenna stiffened and dropped the hand abruptly. Was Rhia somehow involved with the disturbing message she'd received? And the hang up? Why? Anger welled up in her. "Did you see that in your crystal ball?"

Rhia flashed straight white teeth in a serene smile. "Nothing so magical. My friend, Ash'kena, another witch, told me. Would you like to sit down?" She waved a graceful hand at an antique chair and, after Jenna sat, slid into a matching one. She gathered her thick hair and tied it in a knot on top of her head. On anyone else, it would look ridiculous, but on Rhia it enhanced her beauty. "Now, I'll tell you what Ash'kena told me.

"You probably noticed I had a celebration here last night. It's called a fire festival and I have it every June for all of the witches and warlocks in Detroit and surrounding areas. The ritual activities are by invitation only and, as high priestess of the coven, I know everyone who attended. No strangers are allowed into the circle. The party later, however, is open to outsiders.

"Ash'kena comes, but during the party she likes to sit back and observe rather than take part in the festivities. Last night, she climbed up onto my roof and watched from there.

"One person seemed to stand out from the rest. She thinks it was a man, but she's not sure. He didn't seem to be into the party, and was hanging out on the edges. He didn't talk to anyone and he just didn't seem to fit in. So, she watched him.

"At first, she studied his clothes. They were fancier than what we're used to. He wore a long-sleeved, black shirt with big, droopy sleeves, dark leather leggings with black, high boots, and a black vampire-type hooded cape with a red silk or satin lining. His face was made up, too. White face paint with black circles around his eyes that dripped down into black tears. He wore sunglasses, but she could see through them, so she figured they were the yellow kind that you can use to help see in low light conditions."

"Excuse me, Rhia, but I don't see what this has to do with me," said Jenna, although she was uncomfortably aware the man Ash'kena described sounded like her peeping Tom.

Rhia didn't seem to be bothered by the interruption. "After a while, Ash'kena realized he was watching your house. He'd stay in the crowd, but on the edges, and away from the light from the fire and just stare over there. It gave her the creeps. Eventually, she climbed down to get a better look at him and whatever he was so interested in. By the time she got down, he had disappeared, but that's when she saw you sitting in the window with your son."

Jenna tried to suppress a shiver. She stood up quickly and almost knocked over a broom that had been leaning, brush side up, by the door. She caught it in one hand and set it back in place.

"Maybe you should get one of those," said Rhia, head cocked to one side.

"Why?" asked Jenna, although she really didn't want to know. This magic stuff was making her uncomfortable.

"It protects the home from unwanted outside energies." Jenna's eyes locked with Rhia's.

Jenna turned away first and reached for the doorknob.

"Thanks for letting me know about the person at your party."

"It wasn't meant to scare you," said Rhia in a soft voice. "Just to make you aware, so you can take the necessary precautions."

Jenna's shoulders relaxed and she sighed, turning back to Rhia. "Thank-you. I really do appreciate knowing. It's just unsettling to know you're being watched."

Rhia nodded. "I've been through it before, being stalked, and it's no fun. An ex-boyfriend decided he couldn't live without me."

"What happened?" asked Jenna, despite herself.

Rhia lifted her chin and traced a jagged scar that ran across her throat. "He tried to kill me, then killed himself."

Jenna gasped and placed a hand over her own throat. "Oh, my God."

"I don't want that to happen to you. Let me know if you ever need to talk." She stood and walked toward Jenna at the door.

Jenna nodded and reached for the other woman's hand. "Thank-you. I'm sorry I seemed so suspicious. This whole thing is weird and frightening."

Rhia smiled. As Jenna walked through the door, she said, "I'll check my crystal ball and let you know how things look."

Jenna caught the look of mischief on her face and laughed. She waved and made her way home.

As she entered her apartment, the phone rang.

"Hello?" she said. No answer. "Hello?" She strained to hear any background noise, but only a faint hum came over the phone line. "Who is this?" The phone clicked and a dial tone buzzed in her ear.

She slammed the phone down. Within seconds, the phone rang again.

"Who is this?" she yelled into the receiver. "And what do you want?"

"Geez," said a voice, "what a way to answer the phone."

"Everett?" Jenna's shoulders drooped in relief. "I thought you were someone else."

Everett chuckled. "Obviously someone you don't want to talk to."

"Someone's been calling and hanging up." A sudden thought struck Jenna. "How did you get this number?"

"Information."

"But it's unlisted."

"Ve have our vays," he said in a bad German accent. "Actually, it was pretty easy. I called information and told them I was a Mount Clemens detective and I needed to contact you on an urgent matter. I even gave her my badge number and phone number at the station. She was very willing to help. I knew you wouldn't mind if I had your number. You don't, do you?"

Jenna sighed and pushed her heavy curls away from her forehead.

"Of course not, Ev, it's just that I'd rather it wasn't so easy for just anybody to get it."

"I'm not 'just anybody.'" He sounded petulant.

"You know what I mean."

"Did you get Sawyer straightened out?" he asked.

"Yes, Finn and I had a long talk yesterday and he agreed he was being heavy-handed. He promised it wouldn't happen again."

"Don't let him off too easily," Everett advised. "Remember how Angus started?"

"How could I forget?" she answered, although it was easy to forget. The first signs had been subtle, and couched in words and actions of concern and protection: two things she needed desperately at the time. "Don't worry, it's all taken care of."

Chapter Eleven

Jenna riffled through her treasure box, her fingers tripping over the items that had kept her sane in prison. She pushed the cotton aside, then dumped the entire contents of the tin onto the kitchen table. She rapidly separated the items until they were spread out on the table. Perplexed, she rubbed a hand across her forehead.

"Chase," she called.

He emerged from his bedroom and she smiled at his pillow-tousled hair. "Is breakfast ready?"

"Almost. Have you seen the tiny brass teddy bear from my treasure box?"

He shook his head. "I don't remember any teddy bear."

"It's about the size of my thumb and it has a blue ribbon around its neck."

Chase shrugged his left shoulder and sat down at the table. "Haven't seen it, Mom."

She stood and flipped two buttermilk pancakes onto a plate and placed it in front of him. "I wanted to put it on my desk today." She shook her head, bewildered at its disappearance.

"Do we have syrup?" He lathered his pancakes with butter. She handed the syrup to him and sat down with her coffee and toast.

"Are you excited about your first day of work?" he asked between bites of syrup-doused pancake.

"Thrilled. Don't forget, I'll be right downstairs if you need anything and make sure you tell me if you're going out." She watched a drip of syrup make its way down his chin and remembered the three-year-old. "I wish your baseball camp started today instead of tomorrow. I don't like leaving you alone."

"I won't be alone. You'll be right downstairs, remember? I'll be fine, I promise." He wiped his chin with a napkin. "How about if I make lunch for you?"

"You can cook?"

"Of course. I'm not a baby. Do you want Kraft macaroni and cheese, grilled cheese, or peanut butter and jam sandwiches?"

Jenna smiled and kissed the top of his head. "Surprise me."

She smoothed her new cotton skirt over her hips and descended the stairs.

"Good morning," called Finn cheerfully from his alcove office.

She hesitated on the bottom step and surveyed his business look. A crisp white cotton shirt tugged at his broad shoulders and was tucked neatly into navy knit pants. A navy tie decorated with pink and maroon computers completed the ensemble. The overall effect made her catch her breath and took her totally by surprise.

He waved her over and pointed to his computer monitor. "Look at this. Almost all of the computer training companies in Detroit have web pages and offer some kind of online training." He looked up with raised eyebrows. "How are you with web pages?"

"Good morning to you, too," said Jenna with a smile. "I think I can come up with something. Frames or no frames?"

He tapped a front tooth with his finger. "Hmmmm. Let's keep it simple at first, no frames."

She nodded. "What are you working on today?"

He stood and wiggled his shoulders as if to loosen them and reached for his brand-new leather briefcase. "I'm going to drop in on a few potential clients, pass around some of the brochures you made, and see what I can come up with. Wish me luck."

He was halfway out the door when he stopped and turned back to her. "In case of an emergency, or just if you need me, you can call our new cell phone number." He rhymed off the number. Like a child showing off a new toy, he held up a palm-sized piece of plastic. "We can share it. Whoever goes out on a call gets the phone."

Jenna smiled and jotted down the number. "Bring us back some business," she called and watched him skip down the porch steps.

She walked to her own office and logged on to her new computer. She traced her fingers across the pristine keyboard and smiled. At the prison, there had been two decrepit computers shared between 700 inmates. The keyboards and monitors had been covered with years of grime and she had tried to ignore the grit under her fingertips as she typed. Now, her fingers danced over the slippery smooth surface of the keys.

She had learned how to create web pages in prison, but she'd never been able to see what they looked like live. Like most prisons, inmates in the Wayne County Correctional Facility weren't allowed access to the Internet.

Jenna quickly became immersed in her work. She spent two hours planning the layout of their web page, then experimented with backgrounds, fonts, colors and graphics. She still wasn't satisfied when a message popped up that read, "You have mail."

Jenna scratched her forehead. Who would send her e-mail? She'd only gotten the account two days ago and hadn't given her address out to anyone.

She brought up the e-mail program and typed in her username and password. One message sat in her Inbox, but she didn't recognize the sender: Karma. She opened the e-mail, assuming it was from Finn, and recoiled as if the keyboard had suddenly become white hot.

She read: *Remember, Jenna. It's you, me, and destiny. Your Karma.*

"Mom, it's time for lunch," Chase called from the top of the stairs.

Jenna started. She looked at Chase's feet on the stairs, the only visible part of him, and when he started to descend the stairs she hit the delete button.

"Mom?" Chase's head appeared between the banister rails. "You coming?"

She stood on shaky legs. "Sure, honey. I'll be right up." Her eyes strayed back to the computer screen. Who was Karma? And how did he or she get her new e-mail address so quickly?

Jenna climbed the stairs while running a list of people through her mind who would have access to her address. The Internet provider, of course, the printers where they were getting business cards and letterhead printed, and Finn.

She thumped her forehead with the heel of her hand as relief washed through her. Of course, it was Finn. He often spoke of how fate had brought them together again after all these years. She smiled at her own suspicious nature and turned the corner into her apartment where Chase waited with an expectant grin.

After a delicious lunch of Kraft macaroni and cheese and hot dog slices, Chase's specialty, she returned downstairs to resume her web page building.

Several hours later, Jenna looked up from her computer, and rubbed her eyes. She arched her back and groaned as her muscles sprang back into life after sitting still for so long. The roar of a souped-up engine and the slam of a car door made her look out the window beside her desk.

Seconds later, Finn bounded up the steps and exploded into the room. His tie had been pulled away from his neck and his shirt lay unbuttoned at his throat. He looked as happy as a child with a new bike. "We did it! We are ready to roll."

Jenna laughed and stood to meet him, tucking in the stray tendrils of hair that had wriggled out of her ribbon. "What did we do?"

Finn reached for her hands. "We just got our first gig. I visited about fourteen companies today and they all seem interested, but two of them, yes, I said two, need training right away." He clapped their adjoined hands together. "Can you believe it? Our first week in business and we already have sessions booked. We are good, that's all there is to it."

"When is the first session?" asked Jenna. She squeezed his hands. She couldn't believe their luck. If they got good reviews on their first sessions, TechnoTrain would become well known in business circles in no time.

Finn stepped back and fiddled with his briefcase. "Uh, Thursday," he mumbled without looking up.

"What? This Thursday? Finn, we can't do anything this week. We aren't ready. We don't have any manuals prepared, or a training agenda hammered out, or, or anything. What were you thinking?"

Finn looked down at his shoes, then peered at her a little sheepishly. "There are a few minor details we have to work out, but we can do it.

It means working our buns off for the next few days, but they needed the training now or they were going to call someone else."

Jenna rubbed her eyes and let her hands fall away from her face. She straightened her back, squared her shoulders, and took a deep breath. "Okay, let's do it," she said with a smile.

Finn let out a whoop that could probably have been heard in his apartment two floors up. He opened his briefcase and reached for a yellow writing pad. "I'll give you all of the details and then we can split up the sections we need in the manuals. Deal?"

"Deal." They both wheeled their chairs to a conference table in the main room just beyond the foyer. "By the way, I got your e-mail," said Jenna as he spread the materials across the table.

"What e-mail?"

"Come on, you know." Jenna's heart flip-flopped as doubt crept in. "Didn't you send me a message today?"

Finn squinted at her and she knew he wasn't kidding. "No. Why did you think I sent it? Did it say it was from me?"

Jenna opened her mouth to speak, but closed it again. Why had she thought it was from Finn? She busied her hands with the papers and brochures on the table. "Oh, I don't know. It was silly. Someone probably sent it by accident."

"Are you okay? You've gone a little pale. What was in this message, anyway?" Finn turned to face her and brought her chin up with one finger.

Jenna debated whether to tell him about the notes, messages, and hangups she'd been receiving as well as Rhia's warning. She looked into his face and noted the look of strain around his eyes. He had a lot on his mind these days and she didn't want to make it worse.

She laughed uneasily and pulled her chin away. "Nothing. It was nothing. Forget I mentioned it. It was just a silly note I thought was from you. That's all. No big mystery." She reached for a notepad and a pen. "Come on, we have a ton of work to do. First, I need subject, date, time, location, all of the pertinent stuff."

Finn allowed himself to be lured away from the topic, but Jenna could tell from his look he wasn't satisfied with her answer. He let it ride, though, and she was grateful.

It was probably a harmless crank. She had read most stalkers were all talk and no action. Most.

Perhaps she should talk to Rhia again.

At five o'clock, she and Finn moved their work up to her apartment where she could be near Chase.

She opened her door and fell back as if the blast of music was a physical blow.

"Chase, turn down the music," she called, then turned to Finn. "I can't believe how sound-proof this house is."

The music died and Chase appeared at the door. "Hi, Mom. What's for supper? I'm starved."

She kissed the top of his head, which reached her chin already. She wondered how long she'd be able to call him her little boy. "Hi, honey. How does spaghetti sound?"

"With garlic bread?"

At her nod, he rubbed his muscle-hard belly. It amazed Jenna how her pudding-soft baby had changed into a hard body. His enviable stomach was like a wash board and his legs were like a frog's, skinny but strong-looking.

"Do you want some help? I can make garlic bread," he offered.

Jenna smiled. No matter how hard it was to admit, Irene had done a wonderful job raising Chase. He cheerfully worked by her side to prepare their meals, made his bed every morning, and kept his room reasonably neat. All in all, her son was a great kid.

"Why don't you two play cards while I cook?"

"Are you staying for supper?" he asked Finn, reaching for the deck of cards in the end table drawer.

"Sure am. Your mom and I have some work to finish up tonight. Do you know how to play War?"

"Yeah," said Chase with enthusiasm. "I'm the War King."

"We'll see about that."

From her vantage point in the kitchen, Jenna watched the man and boy hunker down on either side of the coffee table. Chase dealt the cards like a pro and the two were soon deep in concentration. Chase laughed gleefully at Finn's scowl each time he scooped the cards his way.

Jenna set a pot of water to boil, prepared the garlic bread and cut up sticks of raw carrots, green peppers, and celery. In prison, all vegetables had been overcooked to the same mushy consistency. If she never saw another cooked carrot, it would be too soon. Luckily, her aversion to cooked vegetables was shared by her son.

"Oh, Mom, I forgot to tell you. Aunt Irene called."

Jenna dried her hands on a towel and stepped into the living room. Her heart slammed against her rib cage. Warily she asked, "What did she want?"

"Aha, that's mine," Chase crowed, sweeping the cards into his pile. His eyes never left the game as he talked. "She wants to spend some time with me."

Jenna gnawed at her lower lip. "How did she sound?"

Chase raised his head. "She's really mad at you, Mom."

Finn looked at Jenna and raised his eyebrows.

"Okay, Sport, you set the table and I'll be right back," he said, leaving his cards in a neat pile on the table. He followed Jenna into the kitchen. When they were out of earshot, he asked in a low voice, "Are you worried she'll do something to Chase?"

Fear for her son created an ache in her chest. Would Irene hurt Chase just to get back at her?

Jenna shook her head and signed. "No, not really, but somewhere in my soul I'm afraid she'll try to take him away. Just disappear." She began to tremble. "I couldn't bear it."

In a move that felt natural, Finn took her in his arms and held her until the tremors stopped. The reassuring thump of his heart beneath her ear helped her relax.

"You could say no," he said.

Jenna stepped back and shook her head. "That wouldn't be fair to either of them. Irene has raised him from a toddler and did a good job. She loves him and she's earned the right to see him."

A pensive silence fell between them.

"What about a chaperoned visit?"

She looked into Finn's eyes. "That's a great idea, but she'd hate it if I were there."

She chewed on her lip again, thinking out loud. "Our only mutual acquaintance is Everett."

Finn snorted at the suggestion, but Chase liked Everett's company and Irene seemed to tolerate him, too.

"Yes, that's perfect. Everett would do it. Thanks, Finn."

His smile reflected his lack of enthusiasm for her choice, but he didn't say a word.

"Mom, is something burning?" Chase walked into the kitchen, nose in the air like a dog picking up the scent of prey in the breeze.

The acrid smell of burnt bread reached Jenna's nose.

"Oh, jeez." She dove for the oven mitts and pulled out the slightly overdone garlic bread.

"Still salvageable," said Finn. "Good nose, Sport."

"Okay, guys. Let's eat."

Jenna served the food up on each plate and they sat down around the table in the small alcove off the living room.

"This is just like a family," said Chase. He slurped up a noodle, flipping spaghetti sauce on his nose and chin.

"Yeah, Mama Bear and Baby Bear…," said Finn.

Jenna stilled, her fork halfway to her mouth. She wondered where he was going with this.

"…and Finn Bear."

Chase laughed. "I hope Goldilocks doesn't come into our house and snoop around."

"And eat all the porridge."

"Oh, that'd be okay." Chase's eyes twinkled at Jenna. "Mom and I don't like mushy stuff."

"No mushy stuff? No bananas? No applesauce? No ice cream?"

Chase and Jenna exchanged a look. "Well, maybe some mushy stuff," they said together, and laughed.

Dinner ended all too soon for Jenna. She enjoyed the feeling of closeness and camaraderie with Finn and her son and wanted to prolong it.

"Chase, can you do the dishes tonight while Finn and I get some work done?"

Chase stood and carried his plate and milk glass to the sink. "What about Aunt Irene?"

"I'll call her in the morning and set something up. After the dishes, you can watch one hour of TV, then off to bed."

Finn and Jenna cleared the table, then spread their papers all around them. They worked until she couldn't see straight and her mind shut down.

At midnight, after she had finally sent Finn home, she fell into bed and let the exhaustion humming through her body carry her away. Her mind drifted as images of the day flitted through her mind. Gradually, the images swirled and changed until a far darker day crept into her dreams.

She was back in her old apartment, the one she'd shared with Angus. Fear and anxiety clutched at her chest. Something in the hall beckoned her, but fear had poured lead into her limbs. She needed to get to Chase.

A caped figure whirled past her and darted away. At the doorway, the person turned back. Shadowed by the doorframe and partially hidden by the hood of the cape, the facial features were indistinct, but she caught a flicker of light. It was short, lasting no more than a fraction of a second, then gone. The figure disappeared from sight.

Jenna bolted upright in bed gasping for breath.

The dream. Or the memory. This time she had no doubt which it was. She remembered the caped figure in her apartment that night. The breath of air on her skin as he or she spun by her; the reflected light; and the feeling of trepidation at what remained.

She massaged her temples and ran her fingers through her snarled curls. What else? What came before that? What had she seen? Her mind clamped tight and refused to let anymore memories stray.

She dropped her hands into her lap and pleated the sheet between her fingers. Two clues could be gleaned from the dream-memory and she reveled in the knowledge they foreshadowed. One, she had not been alone the night Angus was killed. And two, the other person wore eyeglasses. Recalling, Ash'kena's description of the person watching her, Jenna adjusted her theory: they could be sunglasses rather than prescription eyeglasses.

Jenna smiled. For the first time in over eight years, she believed her memory of that fateful night would return. Until then, she'd never be able to prove her innocence, or plead her guiltlessness.

She laid her head on her pillow and tried to let her mind wander, to free itself of the chains that had bound it tightly closed. No new memories emerged.

Sometime before dawn, she drifted into a deep dreamless sleep, secure in the knowledge that she would one day be vindicated.

Chapter Twelve

"So, what's on your mind?" asked Rhia over her coffee cup. She took a sip, then blew on the hot brew.

Jenna ran a finger along the rim of her coffee cup, eyes on the cream swirling in the aromatic Jamaican blend.

Rhia placed a hand over Jenna's, halting its progress. "Talk to me. Is it about the person at my party who was watching you?"

Jenna offered a tiny smile to her new friend. "The caped crusader is only one of the strange things that has been happening lately." She inhaled deeply and felt the sting of incense hit the back of her throat. She let her breath out in a rush. "I think I'm being stalked."

She watched Rhia's face for the disbelief she was sure would appear, but the other woman stared back with concerned eyes. Her nod encouraged Jenna to continue.

"There have been a few things, but until yesterday I just chalked them up to harmless pranks."

"What happened yesterday?" asked Rhia.

Jenna took a sip from her cup and let the rich coffee roll over her tongue. "I got an e-mail from someone called 'Karma.' It said, 'Remember, Jenna. It's you, me, and destiny.' The message itself isn't so bad, but I haven't given my address to anyone. There have been a few other things that make me feel like someone is watching my every move." She flapped a hand. "I know this sounds paranoid."

"No, it doesn't. People ignore their intuition far too often. If something is making you uncomfortable, there's a reason."

Jenna smiled gratefully. "I've been getting hang-ups even though my phone number is unlisted, a note warning me not to move from my old place, and we can't forget the caped crusader."

"Have you called the police?"

"No," said Jenna abruptly. "They wouldn't help me. I don't exactly have a good reputation with them."

When Rhia didn't ask for clarification, Jenna continued. "I've been in prison for the past eight years." She watched Rhia closely for a reaction.

Rhia nodded slowly.

Jenna took a deep breath and decided she needed to trust this woman and be candid about her past. "For the murder of Chase's father."

The woman didn't flinch, grimace, turn away, or do any of the things Jenna had come to expect.

"Chase mentioned something about getting to know you again," said Rhia, nodding. "I just assumed it was a custody battle."

She stood, rummaged in a drawer, then dropped a writing pad and pen on the table in front of Jenna. She paced the room, hands on the hips of her leopard skin pants. "The first thing we need to do is gather information. Where have you kept everything you've received so far?"

Jenna looked up sheepishly. "I haven't."

Rhia stopped moving.

"I've thrown everything out. I didn't think they were important. I might be able to get the e-mail back. I deleted it yesterday, but it sits in the trash folder for three days before it's gone for good."

"Okay, do that, and from now on keep every shred of evidence. Also, I want you to document every incident. Record the date, time, what happened, etcetera, etcetera, etcetera." She moved around the kitchen with animal grace on feet as silent as cat paws.

Jenna scribbled notes as Rhia talked.

"Next, write a list of everyone you think it could be and put a motive, no matter how minor or trivial, beside each name."

"There are only two people, really," said Jenna. "My sister-in-law, Irene, and Billy Channing, an ex-con who lived in my old building."

"What about your business partner?"

"Finn?" Jenna laughed. "No way."

"Are you positive? Stalkers are usually someone the victim knows well. An ex-husband, ex-boyfriend, or it could be someone who's loved you from afar or has something against you."

Jenna felt queasy. "He did say he had a crush on me in high school."

"Bingo. Write it down." Rhia placed both hands flat on the table. "It doesn't mean he's the one, it just means he's a suspect. Who else?"

"Everett?" suggested Jenna weakly.

"Who's he?"

"He's the only person who has believed in my innocence since the beginning."

"Has he ever asked you for a date?"

"Yes. I turned him down."

Rhia raised her eyebrows.

"But we're still good friends."

A hard stare was her only answer.

Jenna grimaced and added his name to the list.

Rhia sat in the chair opposite Jenna and reached for her hand. "There's one other person we have to look at. I know you don't want to think about it, but how well do you get along with Chase?"

"He's a great kid."

"I know he is, but he's had a tumultuous childhood and you've only been reunited a short while. Could he hold a grudge against you for taking his father away?"

Jenna sighed, ashamed of herself for feeling the tiniest bit of doubt about him. "I don't know. I don't think so."

"Did he have access to a computer yesterday when you received the e-mail?"

Jenna's heart felt like a helium balloon had been tied to it. She beamed. "No, he was upstairs all morning. Actually, he hasn't used one since we moved in."

"Good." Rhia grinned. "That's a relief. What's he up to today?" She refilled both coffee cups and pushed a plate of cookies across the table.

Jenna reached for one of the orange disks and nibbled at it before answering. "He starts baseball camp today. I hope he meets some kids from the neighborhood. He's just been hanging around home since we moved here. These are delicious," she said, indicating the cookie. "What are they?"

"Spider cookies."

Jenna's hand stopped inches from her mouth.

Rhia laughed, a full throaty sound showing strong, white teeth. "I'm kidding. They're pumpkin. You should see your face."

Jenna dropped her hand and slanted a look across the table. "You're a real witch, you know that?"

Rhia chuckled. "And proud of it."

The women smiled at each other and Jenna realized this was the first female friend she'd had in years. Even before Angus' death, her friends had dropped away. Her domineering husband had taken great delight in effectively repelling them from her life.

Jenna plucked the writing pad off the table. "What's next?"

"I'm going to give you some strategies for dealing with this nut case. The next time you get a hang-up, dial star, six, nine. That will give you the phone number of the last caller."

Rhia continually traced a finger along the scar on her neck as she spoke.

"Do *not* respond in any way to his or her attempts to contact you.

"Get an answering machine and a second line, but don't tell *anyone* about the new number or even that there is a new number. Except for Chase, of course. He'll phone in on the second line, but for everyone else, you'll let the answering machine pick up. I'll tape the message recording."

At Jenna's raised eyebrows, Rhia explained. "Sometimes stalkers call just to hear the target's voice. This strategy will thwart that activity.

"Finally, you have to research Irene, Billy, Finn and Everett. Find out as much about them as possible. Their families, childhoods, interests, hobbies, everything."

Her dark chocolate eyes found Jenna's. "We'll get this person."

"How do you know so much about this?" asked Jenna.

"I've read books, gone to seminars, and learned as much as possible about my personal safety. I'll never let this happen to me again."

Jenna clasped the pad to her chest as she made her way home. Her head was down, her mind far away, and she almost walked over Everett on the front step.

"Everett, what are you doing here?" She smiled and plopped down beside him.

"I came to take you for lunch." He pushed his glasses up the bridge of his nose with an index finger.

"Too late, but it was a nice thought. I'm just heading back to work." She sighed. "You have no idea how great it is to work in the same building you live in."

"What do you have there?" He reached for the pad. Jenna clutched it tighter.

"Just some notes. Nothing you'd be interested in." Her laugh sounded false to her own ears. "Work stuff."

His eyes searched her face for a moment. Then, he shrugged and bent over to pick a piece of rubber off the side of his aging high tops. "Maybe Chase would like to go out for lunch with me," he said to the sidewalk.

"He's not here. Baseball camp." Jenna lifted the heavy mane of hair off her neck. "Phew, it's hot out here. Why are you here, anyway? Don't you have to teach a class today?"

"Snow day," he mumbled, still playing with his shoe.

"Pardon me? I thought you said 'snow day'."

He sat up and faced her. "That's right. The professors," he sneered, "take snow days all winter, so I decided we should have one on the hottest day of the year." He shrugged. "The students didn't seem to mind."

Jenna squinted her eyes in concern. "Won't you lose your job?"

Everett went back to studying his shoes. "They won't find out. Besides, I have a medical reason."

"You're perfectly healthy," she scolded.

"I have claustrophobia."

She raised auburn brows. "I didn't know that."

"Yeah, ever since I was a kid and my uncle threw me in a doghouse and nailed it shut." The corners of his mouth turned down in a fierce frown.

Jenna inhaled sharply and he turned to her as if seeking comfort.

"No matter what I did, I couldn't get out. I screamed my lungs out. When I slammed my hands on the wall around the doorway, the nails pierced my palms." He held out his hands for her to see. A small scar puckered the skin of each palm.

"Everett, that's horrible. You've never told me. Here you've been there for me through everything and I didn't even know something so important happened to you."

He shrugged and turned back to his shoes. "You had enough to deal with. He was a mean drunk. Anyway, I could feel the unairconditioned room closing in on me today. The heat pressed down on my chest. The walls squeezed my head. I couldn't stand it, so I left." Everett licked his lips. Jenna could see a sheen of perspiration on his forehead.

She recalled Rhia's instructions to find out about Everett's childhood, and realized she had the perfect opening.

A little guiltily, she asked, "Did you live with your uncle?"

"No. He wasn't really my uncle. My mother and I just visited him sometimes, but he always wanted me out of the way."

Jenna felt a deep sorrow at the desolate picture he had drawn. A mother's anger stirred in her chest and she felt overwhelmed by a feeling of protectiveness. She draped an arm over his shoulders and squeezed. "Thank goodness you're a survivor."

She patted his back and let her arm drop. "I have some news that might brighten you up. I've remembered a bit about the night Angus died."

Everett straightened and stared at her.

She smiled. "I knew you'd be as excited as I was. I remembered that someone else was in the apartment with me that night?"

"Wh…" He cleared his throat. "Who?"

Jenna grimaced. "I don't remember that much, just that someone was there. I saw him or her run out the door."

"Do you remember anything about him? Or her?"

"I think the person was wearing some kind of glasses, but a hooded cape covered the face." She sighed.

Everett offered a smile, then scowled when Finn's car pulled into the driveway.

Finn opened his car door, gathered a briefcase from the back seat, and strode toward them.

"Hi, Jenna. Everett." He nodded toward the other man, but the smile he'd sent Jenna had disappeared.

"Sawyer."

Finn offered Jenna a hand. "Ready to go back to work?"

Jenna reached for his hand and grinned. "Yes, Boss."

He gently tugged her up the stairs and she laughed. "I guess it's time to put my nose to the grindstone, Everett. It was nice seeing you."

Jenna turned at the door and caught Everett still staring at them. She waved, then walked through the door into the airconditioned coolness of her new office.

Chapter Thirteen

Karma dropped the phone into its cradle and cursed. Jenna's new answering machine ruined all of the enjoyment. A stranger's emotionless voice with a bland message to leave a number did not fuel the fires of obsession, nor douse the flames. Nothing. Frustratingly unsatisfying. How dare she? Where were the tension and bewilderment? Jenna's voice crying, "Hello? Hello? Who is this? Why are you doing this?" or her silence as she listened for anything that would give her a clue to the caller's identity.

A dry cackle filled the room and the candles flickered in silent response.

The leather diary lay open on the table by the wall, a centerpiece for the collection. Drawing it forward, Karma placed a checkmark beside "E-mail."

Acquiring Jenna's e-mail address had been simple. Child's play. She made the game almost too easy.

Time to up the stakes, to make the game an adventure. A reminder that Karma rules?

The boy? No, not yet.

A visit? A gift?

Yes, a gift.

Karma stood and flicked the brass teddy bear where it hung by its satin ribbon. Cold eyes followed the bear's arc as it swung back and forth like a hypnotist's coin. Finally, the left hand reached up and snagged the bear, squeezing it in a white-knuckled grip as the tack ping-pinged on the hardwood floor.

Only one detail remained to ruin the game. Karma's shoulders tensed. Nothing and no one could be allowed to interfere.

The bear was dropped into a pocket and the pen retrieved.

The guard dog must go. He's sniffing around her constantly. His eyes are too sharp, his nose too keen. Before long, he'll know something's up. The scratching ceased and the pen dropped into the center crack of the diary.

Soon he will be neutralized. Soon.

"Let the games begin!" The shout rang out, bounced off Jenna's photos covering the wall, but never left the room.

Chapter Fourteen

Jenna and Chase scrunched low into the sofa, his head tipped against her shoulder as they took turns reading "Sword in the Stone."

"That'd be cool to turn into a fish," said Chase.

"Wouldn't you be afraid of being eaten by the bigger fish?"

"Naw, I'd be fast. I'd dart in and around the seaweed, duck behind rocks and zoom away."

Jenna chuckled.

"That'd get boring after a while, though. I'd rather be a kid. Or at least an elephant."

She laughed and tapped the book on his head. "You are a kooky kid."

The ring of the phone startled her after the peaceful evening they'd been sharing. She reached her hand out for the receiver, but pulled it back and let the machine pick up. They listened for a voice, but none came. Finally, the monotone signal indicating that the connection had been severed greeted their ears.

Jenna jumped up and dialed star-six-nine, the number Rhia had told her about to get the number of the last caller. She waited while the operator went through her spiel. Jenna agreed to pay the charge and waited impatiently for the number. Her mouth dropped when she heard the operator recite Finn's phone number.

"This can't be," she whispered, as her hand slowly replaced the receiver.

"What's the matter, Mom?" asked Chase, concern creasing his brow.

A knock at the door made them both turn. Jenna's heart thumped against her ribs.

"Jenna, are you in there? Answer the door. Are you all right?" The heavy door muffled Finn's voice, but his deep tones were still distinguishable.

"It's Finn. I'll get it." Chase leaped from the sofa.

"No!" Jenna's firm command stopped him before he was halfway to the door. He turned to face her with a look that asked if she had lost her mind.

Her mind whirled with questions. Why would Finn call and hang up? Was he the mysterious caller? Should she open the door to him? Jenna sighed deeply and pushed her curls from her forehead, her thoughts as tangled as her hair. Rhia had said to trust her intuition. Well, all of her instincts said that Finn was a wonderful person who wouldn't hurt a flea.

She put an arm around Chase's shoulder. "I mean, I'll help you."

If he thought that was strange he didn't remark on it. He reached for the door, unlocked it and pulled it open.

"Hey, Finn. What's up?" said Chase.

Finn's face was creased in lines of worry. He walked into the apartment and swung his head from right to left as if looking for a person who had been holding them hostage.

"Are you all right? Why didn't you answer the phone?" he asked.

"We don't answer it anymore. We let the answering machine get it, because—," started Chase.

"—because it lets us screen the calls," Jenna interrupted, afraid he'd say too much. "You know, so we don't have to listen to any telephone sales people." She wrinkled her nose to show what she thought of telemarketers. "Did you need us for something?"

He ran his fingers through his dark hair and exhaled. "Nothing important. I just got worried when you didn't answer because I knew you were supposed to be home tonight." He waved a hand toward the bay window. "I wanted to tell you to look outside. The moon has a green ring around it. I've never seen it like that."

Chase ran to the window. "Cool, green cheese."

Jenna laughed and peered up at the odd spectacle. "More likely smog, but it is pretty." She looked up at Finn, who stood with them in a tight group. "Thanks for sharing. Would you like to stay for a cup of tea?"

"No, thanks. I'm not quite finished with the changes to our agenda and my taskmaster, or should I say task*mistress*, said she wanted the final product by morning." He raised his eyebrows to her and she smiled.

"That's right. I need those changes before I can finish the handouts for our first session on Thursday. Everything has to be perfect, especially for this one." A business's reputation could be made or broken based on the smallest item and she was determined to get only positive results.

Later, after Finn had gone and Chase was safely tucked in bed, the phone rang again. Thinking it must be Finn, Jenna picked up the receiver with a smile. "Hello?"

Silence.

"Hello, who is this?"

Suddenly, a voice rasped in her ear in a whisper that sent shivers down her spine and raised the hair on her arms. "I can see through windows," the voice recited in a breathy sing-song. "I can see through doors. I can step into your life and walk upon your floors." A dry chuckle punctuated the sick poem followed by a dial tone.

She dropped the receiver as if it had turned into a live, wriggling reptile. Who was calling her and what kind of sick mind enjoyed these senseless pranks? The voice sounded vaguely familiar, but it had been muffled as if the mouthpiece of the phone had been covered with something. She couldn't tell if it was a man or a woman.

Jenna shivered as fear trailed a cold, wet finger along the back of her neck. What did 'I can walk upon your floors' mean? Had the person been here in her apartment? She looked around as if she could spot a sign that her home had been invaded, but it looked the same as always. A little messy near the door, where Chase had dropped his baseball glove and cleats on the braided rug, a few sports magazines on the coffee table, and her work spread out on the kitchen table. Nothing else seemed out of place.

Was it a threat that the person could come here anytime? Finn had just been here, walking on her floor. Everett and Irene had been here before, too.

Jenna reached for the phone and dialed star-six-nine, just as she'd done earlier.

The mechanical voice of the operator informed her that the number was not available. Whoever had phoned must have done so on a cell phone, or somehow had the number blocked.

She dropped the receiver back into its cradle and pressed her lips into a firm line. Up until now, she had been treating the calls and messages as a prank, but this was getting more serious. This call had sounded like a threat and she was determined to put a stop to it.

She wouldn't allow anyone to invade her home and threaten the life she had begun to build with her son. Tomorrow she'd start following Rhia's suggestions. She'd begin investigating Finn, Everett, Billy and Irene. Nothing would be allowed to get by without careful scrutiny. She would find the person responsible.

Jenna slept fitfully that night. Her mind replayed every telephone call, note and e-mail, and inspected them for even the tiniest clue.

The next morning, Finn remarked on her pallor.

She waved away his concern. "I'm fine. I've got a lot on my mind, that's all. What time will you be back today?"

"By noon, I think." He fished around in his briefcase for a moment then handed her a sheaf of papers. "Here's the revised agenda. We can go over it when I get back." He slung a dove gray suit coat over his shoulder and headed for the door in eager strides.

Jenna loved his enthusiasm. She smiled, then let it slip away, momentarily saddened at the thought of Finn as the caller. She shook her head. She wouldn't think about that this morning. The reams of paper piled high on her desk called to her and she sat down to begin another day's work.

By ten o'clock the sun streamed its golden fingers into the room. She relished the feeling of warmth on her back, but the bright rays reflected off her monitor and caused a glare that made it difficult to see what she was working on. Regretfully, she closed the blinds, but opened the front door wide to let in the summer breeze.

While waiting for her eyes to adjust to the gloom of indoor lighting, Jenna glanced around the office, taking in the honey-colored floor, the gleaming conference table, the long windows, the freshly painted walls, and the inspirational prints leaning against the wall in the corner. She jumped up, remembering she had purchased the prints on the weekend and had intended putting them up on Monday. Since then, she'd been too busy and had forgotten all about them.

Now was a perfect time to take a break, grab a coffee, and find a home for each of the seven prints. Within minutes, the handouts she had been working on were forgotten, and she scanned the walls with a decorator's eye. She sipped the freshly-brewed coffee from her "Computer Nerd" mug, a gift from Finn, and hummed a tune from one of Chase's CDs. Contentment seemed to be a palpable thing in the air.

She decided the print with Dale Carnegie's persistence quote should go near her desk. It seemed to reflect her recent struggles and spoke to her heart.

Placing her coffee on the corner of her desk, she hefted the print. She held the poster-sized frame up to the wall and tilted her head to get a better view. She jumped when a pair of well-muscled, tattooed arms encircled her and overlapped her hands on the frame.

"'Most of the important things in the world have been accomplished by people who have kept on trying when there seemed to be no hope at all,'" read the voice near her ear. "I don't know who that Carnegie dude is, but he's right about that. I thought I'd never find you, but here I am." He seemed to think this was enormously funny and brayed loudly.

Jenna wrenched her hands free and slipped under his arms letting the glass-covered picture crash to the floor. She backed away until she bumped into her chair and stared at the ex-con with the same look and feeling as if she'd found a nest of snakes.

Billy Channing leaned against the wall, a toothpick dangling from one corner of his mouth. A pack of Marlboros was rolled up in one sleeve of his snug, white tee shirt. A cheap gold chain stuck unevenly to his sweaty neck.

"What are you doing here?" she cried.

The glass scattered around his feet, crunched as he moved toward her.

"Well, now, I'm here to see you, little lady." The toothpick bobbed with each word.

"What do you want?"

He reached toward her and laughed when she jerked back. He lifted her coffee cup and sipped noisily. His tongue licked his full lips. "Mmmmmm. I can taste your sweetness."

She grimaced in disgust. She'd have to disinfect the cup with bleach.

Her first problem, though, was finding a way to get rid of him. The closed blinds mocked her attempts to search for help outside.

"Why are you here?" she asked through clenched teeth.

"I want to buy some private lessons."

"Fine. I'll have Mr. Sawyer contact you to set up an appointment."

"I don't want no Mr. Sawyer. I want you." He moved a half step closer.

Jenna pretended to check her appointment book. "I'm sorry. I'm totally booked."

"What kind of business is this? Aren't you selling a service? Well," he said with a wink that made her feel like snail slime was dripping down her back, "I want to buy some."

She gritted her teeth and suppressed a shudder. She thought of the phone calls and messages and made a decision. It was time to do some research, no matter how much she wanted him to leave. "Do you even have a computer?"

"Uh, yeah, I got me one, but I need you to learn me how to run it."

"Did you send me an e-mail?" she asked, watching his eyes for any telltale signs of prevarication.

He looked confused a split second before a blank mask fell over his face. "I might have. Sure, it was from me." Billy tongued the toothpick to the left corner of his mouth. "What did it look like?"

Jenna tried to assess if his low computer quotient was an act. She tilted her head and squinted at him. "You *do* know that e-mail comes through the computer, don't you?"

"Well, of course I know that. Who wouldn't know that?" He crossed his arms over his chest and the snake tattoos seemed to crawl from one forearm to the other.

Jenna sensed a lie and decided to set a trap of his own making. "What color paper do you send your e-mail on?"

His eyes skittered around the room until they landed on a ream of seafoam-colored sheets. His cocky grin returned. "Green. I send mine on green."

Jenna sighed, sure she could cross Billy off her list of suspects. The thought saddened her, because it shortened the list to two good friends and her son's aunt.

A wave of fatigue washed over her. She sank into the chair, propped her elbows on the desk, and rested her chin on her clasped hands.

"Billy, I'd like you to leave now. When you get a computer, you can call for an appointment."

He sputtered and opened his mouth to speak.

Jenna held up her hand. "No more games. I've said you can call. Now, I'd like you to leave."

Billy snorted, but turned for the door. "I'll be back," he warned over his shoulder.

She listened to his cowboy boots stomp down the front steps, then click along the sidewalk. When the sound faded away, she got up to close the front door.

She stepped onto the porch and noticed a tiny figure on the railing. When she moved closer, she recognized the tiny brass bear she'd been looking for. Her eyes moved down the street to where Billy strutted toward the bus stop.

Jenna rubbed her temples, a headache threatening. Perhaps Billy couldn't be counted out just yet.

Chapter Fifteen

Jenna hurried around the kitchen. She toasted bread, then slathered it with peanut butter and sliced bananas. With a yank, she retied her bathrobe belt for the tenth time. Her tangled mass of curls sprang out from her head as if she'd been electrocuted, a genetic mutation she cursed every morning. Pulling a ribbon from her pocket, she efficiently tied her hair back before she noticed the peanut butter smeared on one finger. She reached up with the other hand and traced the greasy, sticky mess down a strand of hair. She groaned. Of all days, why did they have to sleep in today.

"Hurry up, Chase," she called. "Everett will be here any minute." She wrapped the sandwich in tinfoil and dropped it in a lunch bag.

The sound of banging drawers came from Chase's bedroom. "Chase, what are you doing?"

"I can't find my ball glove." His voice was muffled as if coming from beneath his bed.

Three strides took her to his door, where she could see a hurricane in process. "Come on, Chase. Everett's going to be waiting for you. Your glove's by the front door."

"Phew. I couldn't go to a Tigers' game without my glove."

"What do you need a glove for? You're supposed to be watching, not playing." She ushered him to the door.

"I'm going to make a great catch. Then, they'll sign me to a big league contract and I'll be able to buy you a new car and a nice house in Grosse Pointe." His grin made her forget that he was running late and she pulled him to her in a bear hug.

"As long as you have a plan," she said with a smile. She kissed the top of his head. "Here's your breakfast." She handed him the lunch bag.

"Toasted peanut butter and banana?" he asked, peeking into the bag.

Jenna wrinkled her nose and nodded.

"Yum."

They heard the short blast of a car horn and Chase reached for his glove. "Gotta go, Mom. See you tonight."

"Have a good time with your Aunt Irene and Everett. Be good. Don't eat too much junk."

"Yeah, okay. See you." He ran to the stairs, slid down the banister to the foyer, and leaped off the top step of the porch on his way to Everett's car.

She smiled and wished she had a quarter of his energy.

When she heard a footstep on the stairs coming down from Finn's apartment, Jenna whirled around and darted for her door, slamming it behind her. She didn't want anyone to see her looking like this, but especially not Finn Sawyer.

They were meeting that morning to debrief from their first training session.

She hurried through her shower, threw on a pair of shorts and a sunshine yellow tee shirt, and appeared downstairs with her hair still dripping.

As she placed her foot on the bottom step, Finn handed her a mug of coffee.

"Ah, you're a lifesaver," she said as she wrapped both hands around the cup and inhaled.

"You look like you need it," he said.

"Thanks a lot."

Jenna peered up at him over the cup. He certainly didn't look like he needed a coffee to wake up. His casual attire was a delicious break from the formal wear of the week, and suited his athletic physique. She allowed her eyes to roam over the snug polo shirt and denim cutoffs. Her insides trembled as their eyes met. His were bright and full of promise.

"I just mean you look pale and tired." He reached out and tucked a strand of damp hair behind her ear. "Didn't you sleep well?"

"No, as a matter of fact, I didn't. I've been having these dreams." If he touched her again, she might have very different dreams. She moved toward the sunbeam warming the floor in front of the window. "We've been so busy I haven't had a chance to tell you. I've been remembering bits and pieces of the night Angus died."

"That's great," he said, then looked at her more closely. "Is that great?"

Jenna chuckled. "Yes, it's great. I keep dreaming of another person in the apartment with me that night."

"Which means you didn't do it." She loved that he automatically assumed her innocence.

"I hope so."

"Who is it?"

She finger-combed her hair with one hand. "The person is wearing a cape and the face is shadowed. I can't even tell if it's a man or a woman. The problem is, once I wake from the dream, I spend the rest of the night wracking my brain for other memories. Hence, the dark circles and pale face."

Finn laughed. "Even tired, you look great, so don't worry about it. Maybe you need something else to jog your memory."

Jenna shrugged.

"What about going back to that apartment? Do you think that would trigger anything?"

She rubbed her eyes, not sure if she ever wanted to see that place again. "I don't know," she said on a sigh. "Maybe. Probably."

"Okay, let's go." Finn reached into his shorts pocket and pulled out his keys.

"What do you mean? Now?" Jenna's heart thumped harder.

"Yes. You've got to put this behind you sometime. Why not make it today?" He jingled the keys and grinned. "You're going to be no good to me if you come in looking like that every morning. You'll scare off all the customers."

"Very funny." The idea of going to the apartment was a little exciting and a lot terrifying. What if she did remember? What if she didn't? She wasn't sure which would be worse.

"Come on, let's go." He nudged her toward the stairs. "I'll meet you in the car in five minutes."

Jenna nodded.

Within ten minutes, they were rolling down Interstate 94 toward Detroit, her mind in turmoil.

To get her thoughts off their destination, Jenna asked Finn about his family.

After a moment of silence, he said, "I'm the baby of a large family, the only one who never quite lived up to his potential."

"I'm sure they don't believe that."

Finn snorted. "Just ask them."

She watched his face, but it was devoid of the bitterness that seemed attached to the words. "Tell me about your sisters and brothers."

"Well, let's see. The first of the over-achievers is Victoria. Heart surgeon."

Jenna whistled.

"Then, Richard, a fighter pilot in the Navy." He glanced at her. "You know, one of the guys who lands on a little ship in the middle of the ocean. Hamilton's a chemist; Philip's an electrical engineer; Elizabeth was a teacher, but now is the youngest Principal in her school district; Pamela's a stockbroker; Catherine's a lawyer; and then," he took a deep breath and exhaled noisily, "there's Finnegan-begin-again who's never quite found his niche." He cast a soft look her way. "Until now."

Jenna offered an encouraging smile. "Tough act to follow, but you're really good at this training stuff. I read over the evaluation forms from Thursday and it sounds like some of them wanted to take you home."

Finn nodded. "At the risk of sounding boastful, I think I have a knack for helping people to learn without making them feel stupid. And I enjoy it." He reached for her hand and squeezed it. "Together we're going to offer the best damn training Detroit's ever seen."

Jenna enjoyed the feeling of his warm fingers, but too soon he returned them to the steering wheel.

"Where was Irene taking Chase today?"

"Comerica Park. The Tigers are playing the Blue Jays. He's thrilled."

"How did Irene take the idea of Everett tagging along?"

She shrugged and watched the scenery change from green fields with the occasional grazing deer to concrete and litter. "She doesn't like anything I suggest."

"What's her story? Why is she so sure you're guilty?"

Jenna sighed. "She has good reason to hate me. By marrying Angus, I took away the only person in the world she trusted." She picked at the hem of her shorts as she thought of the stories Angus had shared before they were married. "They had an absentee father and an abusive mother. Angus defended Irene and, for the most part, kept her out of their mother's clutches. I think the reason she's never married is because of her fears of entering into an abusive relationship. Ironically, Angus inherited his mother's mean streak."

"Wasn't his image tarnished a bit when she saw your bruises?"

"No. Angus often commented on my supposed clumsiness. 'Grace,' he'd call me, mockingly. 'Grace tripped over her own feet again,' he'd say. 'Look at that black eye.' Irene couldn't risk believing her savior had turned into the one thing she feared the most. And I didn't advertise it. A victim's guilt."

"You sound like you're making excuses for her," said Finn in a disbelieving tone. "After all she's put you through, I'd think you'd feel a little more vindictive toward her. Didn't she lie at your trial?"

She nodded. "I feel more pity than anything. She's had a rough life. I can't blame her for the wrong turns my life has taken. I made the mistake of marrying him."

Jenna looked up and realized they were in the Ferndale area of Detroit. "Turn right at the lights." She guided him toward the five-story building where her life had changed so dramatically.

Finn parked in front and turned the ignition off. The engine's rumble faded away, but neither of them opened the car door.

Jenna stared at the front of the building, held in place by disconcerting visions of Angus stomping through the front door. She glanced at Finn, grateful he wasn't pushing her. "I guess we should go in."

"Are you ready for this?" His voiced washed over her like melted caramel, soft, warm and comforting.

"Do I have a choice?"

"Yes."

She grinned at him. "Yes, I do. Let's go."

She was the first to the super's door, but hesitated before knocking. "Mrs. Van Nesslund doesn't like loud noises," she whispered. She tapped lightly with one knuckle and listened for the shuffling sound that would announce the aging landlady. She leaned one ear closer to the door, then leaped back when it was flung open.

"You kids are g...oh, sorry lady." The man stuck his cue ball smooth head into the hall, looking both ways before drawing it back like a turtle in its shell. "We've got some young hooligans who think it's really funny to see me answer the door." He yawned hugely, displaying several gold teeth. "What can I do for you?"

"Is Mrs. Van Nesslund here?"

"No, ma'am. She up and died about four years ago."

"Oh."

Finn cleared his throat. "We'd like to see one of your apartments."

"Sure, I've got an opening on the fourth floor. Let me get my keys."

"Actually, we're interested in apartment three-twelve."

The man frowned. "I've already got a tenant in there, but the one on four is just like it."

"We'd like to look at three-twelve, if you don't mind."

"I can't just let strangers into someone else's apartment."

Finn pulled out his wallet and handed over a twenty.

The bald man shuffled from one foot to the other. "Well, she is away for a few days."

Another twenty changed hands.

"Okay, let me get my keys."

Jenna and Finn followed him into the elevator. She tried to ignore the smell of cooked cabbage and sweat emanating from the thick body beside her. All three watched the lights until the door opened on the third floor.

She turned to the right and stopped at the second door on the left. The landlord gave her a strange look, then jiggled the key in the lock until the door swung open.

She didn't move. Her eyes focused on the short hall that led to a Hollywood kitchen. In her mind, she added a dried flower wreath to the wall and a yellow hooked rug to the floor by the door. The place suddenly felt like her lost home.

She crossed the threshold and stepped into a past painted with a strange combination of pleasant and horrific memories. The kitchen where Chase had taken his first steps; the corner of the table that had left a scar under her left eye after one of Angus' rages; the tiny bedroom down the hall where she'd sing lullabies to her baby and the other bedroom where her husband delighted in proving his domination.

Jenna walked down the hall with trepidation. She peeked around doorways and corners as if she might see Angus' ghost appear or his crumpled body lying in a pool of blood, half of his neck obliterated. She had no trouble recalling that scene. In truth, it had been in her nightmares for months after the event, until her own survival took priority.

Now, she looked around and only saw white walls, bright airy rooms, colorful duvet covers, and attractive strangers smiling at her from framed photographs.

She returned to where Finn leaned against the wall by the door.

"Anything?" he asked.

She shook her head. "Nope. Nothing new." She took his arm and smiled up at him. "It was a good try, though. Thanks."

That night, the dreams came with unprecedented ferocity, one on top of the other. Finally, near dawn, Jenna awakened to a loud explosion near her ear and shot up in bed.

Chapter Sixteen

Jenna dialed Finn's number with trembling fingers. She had waited a few hours, hoping a hot cup of herbal tea would calm her nerves. Although the soothing effects of chamomile had lessened the nausea, her hands still vibrated from shock.

"Finn?" She tried to choke back the sudden urge to cry at the sound of his voice, and put a hand to her eyes. "I think I killed him. I killed Angus." A sob caught in her throat.

"Jenna? Are you okay? What happened?" Finn's deep tones wrapped around her like a warm blanket.

She closed her eyes and imagined that she stood within the safety of his embrace.

"I had another dream. This time I couldn't see anything, but I heard a gunshot. The sound exploded in my ear, and I could feel the heat of the gun on my cheek, so I must have pulled the trigger." Jenna groaned. "My God, I'm a murderer. How will I ever tell Chase?" She glanced at his closed bedroom door and thought of rending the special relationship she had built with him. Fresh tears trickled from her eyes.

"Jenna, listen to me. You did *not* shoot Angus." His voice sounded firm and full of conviction.

She wanted to believe him, but couldn't. "How can you know that? I'm so scared."

"Someone else must have been standing close behind you. Stick your hand out as if pointing a gun at someone. Go on, do it."

She felt a little ridiculous, but she did as he asked. "Okay, it's out there."

"Is the gun hand anywhere near your face?"

"No."

"Then, how would you feel the heat of it on your face?"

"Oh," she said. The first mists of relief began to spread through her body as Finn's common sense interpretation sank in. Her shoulders relaxed and the pain in her chest faded to a small knot. "Oh."

"Feel better?" He still sounded concerned.

"Much. Thank you. I guess I was just so distraught I couldn't think straight. The dream was so real and I thought it could only mean one thing." She shook her head. "I'm lucky I have you to interpret my dreams."

Finn chuckled. "Happy to be of service, ma'am. Now, how about we get out of here today?"

"What did you have in mind?"

"I think you and Chase and I should go hiking at Fern River Falls. Have you ever been there?"

"No, although I've heard of it."

"It's gorgeous. Water rushes down a narrow river, pours over the rocks, and falls about forty feet. There are trails all over the park. We could take a picnic and eat by the river. What do you say?"

Finn's enthusiasm created a longing in her to go back, back to the hikes she'd taken with her father, following the trails along the meandering creek that ran through their farm. She sighed. Those were the halcyon days of childhood, before she went away to college, and before she received the devastating news of her parents' deaths in a car accident. Grieving and lost, she'd fallen into the consoling arms of her English professor, Angus McDougall. And set up the mistakes that would follow her for the rest of her life.

Jenna shook off the past. "We'd love to go. I'll pack a picnic for us. Any special requests?"

"Just y...no, nothing special. Call me when you're ready."

"Okay. And Finn?"

"Yes?"

"Thanks. I really appreciate your confidence. I need that right now."

"Hey, don't thank me. I can't help the way I feel. It doesn't take a psychiatrist to know you could never kill anyone. Now, let's forget all that and have some fun." Sometimes, he sounded as young as Chase and she loved that about him.

Jenna set down the receiver and padded to Chase's door. She peeked in the room, past the trail of yesterday's clothes on the floor, to the sleeping child in the bed. Chase lay on his side, curled in a fetal position, with his right thumb between his lips. Her heart squeezed as she watched him. He had stopped sucking his thumb when he was two, but obviously reverted back to this one comfort when he lost his mother. She sat on the side of the bed and smoothed the long wisps of hair back from his face.

Slowly his eyelids fluttered open. He rolled onto his back and stretched his arms over his head. "Hi, Mom," he said sleepily, after curling onto his side again.

"Good morning." She kissed his forehead. "How would you like to go hiking today?"

Suddenly he was wide awake and sitting up. "Yeah!"

She laughed. Chase loved to do anything out of doors, but he hadn't had much exposure to it because, he said, Irene was allergic to bees and avoided plants and trees where they might congregate. Luckily, she had allowed him to sign up for scout camp where he'd been able to commune with nature from sunup to sundown.

They arrived at the park shortly before ten and set off on one of the trails that followed the rushing river on its way to the falls. Eventually, they turned a bend in the trail and the roar of the falls stopped them. They grinned at each other, all three reveling in the power of nature, and set off again, hurrying to the lookout over the cascading water. The power of the hurtling faucet shook the ground where they stood in awe. The river plunged down the ravine where it became a churning cauldron and finally surged ahead on its race to the lake.

"Wow," said Chase in a whisper barely heard above the sound of the falls. "That is so cool."

Jenna and Finn looked at each other over Chase's head and grinned. "It sure is, Chase," said Finn, patting his back. "It's definitely cool. Who's hungry?"

A chorus of 'I am' greeted his question and they moved on to look for a perfect place for lunch. Around noon, they found a secluded spot on a peninsula that hadn't yet been washed away by the swiftly moving water.

Finn and Chase dug in as if they hadn't seen food for days. Jenna kept filling their plates until they rolled back in the grass and groaned. After helping her clear up, they crawled away to the water's edge. She leaned back on her elbows and watched them point at minnows and a chubby beaver that dove in from the far bank.

If she squinted her eyes, she could almost imagine they were a real family. Not the kind where caresses were shrugged away, and fists replaced kisses at the slightest or no provocation.

Heartwarming memories of outings with her parents floated through her mind like misty watercolor scenes. Picnics in the park, cross-country road trips, cool fall days at the fair, and ice skating on the pond. With no siblings, Jenna was showered with undiluted attention and she loved spending time with them.

"Hey, Sleepyhead, what are you smiling about?"

Jenna opened her eyes and peered up at Finn and Chase. "I was dreaming that two big strapping males would escort me back to the falls for one more look."

Her son grinned and looked around. "Don't see any. Will we do?"

She laughed. "You'll always do."

Finn took one of her hands and Chase the other and they pulled her to her feet.

They spent the rest of the afternoon hiking and dragged themselves back to Finn's car in the late afternoon, tired and happy from a day outdoors together.

After stopping for hamburgers, they returned home to the house that had become Jenna's haven.

"Why don't you jump into the shower, Chase, and then, off to bed. You've got an early day tomorrow at baseball camp." She herded him into the bathroom, his puppy smell filling the tiny room and taking her back to his toddler days.

She rejoined Finn and they settled on the window seat, his arm along the ledge behind her. Jenna felt safe and relaxed.

"I had a wonderful time today," she said, almost shyly, drawing her knees to her chest.

Finn reached out a gentle hand and traced a finger from her ear to her chin. "Me, too," he said in a whisper that sent heat through her veins. He placed one finger under her chin and drew her closer until their lips touched in a gentle brush.

Jenna kept her eyes closed as sparks shot to the core of her being. She felt the pressure of his mouth again and a low moan started deep in her chest as his tongue flicked between her lips. She could drown in the sensations that were overtaking her body.

Sanity returned, clawing at the cotton encasing her brain, as the shower stopped with a squeak of the tap.

Jenna placed a hand on Finn's chest. "Finn, I can't do this. I'm sorry. I'm just not ready."

"It felt like you were ready to me," he said with a devastating grin that made her want to change her mind.

Jenna offered a wry smile. "It's not that I'm not tempted. I'm definitely attracted to you, but when I'm ready I want to do it right, with all my heart. I don't want to wonder if I'm making another mistake. I've made enough of them."

"You've paid for those mistakes. Can't you move on?" His quiet voice encouraged, but held no criticism.

She shook her head. "Not yet. Our working relationship is going so well, I'd hate to mess it up." She placed her hand on his. "Can you accept that, at least for a while?"

He smiled. "Of course. You can take as long as you need. I'll still be around when you come to your senses."

She smiled, relieved.

Finn stood. "I better go." He leaned down and pecked her cheek, then let himself out.

After she tucked Chase into bed, she snuggled into her Princess Anne chair with a cup of tea and an afghan, and replayed the day. Her mind wrapped around the blooming relationship between Finn and Chase, the fun the three of them had together, and Finn's lips as they caressed hers. Pushing him away had been more difficult than anticipated, but she was relieved that he was prepared to wait. Jenna nestled deeper in the chair and allowed her body to relax, content to listen to the soft hum of cicadas in the trees outside her window.

Her peace was short-lived. With an explosion that shocked her from the chair and made her heart nearly jump out of her chest, a rock crashed through the window and landed at her feet in a spray of glass.

Chapter Seventeen

Jenna stared out at the darkness through the jagged maw of the window. The thought of an evil force creeping into the room propelled her to the phone. Shakily, she dialed Finn's number.

"Come on, come on," she whispered, keeping a fearful eye on the gaping wound in her wall. "I know you're there. Pick up."

The ringing continued, unanswered.

She pressed the disconnect button and started to dial Everett's number.

"Mom?" She heard Chase's sleepy voice and cradled the receiver, then hurried to his room.

Chase sat up in bed and squinted from the glare of the hall light. His hair stuck up in several directions. "What happened? What's all the noise about?" He rubbed his eyes.

"Nothing, honey." She tried to think of something plausible that wouldn't frighten him. "I…I broke the window by accident, but it's okay." She held up both hands. "Look, I didn't even cut myself."

He slanted her a look. "How'd you do that?"

She faked a laugh. "Clumsy, I guess. Just call me Grace." At his look of confusion, she explained, "You know, graceful. Oh, never mind. Lay down and I'll tuck you in. I'll have it all cleaned up in no time."

She kissed him good night and crept from his room, closing the door behind her.

She headed for the phone again, but a knock at the door stopped her. Jenna's heart pounded and she wiped her damp palms against her shorts. She inched toward the door and leaned her ear against it. She nearly jumped out of her skin when the person outside hammered on the door again.

"Who is it?" she called.

"It's Finn. Who else? Let me in." The thick door muffled his voice.

She threw back the deadbolts and peeked through the crack left by the chain lock. Satisfied it really was Finn, she slid the chain off, opened the door wide, and let him limp into the room. His feet left pebbles of mud on her floor and the broken glass crunched under his weight.

"Where were you?" she asked, staring at his muddy shoes. "Someone threw a rock through my window and I tried to call you, but there was no answer." She tried not to use an accusing tone, but heard it creep into her voice.

"I was outside." His face was streaked with scratches and a long red line ran down his left arm.

"What?" Jenna shook her head and rubbed her scalp fiercely trying to understand what had just happened. "Why would you be outside?"

Finn's eyes scoured the room as if looking for an intruder. "I thought I saw a light glinting off something in the bushes. It didn't look right, so I decided to sneak down the back steps to get a closer look. I only made it half way when I heard the crash. When I jumped off the stairs, I twisted my ankle, but I saw someone running across the lawn. I chased him to the end of the yard and across the creek, but lost him in the woods."

"So it was a man?" That would narrow the field a bit.

"I couldn't tell for sure. I just assumed." He turned to her, seemingly satisfied that no enemy was hiding in the corner or behind the sofa. "Are you okay?"

"Yes, I'm fine. A little shaken, but unhurt."

"Good. I'll be right back."

"Where are you going?" she called, but he had already sprinted out the door, moving remarkably quickly for a man with an injured ankle.

Within minutes, he returned carrying an expensive camera.

Jenna stared. "What are you going to do? Take pictures? Are you sure you didn't hit your head while you were out there?"

Finn laughed, but sobered quickly. "I found this in the garden."

"Why would any...oh. Oh, no." She didn't want to think it much less put it into words. "The person was taking pictures of us? Oh, my God." She put her head in her hands. "Who is it? Who is doing this?"

"What's that on the rock?" He pointed to the corner where the missile had come to rest. He picked it up and, for the first time, she realized it was wrapped in paper, an unnerving gift from the vandal. She took the camera from him and set it down while Finn peeled the page back and smoothed it on the coffee table. They sank down onto the sofa.

"Oh, my God," she whispered again.

"Shit," muttered Finn.

The message, written in red nail polish, stared up at them: "You're mine."

"What the hell is this?" asked Finn. "What's going on, Jenna?"

She kept her eyes on the note. "What do you mean?"

"Come on. You come to work looking pale several days a week, you jump at every sound, and now you get a rock tossed through your window *with a note*." Finn ran his fingers through his dark hair. "Level with me."

Jenna sagged. "I don't know." She scrutinized his concerned green eyes and made a decision. She had to believe her own intuition and right now it was screaming that this man was hero material, not the sniveling coward sending anonymous messages. A feeling of relief flowed through her at the thought of sharing the burden with him. She smiled sadly. "Someone's trying to drive me crazy." She told him about every strange thing that had happened over the past few weeks.

"Why didn't you tell me?"

Jenna pulled her lips in and scuffed a toe on the braided rug in front of the sofa.

"What?" he asked, looking confused. She watched his face as shock replaced confusion, then quickly changed to hurt. "You didn't think I…? No, you couldn't…" His consternation was so profound, he seemed unable to complete a sentence. "Why?"

She sighed. "It's not that I really thought it was you, it's just that Rhia said I should be careful until I could absolutely rule you out. We're sure it's someone I know, possibly someone I'm close to." She placed a hand on his forearm and felt the muscles tense. "I'm sorry. Really. You understand, don't you? You know I find it difficult to trust my own judgment about people. I had to be careful. After all, I haven't known you for very long."

"Only since high school."

Jenna sniffed. "I didn't know you in high school. I knew your sister."

"Well, I knew you." He sounded like a sulky child.

"Finn, I can't afford to have anything happen to Chase or me. We just found each other. I'm sorry if your feelings are hurt. That wasn't my intention, but I have to put our welfare first. Chase has already had to deal with the consequences of my mistakes. I can't let it happen again."

He traced the letters with the side of his thumb, his silence becoming a discernible presence in the room.

"Come on, it's nothing personal. Say you understand."

He shrugged. "I guess."

"Good. Now, do you think we can get fingerprints off the camera?"

Finn scowled. "Damn. Not now. I didn't even think of that. My fingerprints are all over it now."

Jenna shook her head. "It doesn't matter. I really didn't want to get the authorities involved anyway."

"Jenna, that's silly. We should get this on record. They might be able to do something."

"No. Just leave it, Finn. I don't want my name on any official police records." She stood and paced the room, her long strides gobbling up the distance between wall and sofa. Finally, she stopped in front of him, hands on hips. "Okay, here's what we're going to do. While I clean up the glass, you can cover the hole. Then, in the morning, we can replace the window and get the film developed. Maybe the photographs will give us some clue to the identity of the creep who's doing this."

Finn stood and wrapped his arms around her stiff body, until she melted against him. "Okay, we'll play it your way," he murmured in her ear. He held her away from him and offered an encouraging smile. "Do you have any plastic?"

They worked side by side repairing the damage. By midnight, the floor was free of glass and the plastic covering the window crackled with every gust of wind.

"Thanks, Finn. I'm so glad you were here for me." She yawned. "I'm whipped. I'll see you in the morning, okay?"

"I'm not leaving, Jenna." Finn sat on the couch and put his feet on the table.

"Pardon?" She was too tired to play games.

"I'm staying here tonight. And, I think I should stay every night until we catch this guy."

She sighed. "We don't know if it is a guy, and you're certainly not moving in here with us." She glanced at the black plastic where her window should be. It shook and snapped as if an incorporeal force pushed from the other side. She shivered. "Well, okay, but just for tonight." She found a blanket and pillow for him and left him to his night-time vigil.

Jenna stretched out under her comforter and snuggled into the soft mattress. Fatigue, both emotional and physical, soon allowed the dream world to take her away from the grim reality of the evening.

She played pat-a-cake with a three-year-old dream-Chase and they giggled together. He threw his teddy bear at the window and laughed as shattered glass rained down on them. The glass shower sounded like the Fern River Falls.

Then, Angus appeared, berating her for breaking the window. He stomped toward Chase's room and she looked down to find her arms empty. Fear clutched her heart. She couldn't hear his words, but he yelled loud and furiously and she knew he was going to hurt Chase. Before she could move to protect her son, he whirled around and seemed to look past her. An explosion sounded in her ear and she felt a familiar whisper of heat against her cheek.

Jenna jerked. Slowly, the remnants of sleep drifted away and she realized Finn was sitting on the side of the bed holding her. The heat of his body scorched her cheek where it pressed against his bare chest.

"Finn?" she said, sleep still clinging to her mind like droplets of dew on a spider web.

"Are you okay?" His voice rumbled in his chest and competed with the thunderous rhythm of his heart echoing in her ear.

"Why are you in my bedroom?" His arms felt so comforting she couldn't pull away.

"You called out in your sleep. Another nightmare?"

She nodded. "This time Angus looked over my shoulder just before the gunshot."

"More proof that you weren't alone." He cursed. "Someone must have seen something that night. Did the police interview your neighbors?"

Jenna pulled back slightly and looked at him, but night shadows obscured his features. She concentrated on his arms and his soothing voice. "I doubt it," she said. "They thought they had their murderer."

"This week we'll go back and ask around." She felt him shrug. "You never know, we might get lucky."

"We should talk to Wim Vandermeersch. Angus used to call her 'the building busybody' because she kept an eye on everyone. If anyone knows anything, it's Wim."

They agreed to visit Jenna's old neighbor and Finn left her to return to the couch. He was gone by the time she woke in the morning.

After sending Chase off to baseball camp, Jenna descended the stairs and sat down at her computer. She had already started worrying by the time Finn arrived an hour later, breathless and waving an envelope in the air.

"I got the film developed," he said, "from the camera in the bushes. You won't believe this." He dumped the photos onto her desk.

Jenna flipped through the pictures quickly, then again more carefully, inspecting them with deliberate attention. Her chest tightened with each glossy print. Finally, she fanned them out like a deck of cards and looked at Finn.

"They're all of me. Some from our trip to the falls and others from my apartment, which scares the hell out of me."

Chapter Eighteen

The digital clock on the desk revealed that it had been less than ten minutes since Karma entered the candle-lit haven, yet it looked like a band of demons had whirled through, leaving a path of destruction in their wake. Unleashing the fury on 'the Jenna room' should be cathartic, but the anger still simmered, a dark boiling cauldron of venom in the soul. Each day it built, as the prize remained out of reach and moved even further away than ever.

Her belongings cluttered the floor the way her image cluttered Karma's mind. Other thoughts came and went, but she stayed…forever.

The most recent photos were gone along with a camera too expensive to lose. With that thought, a muddy shoe shot out and kicked a stuffed turtle out of the way. The toy, a ridiculous memento from her first year of marriage, slid across the floor and checked up against the diary.

Catching sight of the journal, Karma stooped to retrieve it, carefully dusting away splinters of pink glass. The book, returned to its place in the center of the table, smelled of baby powder. Jenna's scent.

"The better to track you, my dear," Karma rasped, then howled at the jest.

Frustration soon returned the scowl. After all of the hours of waiting, the careful planning, it was too much to lose the coveted photos. Too much!

The sound of a fist repeatedly slamming against the table filled the room and shook the flimsy structure.

Finally, silence reigned, peace descended like a comfortable cloak, and a plan began to form. Karma's lips curled back in a feral grin. No more time could be wasted on regrets. It was time to look toward the future with an eye on the prize. Yes, the prize.

Chapter Nineteen

The wipers on Finn's Barracuda slapped away the rain, sending thick rivulets across Jenna's window. The monotonous thwump, thwump of the blades mimicked the thoughts bouncing around Jenna's mind.

What would Wim tell them? Had the police questioned her? Would she have any information to help them make sense of her dreams?

"We're here."

Jenna looked up and realized the deep rumbling of Finn's muffler had stopped. The thrumming of rain on the roof reminded her of camping with her parents and she nestled back in the seat with a smile.

"Mrs. Vandermeersch's probably wondering where we are." He glanced at the Timex on his right wrist. "We're a few minutes late."

She laughed. "Don't worry, she knows we're here." She pointed to the ground floor apartment beside the front door where a rain-blurred gray-haired woman peered back at them. "Wim doesn't miss a trick."

"Let's make a run for it."

They dove out of the car and ran for the front door, leaping over puddles like children as they went.

As Jenna raised her hand to knock, the door opened and a big-boned woman greeted them with a soft smile that seemed out of place on the severe face.

"Jenna, my dear." She enfolded Jenna's hands between her own large ones.

"Wim, how have you been?"

"Please come in. We don't want the neighbors nosing into our business."

Finn made a noise that sounded suspiciously like a snicker, but turned into a cough at the reprimanding look from the former school teacher. Jenna hid a smile and followed Wim into the room.

She looked around in awe. Spiral-bound notebooks, lined up with military precision, stood on floor-to-ceiling bookshelves and covered every inch of wall space. Flat shelves sat on support brackets above the door and the lone window. The wood sagged under the weight of more notebooks held upright by heavy clay bookends obviously fashioned by childish hands. Wim led them to the aging furniture huddled in the center of the room.

Jenna made the introductions, then added, "Finn's been helping me try to find out what really happened the night Angus died."

"He's been a big help already, hasn't he?"

"What do you mean?"

"Well, the super was certainly happy with the 'tip,' shall we say, that Mr. Sawyer gave him last week." She leaned her large frame toward Finn and whispered, "He would have done it for half. He's a greedy little pig."

"As it turned out," said Jenna, "it wasn't all that enlightening anyway."

"Perhaps I can help. What would you like to know, my dear." While she spoke, she periodically glanced out the window and jotted notes, all without seeming to miss a word in the conversation or a movement outside.

"I've never been able to remember what happened that night, but I've been having dreams that don't seem to fit with the story the DA sold at my trial. We've decided to do a bit of investigating on our own. Do you remember anything about that day?"

Wim chuckled, a sound she kept deep in her throat. "I remember everything about that day. Forty-eight people entered through the front door, thirty-six of which took the elevator. A titian-haired beauty arrived at eight-forty-six. She entered Sam Jensen's apartment down the hall and didn't emerge until three-oh-five."

She stopped mid-sentence and peered at Finn whose face held a look of skepticism. Her steel-blue eyes pierced him to the spot.

"Do you have a problem, Mr. Sawyer?"

Finn squirmed. The spindly chair squeaked with every movement. "No, ma'am. It's just, well, it was over eight years ago and you're talking as if you remember it like yesterday."

She pushed to her feet and hobbled to the bookshelf beside the door on feet distorted with bunions. Her fingers walked along the spiral bindings, periodically sliding a notebook out and fitting it back, lining up the spine with its neighbors and moving on. After three minutes of silence, she made her selection, gently turned the pages and handed the booklet to Finn.

She eased into her rose-colored armchair, laid her head back and closed her eyes. Her eyeballs moved back and forth beneath her eyelids as if reading.

"Little Harry Phelps woke me up this morning when he threw the Detroit Times at my apartment door. It's overcast today and the air feels heavy. A full moon is still in the sky, even at seven in the morning.

"Mrs. McAuliffe left for work at seven-oh-five wearing a new yellow slicker, a birthday gift from her grandson. Mr. McDougall was next, the usual grimace on his face. He had a little piece of tissue stuck to his neck. He'll be angry when he realizes it's still there. His assistant picked him up, but won't have the nerve to tell him. At seven-fifteen—"

"Wait," said Finn, looking from the Dutch woman to the book and back to her.

Wim opened her eyes.

"You're reciting that verbatim." His voice was full of awe. "How...?"

"Mr. Sawyer, I wrote every word on those pages. As you can see, I have a keen eye for detail and an excellent memory. I record every detail of my life and frequently review my journals. When I saw you two here last week, I reread my diaries from the period Jenna lived here, to refresh my memory. I am a student of the human condition, Mr. Sawyer. To simplify, I watch people."

Finn finally closed his mouth.

"Now." She interlaced her thick fingers and lay them across her middle. "You may either read about every trivial detail of that day, or you can allow me to separate the wheat from the chaff and offer you only the golden kernels."

Jenna struggled to suppress a smile. "I think we'll go for gold. Thank you, Wim."

The old woman nodded at Jenna and resumed her speech. "Mr. Hunter arrived at six-thirty and a few minutes later, your husband was dropped off. He got out and slammed the door, not unusual for him. On the way up the steps, he dropped his briefcase and cursed loudly. He took the elevator.

"Next, a woman arrived whom I didn't recognize. She took the elevator to the second floor." She turned her head to Finn as if he doubted her information. "I looked through the peephole and watched the elevator lights.

"Another person entered the building through the service door at the back, which was always locked. I didn't see that person arrive, but I knew someone was there because I heard the squeak of the door. I peeked out the peephole again and saw a person in a long black cape (like something from a theater group) go through the door to the stairway. I couldn't see any distinguishing characteristics because the hood was up, covering the hair. Not tall, not short.

"About ten minutes later, I heard a muffled bang, like a firecracker. The police and emergency people arrived twenty-three minutes after that and took Mr. McDougall away. And then they led you out, Jenna, carrying your beautiful baby. It nearly broke my heart." She dabbed at her eyes.

Jenna leaned forward. "Did you see the person with the cape leave?" she asked.

"No."

"Did the police talk to you?" asked Finn.

"I waited a few days and, when they didn't arrive, I went to them with my journal. They weren't interested. After a cursory glance, they said they had all the information they needed, thanked me and herded me out."

Jenna smiled and squeezed the woman's hand. "Thanks for trying, Wim."

Soon after, Wim escorted them to the door. She placed an arm around Jenna's shoulders.

"I don't want to upset you, dear, but someone has been snooping around asking questions about you."

Jenna felt the blood drain from her face. "Who? Who was it?"

"He didn't say his name, but he looks like trouble comes looking for him, no matter where he hides. He had hideous snake tattoos on his arms, an earring in one ear, and black, plastic sunglasses. Quite tough looking, in a cocky sort of way."

"Billy," muttered Jenna.

"Who?" asked Finn when they were back in the car and rolling toward home.

"Billy Channing. He's an ex-con who lived in my old apartment building on Lecaron. Remember? He's the one who made me drop the picture frame. I told you about that."

"Why would he be asking about you?"

She sighed and rolled her eyes. "For some reason, he seems to think we'd make a dream couple. Two ex-cons making it together on the outside." She swept her hand across the windshield as if reading a marquee.

"Maybe I should pay him a little visit," said Finn, his chin jutted out an extra inch.

Jenna grabbed his arm. "No, you will not! I don't know what he was in prison for, but it wasn't for anything pretty."

"He must be the one who's been hanging around in our bushes."

"Not necessarily," she said. "Maybe I'm wrong, but I assume the person who's taking the pictures is the same one who's been sending me e-mail. Billy didn't seem to have any idea about computers, though he tried to fake it."

Finn and Jenna worked in the office for the remainder of the afternoon. That evening, when Chase asked to go to a friend's house in the neighborhood, Jenna decided to visit Rhia.

She told Rhia about finding the camera and expressed her relief that they could scratch Finn's name from their list of suspects.

Rhia remained silent. She flipped through the photographs quickly at first, then again more slowly.

Jenna wrapped her fingers around the dewy glass of iced tea. The rainy day had turned into a muggy, clinging evening. She enjoyed the coolness against her fingers and allowed the chill to work its way up her arms.

"So you can see," she said to Rhia, a bit smugly, "that Finn couldn't have anything to do with this." Jenna felt vindicated that her instincts had been correct about him.

Rhia's eyes lifted from the photos fanned across her kitchen table. "How do you get that? There's nothing here that proves that."

"Rhia," Jenna cried, "Finn was with us all day, so how could he have taken the pictures?"

Rhia crossed her arms on the table. Her butterscotch skin glistened from the humid weather, which only enhanced her beauty. A few damp tendrils clung to the side of her neck. "Okay, I'm going to ask you a few questions and when I'm finished, you tell me if you still think he's innocent."

She sounded unsettlingly like a lawyer. Jenna sat back in her chair, not sure she wanted to play this game.

"Where was he when you tried to phone him? Did you see another person in the bushes? Did you see Finn chasing anyone? Were there other fingerprints on the camera?"

Jenna chewed the inside of her cheek and drew her eyebrows together until a pain throbbed between her eyes.

"Was Finn carrying anything while you were hiking?"

Jenna nodded. "A backpack."

"Do you know for a fact that there wasn't a camera in the backpack trained on you the whole time?"

Rhia's questions stabbed at her like tiny knives, drawing blood with each thrust.

"You really have no evidence at all, other than his word. Did you notice that none of the photos are of Finn?"

Jenna's eyes dropped to the pictures.

Rhia was unrelenting. "What if he's obsessed with you and wants to make you dependent on him to keep you near. Think about it, Jenna. He arranges it so he works with you, so you share a house, and didn't you say he slept in your apartment last night?" She ticked off each point on her fingers. "Sounds to me like he's got it made. If that's his plan."

Jenna's spirits sank to the tips of her unpolished toes.

"If Finn wanted you to need him, he's done a great job. Who did you call when the rock came flying through your window?"

"Finn," she muttered.

"If it is Finn, his plan is working brilliantly, don't you think?"

"Normally, I'd call Everett, but with Finn being so close…"

Rhia patted her hand. "I know you don't want to hear this, but you have to realize, in these cases, it's often a person close to you. He or she could easily divert your suspicions to someone else. Don't underestimate this person's intelligence."

Chapter Twenty

Finn paced in front of his suitcase near the door and ran a hand through his hair. "I just don't feel right leaving you here alone."

"You don't have a choice. One of us has to attend the conference in New Orleans, and I can't leave Chase." She smoothed his hair, straightened his psychedelic tie, and patted his lapels. "It's only three days and you'll be back before you know it. We'll be fine. You're going to make some fantastic connections there. I can feel it."

The corner of his mouth curved in a reluctant grin. "It does sound good."

Jenna watched him run down the front steps. He turned and waved his briefcase before he jumped into his car and roared off.

A feeling of guilty relief swept through her. She loved spending time with him, but right now it was easier to be alone than to wonder about every move he made.

She wanted to blame Rhia for planting suspicious thoughts in her head, but Jenna knew she was right. Until they identified the stalker, she couldn't trust anyone.

Stalker. The word made her shiver. She hadn't really thought of the person quite like that before, but it seemed appropriate after seeing the photographs.

She trudged upstairs, thoughts of Finn heavy on her mind.

"Are you ready to go, Mom?" Chase stood in the doorway, dancing from one foot to the other in his excitement. "You're going to love the game. We're getting really good."

"I just have to find my baseball cap," said Jenna, looking around the room. She slanted him a look. "And my pom-poms, and my cheerleader's skirt."

"No way."

She laughed at his horrified expression. "Okay, I'll leave my pom-poms behind, but I'm wearing my Tigers cap. Don't you have to leave now? I thought you had a short practice before the game." She started to tuck her thick hair under the cap.

"Yeah, but I wanted to tell you that Aunt Irene called."

Jenna's hands stilled. "Oh? Is she coming to your game?" It would be so much easier if the woman just stayed away, but Jenna knew that wouldn't happen.

"No, she sprained her knee. The doctor says she has to stay off it for a few days."

She visualized Finn chasing the stalker through the woods. Holes, hollows, rocks, and roots littered the ground and could make running a problem. "How did she hurt her knee?"

"She said she stepped in a rabbit hole in her back yard. Anyway, she said to tell you to be careful."

Jenna's chin came up. "What did she mean by that?"

He shrugged one shoulder. "I don't know. Maybe she thought you should watch where you're going. She's a worrywart, you know. Gotta go." He was halfway out the door when he turned back. "You'll be there, right? You're coming?"

She kissed his cheek. "Of course. I wouldn't miss it for the world."

Now that Chase was gone, she allowed her anger to simmer. What did Irene mean, 'be careful'? Was that a real threat or just a ploy to make Jenna uncomfortable? The nerve of her to send double-edged messages through Chase. Jenna didn't believe for an instant that her sister-in-law had suddenly begun worrying about her welfare. She would have to lay down some ground rules if Irene tried that trick again.

She tucked the last strands of hair under her cap. A quick look in the mirror brought a sigh to her lips. Her thick hair filled the hat and left a huge bulge on top as if her head was swollen like an alien invader. She ripped the hat off and allowed the mass of curls to hang loose, then plunked the cap on again and left the apartment.

Jenna enjoyed the warm sun on her back as she strolled to the park. Every year the town gave awards to the most beautiful and most original gardens and the homeowners had outdone themselves. Multi-colored petunias vied for attention with coddled rose bushes and English-style gardens full of perennials. She raised her face to the sky and inhaled the sweet potpourri of wild and domestic flowers intermingled with fresh-cut grass.

With only the faint sound of sneakers slapping against the pavement, Everett appeared by her side.

"Another snow day?" she asked with a grin, surprised but pleased at the company.

"No, the prof decided he wanted to get off his fat butt and teach a class instead of me doing all the work. So, I'm free." He tugged at his shirt sleeve, then pulled it down to his wrist again.

"Lucky me, but why are you here? Did you know Chase had a game today?"

He nodded. "Irene told me."

At her look, he hastened to explain. "I check up on her from time to time. She doesn't have anyone now, and I feel sorry for her."

She didn't feel at all sorry for the woman at the moment, but she smiled and said, "That's sweet of you."

They entered the ball park and found a place at the top of the stands where they had a clear view of Chase's dugout.

"Aren't you a little warm?" asked Jenna, eyeing his long-sleeved shirt.

He shrugged the same way Chase had a half hour earlier. One shoulder. "I'm okay."

"And what did you do there?" She pointed to the bandage on his chin.

"I sliced off a layer of skin while shaving. It's nothing. Look, they're starting. Chase will be happy. He's playing shortstop today."

The parents in the stands cheered and applauded as the home team took the field. Chase found them in the crowd and gave a small wave of his glove. He looked like he was trying to keep a grin off his face.

"He's thrilled you're here," Everett said.

Tears threatened and she swallowed a lump in her throat. "Me, too."

Chase got the first two outs and, after a pop fly to center field, his team hustled in to take their turn at bat.

"Everett, can you do me a favor?"

He sat up taller. "Of course. You know I'd do anything for you." He seemed inordinately pleased and eager to help.

"Remember Billy Channing? The guy you had a run-in with in my old apartment building?"

A scowl wrinkled his forehead. "What about him?"

"Oh, Chase is up to bat. Yay, Chase!"

Everett's eyes were slow to leave hers and he seemed to have lost pleasure in the event. Jenna didn't let his sudden mood distract her. She clapped and called out encouragement as Chase fouled off one ball after another. Finally, he took a mighty swing and the ball sailed over the left fielder's head.

"Go, Chase, run, run!" Her voice was drowned out by the screams of the coaches and players, but she stood so he could look up and see her when he crossed home plate. She waved an arm and whistled, and he gave her the thumbs up sign, a huge grin splitting his face.

Everett remained seated. When she sat down, still glowing from Chase's home run, he asked, "What's he done?"

"What? Oh, Billy, right. I'm not sure he's done anything, but I wanted you to find out about him." She sighed. "Someone's been making a pest of him- or herself, and it may be Billy."

"What do you mean 'a pest'? Has he been bothering you?" He seemed ready to leap off the stands and find the man.

She placed a hand on his arm. "Well, he came to the office once, but that's not it." She took a deep breath, ignoring Rhia's warnings about suspecting everyone, including Everett, and plunged on. "Someone's been following me. They've hidden in our bushes and taken pictures. I don't think Billy could afford the film for a camera, let alone an expensive piece of equipment like that, but I need to know for sure. Do you think you could check him out? See what he's up to these days?"

"That scumbag," he muttered. He patted her hand and his lips moved in what was supposed to be a reassuring smile. "Don't you worry. I'll protect you. I'll find out what this guy's up to."

The next time Chase got up to bat, Everett yelled as loudly as Jenna. "Watch the ball, Chase. Keep your elbow up. Step into it," he called.

A woman in front of them turned and smiled. "Your son is really good."

Everett nodded. "Yes, he's a natural."

Jenna frowned, but didn't scold him for not correcting the woman. He probably wanted to avoid a long explanation. She shrugged and turned her attention to the game.

Chase's team won by four runs and he was jubilant as they walked home. "Did you see my home run, Mom? That ball just flew off the bat." He mimed an enthusiastic swing and spun himself around.

"How could I miss it? It was huge."

Everett chuckled. "The next Al Kaline."

Chase bounced ahead and Everett and Jenna sauntered toward her home.

"Are you planning some advertising for the business?" asked Everett.

Jenna tilted her head. "No, we're starting off with just a few clients until we get our feet under us. Why do you ask?"

"Uh, no reason."

She looked at him suspiciously. "Come on, why did you ask about advertising."

He shrugged. "It's just that I saw Sawyer buying a camera in Detroit a few weeks ago. I just assumed he wanted to take pictures for your pamphlets or something. Maybe he's going on vacation."

She tried to hide her discomfort. "As a matter of fact, he is on a kind of vacation. He's gone to New Orleans for a training and staff development conference. Maybe he wanted to bring us back some pictures."

"Yeah, maybe. When will he be back?"

"Saturday night."

He smiled and showed his tiny teeth peeking out of pink gums. "Chase," he called. "How would you like a pizza for supper tonight? We can celebrate your win."

"Yahoo," the boy yelled. "Can we, Mom?"

Jenna sighed. She wished Everett had checked with her before offering the treat to her son. She already had chicken set out to thaw.

She looked at Chase's expectant face and knew she couldn't reject the offer. "Sure," she said with a smile.

"We have to fatten that boy up, if he's going to play major league baseball. Right, Chase?"

"Right, Uncle Ev. Can you play catch with me this afternoon while Mom's at work?"

"I'd love to." He turned to Jenna and added, "That is, if it's okay with your mom."

Once again, she felt like she was being put in a position where she couldn't say no. "Okay, but only if you do your chores first."

He turned to Everett. "I have to clean my room, then I can go out. Will you wait?"

Ev nodded.

They entered the house and Chase led his 'uncle' up the stairs while Jenna sat at her desk and checked her e-mail. She breathed a sigh of relief when no new messages appeared from Karma. They had become a daily occurrence and she dreaded every one.

For the next few hours, she immersed herself in her work until she smelled the rich aroma of Italian sausage and tomato sauce laced with Italian herbs. She looked up when a pair of scuffed Nikes appeared by her desk.

"You order a pizza, lady?" The delivery boy's green hair stuck out in spikes like the Statue of Liberty's crown.

"I'll get that," said Everett. He stepped onto the bottom step and reached for his wallet. "Are you coming, Jenna? We've got a hungry boy up there."

"I'll be right up."

When the delivery boy left, Ev locked the front door and she packed up her work. She joined him on the stairs and they entered the apartment together.

Chase had set out plates and napkins and, within seconds, they were enjoying their first savory bites of pizza.

"I like your apartment," said Everett between mouthfuls. He nodded toward a corner of the room. "Why are your books on the floor?"

Jenna twisted her lips. "I haven't had time to get a book shelf. It's hard without a car. Finn would take me, but he's been so busy I hate to bother him." Besides, she wanted to do it herself.

"You could have asked me." He put his pizza down and forced her to look at him.

"You've already done too much for us. I can't keep relying on you for everything."

"Sure, you can."

Jenna shrugged and returned to her pizza. She worked hard for her independence and didn't want to turn to a man every time she needed something. "I'll get it done."

After a boisterous game of Monopoly, Chase headed for bed and Everett left for home. Jenna waved from the front window. He seemed happier than he'd been in years and she was glad for him. Maybe he was getting closer to the promotion he'd been waiting for, or perhaps he'd found a girlfriend. Irene? He'd been seeing her a lot lately. Wouldn't that be nice for everyone. It would give Irene something better to do than to try to make Jenna's life hell, and it would put some enjoyment into his life and possibly raise his self-esteem. She smiled and pulled the blinds down to hide the night.

The next morning Jenna woke to the sound of the doorbell. Finn had rigged it so that a caller could ring either Jenna's or his apartment. Still muddled by sleep, she threw on a robe and peeked out the front window. Everett's car stood in the driveway.

"What on earth is he doing here?" she muttered as she made her way downstairs.

She tried to pat her hair into some semblance of normalcy, but gave up when it insisted on springing out on all sides. She opened the front door and leaned against the jamb.

"Good morning," he said, too sprightly for six o'clock in the morning.

He held a long flat cardboard box under one arm and an assortment of tools in a leather pouch in the other hand.

"What are you doing here this early?" she asked. She tried to hide a yawn with one hand.

"I have to teach a class at eight-thirty," he said, "so, I wanted to get this finished before I went in."

"Get what finished?" She felt like she had missed something along the way.

"Your new bookshelf?" He jiggled the box slightly.

"My what?"

He squeezed his way through the doorway and headed up the stairs. "You said yesterday you needed a new bookshelf, but it was too hard to get without a car, so I went out and picked you up one. I'll put it up this morning."

"Everett, I didn't mean for you to get one. I would have done it eventually." She followed him up the stairs, talking to his calves.

"I know, but it's easier for me to do it. You should never be ashamed to ask for my help."

"I'm not ashamed," she spluttered.

"Okay, too proud, then. I like to help you." He stood back while she opened her apartment door. "Now, where do you want to put this thing?"

Chapter Twenty-One

On Saturday morning, Everett was back and he insisted on taking them to the zoo. Although he and Chase seemed to enjoy themselves, Jenna was distracted by Finn's imminent return. She couldn't help wondering why he would buy an expensive camera and if that had anything to do with the one he said he found in the bushes.

Also, she seemed to be free of the stalker's pranks since Finn's departure. What did that mean? Was that a coincidence?

She missed him and couldn't wait to see him, yet at the same time she dreaded it.

"Where to next?" asked Everett, breaking in on her thoughts.

Chase climbed into the roomy front seat between her and Everett. "Home, please," she said. "Finn will be back soon and I promised him dinner at our place tonight."

His mouth turned down. "You shouldn't let that guy in your apartment. I don't trust him."

"Everett, Finn's been wonderful to us." She stopped short of saying she trusted him implicitly. She *wanted* to trust him. That should count for something.

Everett remained silent during the trip home and, since Chase had a new jungle book to leaf through, it left Jenna time to think about how she'd broach the subject of the camera with Finn.

They pulled into the driveway behind the lime-green Barracuda.

"He's home!" cried Chase. "Let me out, Mom. Thanks Uncle Everett." He bounded up the stairs.

"Thanks for everything, the trip today and the bookshelf," she said over the roof of the car. "We're so lucky to have a friend like you."

He looked at the door through which Chase had just darted, and grunted.

"Oh, don't worry about him. He's just excited about seeing Finn. He's lucky he has two men to choose from."

"So do you."

Jenna laughed. "Hopefully, I don't have to choose between you. I'd like to keep you both as friends. Bye, and thanks again." She walked into the house and didn't hear his car roll away until she was halfway up the stairs to her apartment.

She decided to put off her discussion with Finn until after Chase went to bed.

As she opened her door, she heard a sound like a dying elephant.

"Look, Mom. Look what Finn brought me." He held a brass toy trumpet in one hand. "It really works." He blew into it and the horrible sound filled the room.

Jenna rolled her eyes. "Thanks a lot."

Finn laughed. Her heart tripped at the sound of his rich, melodious laugh. His eyes seemed greener than ever before.

"What did you get for Mom?" Chase's excitement was palpable.

"Chase," she reprimanded.

Finn dug into the inside pocket of his suit coat and pulled out a long blue velvet box. He handed it to her and looked as eager as Chase for her to open it.

Carefully, she opened the hinged lid and pulled out a silver bracelet adorned with tiny silver charms. Miniature trumpets, saxophones, and flutes dangled from the woven chain and caught in the light.

"Oh, Finn, it's beautiful."

Chase grunted and muttered, "I like mine better."

She chopped vegetables for a stir fry and listened with half an ear as Chase talked to Finn about Margie, the lone girl on his baseball team.

"She's awesome. She runs faster than most of the guys."

This was the first time she'd heard Chase mention Margie and it worried her that he was growing up too fast. She didn't want him to be interested in girls yet. As selfish as it seemed, she wanted to be the most important female in his life, at least for a few more years.

"Really?" said Finn.

"Except for me, of course."

"Of course. Have you asked her over here to play?"

"No way. She's a girl," he said, as if that explained everything.

Jenna smiled to herself and breathed easier. That's my boy.

Once again, Finn's presence seemed to create a family atmosphere. They laughed and chattered and exchanged news as if he'd been gone for weeks. Jenna let Chase stay up later than usual, but by ten o'clock he had drifted off to sleep, curled up on the sofa between them, his head on her lap.

"Now, you can tell me what's on your mind," said Finn. He turned sideways on the couch, so he could look directly at her.

"What do you mean?"

"I mean you've been acting funny all night, staring at me as if trying to read some secret code through my skin."

She sighed. "I'm sorry. I didn't mean to be rude." She looked down and brushed a hand across Chase's silky hair.

"I'm not worried about your manners. What is it?"

She looked into his eyes and took a deep breath. "Did you buy a camera a few weeks ago?"

Finn's body tensed. "No, why?"

"Have you looked at cameras lately?"

"No. What's this all about?"

Jenna rubbed her forehead. "Everett said he saw you buying a camera."

"Well, he's lying. I haven't bought one."

"Why would he lie?"

"Heck if I know. You tell me."

Neither said a word. She continued to smooth Chase's hair, her lips pushed out, frustrated at the impasse.

"Wait a minute," said Finn. "Did you tell him about us finding the camera in the bushes?"

"Well, yes, but that was before."

"There you go. That's your answer."

"What answer?"

"He's just trying to make you think I'm the one with the camera, that I'm the person following you." He shook his head. "I'm telling you, that guy is a piece of work."

"I know you don't like him, but…"

"Jenna, he's trying to mess with your mind. You don't believe any of his baloney, do you?" At her silence, he threw his arms in the air.

"Finn, he's a friend of mine and, as far as I know, he's never lied to me before."

"So, you believe him over me."

"I didn't say that."

"Then, what are you saying?"

"I don't know!" she yelled in confusion.

Chase fidgeted in his sleep.

"I don't know," she continued in a whisper. "I'm so confused. I don't understand why any of this is happening."

"Let's look at this logically," he said. "How could I have taken those pictures? I was with you the whole day?"

"You weren't in any of the pictures. You could have had a camera hidden in your backpack."

He gasped. "You really think it's me."

"No, I don't," she said, shaking her head. "But, I can't rule you out, either. That's the problem."

He stood and glared down at her. "Then, why the hell am I in your apartment if you don't trust me? I shouldn't even be here." He strode to the door and stormed out, slamming the heavy wooden panel behind him.

Chase jerked awake. "Where's Finn?"

"He had to go home, honey. Let's get you to bed."

Jenna's sleep was anything but restful that night. Dreams skittered in and out like mice gnawing at the edges of her mind. Snatches of days merged in a strange conglomeration that made no sense upon awakening.

She got out of bed before sunrise and sat on her window seat with a cup of tea to watch the sky turn from black to mauve to rose and, finally, to gold as the sun gave birth to a new day.

At seven o'clock, Finn appeared on the back lawn. Shoulders hunched, hands in his pockets, head down, he presented the picture of dejection. Jenna's heart shimmied as she thought of the hurt her mistrust had caused him.

She leaned her head against the window and contemplated rapping on it to get his attention. He moved away from the house, a backpack slung over one shoulder, and she let him go. Nothing had changed. She couldn't take back her words or pretend she trusted him implicitly. It wasn't true, no matter how much she wanted it to be.

He crossed the yard, leaped over the creek, and disappeared into the woods behind the house. She waited for an hour, the tea in her mug cooling, but he didn't return.

When she heard Chase stirring in his room, she went to the kitchen to start breakfast. Irene's seemingly innocuous warning flitted through her mind. She wondered how much Chase knew about his aunt.

"Mmmm. What's that?" he asked. He slid into his seat at the table.

She placed the plate in front of him. "Belgian waffles."

He plucked a strawberry and licked off the whipped cream, then dipped it again. "Aren't you having any?"

Jenna shook her head. "Not hungry right now. I'll eat later."

He dove into his breakfast, elbows high in the air as he cut and skewered with knife and fork.

"Chase, does Aunt Irene have a computer at home?"

"Mmmhmm," he said, his mouth full.

"Can she get the Internet and e-mail on it?"

He nodded and licked whipped cream from the corner of his mouth. "She works at home sometimes and her boss sends her messages. She let me try it once."

Jenna poured him a glass of milk and tried to sound nonchalant. Her first suspicions were confirmed. Now, for the rest. "Do you know if she kept any of your father's things?"

He swallowed and scrunched his face. "I wasn't supposed to go into the spare bedroom."

"But did you?"

He stared at her a few seconds, obviously wondering if he'd get into trouble if he told her the truth. He set down his fork and nodded. "I wouldn't have, but sometimes I'd see her come out of that room and her eyes would be all red as if she'd been crying. So, I went in."

"What did you see?"

He shrugged. "A bunch of books, some clothes, like suits and ties, black shiny shoes. You should have seen these shoes. They were huge!"

Jenna pictured Angus' long white feet and the black leather shoes he polished every morning before leaving for work. She smiled. "What else?"

"Papers and stuff. A watch."

"What made you think they were your father's?"

"I didn't know at first, but then I saw a paper on the wall. In a frame and covered with glass, like it was a picture, but it was just a paper. I saw my name on it. Well, not my name exactly, but it said 'McDougall'. Angus McDougall. That was my father, right?"

"Yes."

He sighed. "I asked Aunt Irene, but she got really upset."

"Did you see any writing paper and envelopes with your father's name on them?"

"No. I only went in there once, because Aunt Irene locked it after that." He tilted his head. "Why all the questions, Mom?"

Jenna sat back in her chair, only now realizing she had been leaning in, eager for every tidbit of information. "There are a few things that belonged to your father that I think you should have." That was true, but he didn't need to know the other reasons for her interest.

"Like what?"

"Well, the watch, for one. The university gave it to him. He was very proud of that watch. Are you finished?" She reached for his plate.

"Yup. Can I..." He stopped at the sound of the doorbell. "I'll get it," he said and ran from the room.

Chase returned a few minutes later holding a long white box. "The man let me sign for it," he said proudly. "He said they're flowers. Can I go to Jason's house?"

She kissed him goodbye and watched him race out the door. Flowers clearly didn't hold any interest for him.

Jenna turned her attention to the white box. Perhaps Finn had forgiven her and had sent them as a peace offering. Eagerly, she lifted the lid. And cringed.

White roses. Angus' favorites. A flurry of images flashed through her mind. Dark mahogany caskets, draped with huge bouquets of white roses, symbols of sorrow; an overwhelming feeling of dread and helplessness as she watched her parents being lowered into the cold ground; Angus' macabre glee at the way her face paled every time he brought them home, pretending to offer a loving gift.

A pink note nestled among the barbed stems. With trembling fingers, she turned the note over and shuddered. As she yanked her hand away, a thorn pierced her finger. A drop of blood fell onto one of the flawless petals, a crimson tattoo on white skin.

She pressed her finger to her mouth and tasted copper. Who could have known the exact words Angus used when he'd accused her of flirting with another man. 'REMEMBER WHO OWNS YOU' was written in block letters on the pink paper. Angus would scream those words over the phone from his office, then again later in their apartment where he could punctuate his words with brute force.

Would he share that with his assistant? His sister? Complain of his wife's disloyalty to an understanding ear?

She nodded. Irene would enjoy and encourage that kind of confession.

Jenna closed the box and resolved to be more wary of the woman who seemed to have access to all of her failed and tattered dreams.

Chapter Twenty-Two

Karma sniffed the single white rose and placed it gently in a vase on the table. The pale petals danced in the flickering golden candlelight.

A sneer crossed Karma's face. This latest intervention, the roses, should have been unnecessary. It could have been all over, a satisfying end in place, but Jenna persisted in encouraging the guard dog. That couldn't be allowed. She must pay for her transgression.

A smile of satisfaction replaced the sneer. The message on the note had come from a long-forgotten memory that had resurfaced in a moment of pure brilliance. Angus hadn't been reticent about sharing his feelings about his young wife. With a little nudging, he had been quite willing to brag about his 'ownership'. Like a dog, she belonged to him. Pavlov's dog. She still trembled whenever she saw white roses.

Karma spat on the floor. Such games only delayed the inevitable. Anger rose, hot and red, threatening to boil over.

With a force of will, Karma sat in the over-stuffed easy chair facing the montage of photos on the wall. Enlarged to life-sized, Jenna's face had been caught and held in a myriad of emotions. She squinted in the sunlight, laughed down at her son, and spent quiet moments reading on her windowsill. All were caught by Karma's camera. A favorite was the age old yin-yang symbol, two opposite energy forces, representing the balance and harmony which exists in all nature. The yin side, the dark, breeding, cold, wet side, held Jenna's profile. On the inverted yang side, the active, warm, bright, procreative side, Karma's profile faced hers. Karma knew their lives were interwoven, their destines entwined. Now, she must realize it, too.

Nothing could stop the momentum of their collision. Not even the guard dog.

Chapter Twenty-Three

A daisy was thrust under Jenna's nose. The earthy scent of wildflower meadows filled her senses. She looked up from the array of papers that covered her desk. Finn stood beside her desk, a shy smile curving his full lips.

"I picked a bunch of daisies, but I plucked the petals from the rest. You know, 'she hates me, she hates me not.' It's taken me three hours to get up the nerve to give them, it, to you."

Jenna sighed and stood to accept the flower from his outstretched hand. "I'm so sor…"

He held up his hand. "I'm the one who's sorry. I understand why you feel you have to suspect everyone. I don't agree with it, but I understand it."

At Jenna's questioning look he continued.

"I went for a long hike yesterday and thought about everything that's happened and what you said."

She smiled. "And you had an epiphany?"

"No, I still didn't understand it, so I went to see Rhia."

"To ask her to explain it to you?"

"Heck, no. I went over to tear a strip off her for filling your head with fear and garbage."

At her look of outrage, he ducked and raised a hand to shield his head.

"I know, I know. I'm a jackass, but I've seen the error of my ways. Believe me, that woman can take care of herself."

Jenna swatted him with the daisy, sending petals fluttering to the floor. "She put you in your place, did she?"

"To put it mildly. She started ranting and poked her fingernail into my chest with every point she made." He rubbed his chest, as if it still pained him. "I had to call 'uncle' or she would have boiled me in her eye of newt soup."

"Good for Rhia."

"You women always stick together, don't you?"

Jenna nodded solemnly. "It's a rule."

"Figures. Anyway, after she calmed down, we had a good talk and she convinced me that it's in your best interests to treat everyone like a suspect. She said that most stalkers are someone the woman knows."

Jenna nodded.

"Scary stuff, but it's not me." His eyes searched hers.

"I know."

Finn's strong white teeth flashed in a smile. "Good."

"I went to see Rhia yesterday, too," said Jenna. She brought the tattered daisy to her nose and peered over it.

"I saw the roses. She seems to like them."

Jenna shuddered. "She can have them."

Finn's eyebrows drew together. "Another gift?"

She nodded. To prove that she really did trust him, she fished out a note from a cookie tin that had been pushed to the back of her top desk drawer and handed it to Finn.

He scanned the note quickly. "Holy shit," he muttered. "This sounds just like Professor McDougall."

Shock radiated from Jenna's fingertips to her toes. Her mind numbed. Finn had never even mentioned meeting Angus before, and now he sounded like he knew him. She felt like she had entered a parallel universe, one where an impossibly insane event suddenly became possible. She cocked her head to one side and tried to breathe evenly. "How do you know what my husband sounded like?"

He snorted. "Anyone who ever took a course from him knew how he felt about his wife. He always emphasized 'my' when talking about you, as if warning everyone else off. I figured that was why you dropped out after you got married. His jealousy couldn't handle you being surrounded by young college men."

Her consternation over his original statement warred with the need to respond to his faulty theory about why she left school. She would have explained that she and Angus had made that decision together, but his assumption made her pause. Angus had always been a master at manipulating situations. She remembered him asking her very simply, 'Do you want to be a good wife, or a good college student? You can't be both. It's your decision, of course.' And it had been her decision, but he knew how desperately she needed someone to love. After the death of her parents she had been cast adrift in a world that suddenly seemed empty of love and comforting arms. Angus had offered that at a price, and she had been eager to pay it.

"I didn't know you went to the university. Why didn't you mention that before?" she asked. Anger had seeped into her voice. Exactly what kind of game was he playing?

Finn shrugged and turned toward the window, his eyes obviously seeing something other than the golden light pouring in and creating a honey pool on the floor.

"I only went to school for one year, then I dropped out. I figured you didn't need to hear anymore about Angus than you had to, so I never mentioned it." He glanced at Jenna. "Now don't look like that. There's nothing suspect in this. I was a kid who took a course from your husband. I had a few conversations with him. I didn't like his whole domineering attitude, so I tried to avoid him as much as possible."

She allowed him to take her hands, the daisy bending toward her as if pleading his case. "Look, it's nothing. Really," he cried, his voice higher in anxiety. "It's just Finnegan Begin-again striking again. I told you, that's the story of my life."

Jenna nodded and molded her face into a smile. It felt stiff, like cold plasticine. She tried to ignore the anvil sitting on her chest. She hated to doubt him.

"I shouldn't have told you. Now, I'm back on your black list."

"No, no, it's okay. I just have to get used to the idea that you had a connection with my husband." She took a deep breath to dispel the sensation of being kicked in the stomach. "I had another dream last night."

Finn's eyebrows jerked up as if pulled by an invisible puppeteer. "Anything new?"

She ran her fingers through her auburn mane. "I dreamed I was scrambling for the gun in Angus' nightstand. I was afraid. So afraid." She wrapped her arms around herself and Finn moved closer. "But not for me, for...I don't know. I felt this overwhelming sense of foreboding. I can't explain it."

"Did you touch the gun?"

Jenna sighed. "Yes. I remember picking it up, holding it. It was heavy, so heavy. I was surprised at its weight. I'd never touched it before."

"That still doesn't mean you shot it." Finn rubbed her back, a comforting presence to ward off the memories that brought goose bumps to her arms.

"No, but that was the gun that killed Angus, and my fingerprints were on it."

"And the police convicted you on that?"

Finn's naive statement brought a smile to her lips. "You have to admit, it's pretty damning evidence."

"Totally circumstantial."

"They also had Irene providing them with a motive. She said that we fought all the time, which was true, and that I had threatened to kill him, which was a lie."

He shook his head. "What are you going to do?"

"I don't know."

"Have you thought of digging up the records from the case?"

Jenna tried to suppress an unladylike snort. "I'm quite sure that any shred of evidence that could have cleared me is long gone."

"Now, that's a cynical attitude."

She straightened her spine. "You try spending eight years of your life in prison for a crime you didn't commit and see if you have faith in the system."

"Point taken. I'm sorry."

Jenna waved away his apology and moved toward the window. "What I need," she said, half to herself, "is to talk to a real person. Someone who was there."

"The detectives on your case." Finn had followed her to the window and stood directly behind her. He brushed aside her hair and gently rubbed the knotted neck muscles with his thumbs.

She groaned with pleasure, warm sensations crawling down her spine, and tried to remember their conversation. "Yes, but they won't talk to me."

"Why not?"

She twisted her neck to look up into his face. "If you helped put a person away for murder, would you want to talk to them?" She laughed and turned back to look out at the yard. "I wouldn't. I'd be afraid they were coming to kill me. Or to exact revenge," she added, dramatically.

"It's worth a try."

"It would be a waste of a trip." His thumbs made tiny circles from her ears to her shoulders, sending relaxation ripples through her taut muscles.

"What do you have to lose?"

She shrugged. "Nothing, I guess."

"Great, I'll take you in on Saturday."

Finn pulled her against his chest. She jerked when she felt his warm breath and lips on her neck, but soon melted under his caress. A tiny corner of her mind cried out, 'Stop! What are you doing? You don't know if you can trust this man.' She ignored it and twisted in the arms that had encircled her. She raised on tiptoe and offered her mouth.

Their kiss was sweet, deep. Jenna's entire body hummed with sensation. He tasted like toothpaste and coffee. He felt like total man in a chambray shirt. She arched toward him and felt his hands gliding over her back, drawing her closer.

The shrill ring of the telephone startled them apart.

Finn groaned. "Just leave it," he said, and reached for her again.

"I can't," said Jenna. "It might be Chase. Sometimes he forgets to use the second line." She hurried to the phone.

"Hello?"

"Jenna? Did you have to run to the phone? You sound breathless." Everett's voice brought her down from her brief ride in the clouds.

"Hi, Everett." She watched Finn's face darken. "What's up?" She flipped a pen through her fingers like a tiny baton.

"I looked up your admirer yesterday."

Her hand stilled. "Pardon? What admirer?" Did Everett know who was tormenting her?

"Billy Channing. Remember, you asked me to find out about him."

"Right." Jenna exhaled and let the tension trickle from her body. "Did you find anything?"

"He won't be bothering you again."

Alarm raised her voice. "Everett, what did you do?"

He chuckled. "I didn't have to do anything. The dunce did it to himself. The cops picked him up again."

"What did he get caught for this time?"

"Stealing from a security company."

"What could he possibly want from a security company?"

"A computer. Actually, just a monitor. The dumb ass didn't know he needed the CPU, too." Everett seemed to find the other man's ignorance hilarious.

Jenna felt a twinge of guilt. She had told him to come back when he had a computer. Surely, he wouldn't think she meant he should steal one.

Chapter Twenty-Four

Jenna trembled as she climbed the pitted concrete steps to the High Street Police Station. She stilled the tiny voice urging her not to cross the threshold. The last time she'd been here, they had taken away her freedom and her son for eight years.

"It's different now," she muttered.

"Pardon?" asked Finn. "You okay?"

"Sure, sure." She inhaled deeply and exhaled. Her bangs fluttered.

He reached around her to open the door and coaxed her forward. They stepped into the room and Jenna wrinkled her nose at the smell of sweat, stale cigarettes, and old booze. There was barely an inch of space on the benches to the left and right of the door.

A woman in stiletto heels and a tube top sat nearest the door, a bored expression pulling down the corners of her painted mouth. She filed her nails and ignored the grimy bag lady beside her who threatened to fall off the bench in her sleep. Two youths with identical Satanic tattoos glared at them. She looked away and was grateful for Finn's solid presence behind her.

His hand on her lower back pressed her toward the huge raised desk behind which sat a uniformed officer whose expression dared anyone to bother him. His nametag said he was Sergeant S. Fryfogle.

Jenna would have held back, but Finn had no such reticence.

"Excuse me, sir."

The officer turned the page of his newspaper, but didn't look up.

Finn leaned his hands on the edge of the desk. "This will only take a minute. If you wouldn't mind."

The Sergeant put down the paper, scratched his balding head, and scowled at Finn. "Are you blind?"

"Funny you should ask," said Finn, a huge smile pasted on his face. "I'm not blind, but I sure am looking for someone. We'd like to talk to a couple of detectives."

A nod toward the stairs told them where to go. "Help yourself. Second floor."

He started to pick up the paper again, but Finn's hand held it down. Jenna flinched at the daggers the man was throwing with his eyes, but Finn kept his hand firmly in place.

"Two specific detectives. Mickey O'Grady and Judy Farandino."

Sergeant Fryfogle's face hardened at the woman's name and his eyes drilled Finn's. "What do you want with Judy?"

"We have a few questions about a case she was on a few years back."

"Well, you can't talk to her," he said gruffly and cleared his throat.

"Why not?"

"She's dead. Some scumbag stabbed her six months ago."

Finn withdrew his hand, but didn't move away from the desk. "I'm sorry."

"Yeah, everyone's always sorry." He seemed to lose interest in his newspaper. He folded it and stuffed it under his desk.

"What about Mickey O'Grady? Is he still around?"

"Nope. Retired."

"Where can we find him?"

"You can't."

"We just want to talk to him. Ask a few questions."

"That's what they all say. Next thing, I read a headline: Cop Found Dead in Home." He kicked the newspaper under his desk for emphasis.

"Look," growled Finn.

Jenna could see his frustration level was rising with each word. She stepped forward. "Excuse me, Sergeant Fryfogle. We're terribly sorry to bother you. I understand why you can't give out his address." She smiled and looked around the room. "You must get a lot of crazy people in here."

A tiny grin tugged at one corner of his mouth. He nodded. "You're right there, ma'am. A lot of crackpots."

"It must be difficult being a police officer, always putting your life on the line."

He nodded again. "It's tough."

"I don't want to breach Mr. O'Grady's security. I know that's important, so perhaps you could just give me his phone number."

"Nope, can't do that either."

Jenna gritted her teeth. A man with long fingernails, a blonde wig, and a pink skirt yelled in a falsetto voice, "Stewie, I've been waiting for hours."

"Shut up, Raquel," shouted the Sergeant. "You'll get your turn." The man flounced back to a bench, tottering on three-inch heels.

"Sergeant Fryfogle, it's very important that I speak to Detective O'Grady about a case he ran. Is there anyway you could help us out?" Jenna wished she could flutter her eyelashes or shed a tear or two, but she'd never been much for artifice. She offered a wide-eyed gaze instead.

He looked at her and sighed. "I guess I could call him, see if he wants to talk to you."

She brightened and smiled hugely. "That would be wonderful. Thank you so much, Sergeant."

Finn squeezed her hand while the Sergeant carried on a low-voiced conversation into the phone. Finally, he thumped it back into its cradle.

"He says you can go out there right now," he said angrily. "Loneliness has eaten all of his brain cells, the silly fool."

"Could you write his address down for us?" asked Jenna.

"No. Not until I see some identification. From both of you," he added, giving Finn a hard look. "If anything happens to Mickey, I'm coming after you two personally."

They dug out their wallets and flipped them open for him. He wrote down their names and address and shoved the paper into his front pocket. Still muttering about his foolish friend, he spun a Rolodex and pulled out an address card. He jotted the address on a piece of paper, folded it, and handed it to Jenna.

A half hour later, on a pampered fragment of land, they found O'Grady's bungalow. The other homes along the street sagged in neglect, hobos flanking Harriet Nelson.

They skirted the picket fence, passed neat rows of marigolds, and rapped on the freshly painted front door.

"Boy, this guy doesn't have enough to do," whispered Finn.

Albert Einstein with a perm answered the door. "Come in, come in."

Jenna tried not to stare at the white hair that bloomed from his head. Big hair, her mother would have called it. Faded red strands streaked his walrus mustache.

"You must be the couple from the station. Yes?" His gravelly voice held the trace of an Irish accent.

"Me da was a shipbuilder," he said. He waved a hand at the miniature sailing vessels on every level surface around the room. "Come see what I'm working on."

"Actually, can we…" Jenna started, but he left the room, leaving them no choice but to follow.

He led them to a small room off the kitchen where a partially built schooner awaited his touch. The boat was no taller than a juice glass. "Watch this," he said, his voice laced with excitement. He pulled a tiny thread attached to the mast and the boat collapsed into a narrow row of sticks.

Jenna gasped. "Oh, no, all that work."

He laughed and pulled the string again. The vessel reconstructed itself.

Jenna walked around the table and realized the vessel hadn't broken apart, but had been carefully designed to fold in on itself.

"What do you think it's for?"

She looked up at the detective, his eyes dancing beneath white bushy eyebrows.

Finn squinted his eyes and stared at the model, lips pursed. "It's to put a ship in a bottle," he said finally.

"Bingo!" yelled Detective O'Grady. "Excellent. Go to the head of the class." He reached for a whiskey bottle under the table and plunked it on the workbench. "This bottle, to be precise."

Finn squatted to get a better look. "That's awesome." He sounded like an eight-year-old.

The detective thumped his chest. "I designed it meself."

Jenna groaned inwardly. The two men could be standing here for hours if she didn't steer them back toward the purpose of the visit.

"Detective O'Grady, would you mind if we asked a few questions about one of your cases from eight years ago?"

"Oh, sure, sure. Be patient, lass, we'll get to that. Would you like a cup of tea?"

"N...," she started.

"Yes, that would be very nice. Thanks," said Finn.

He and Jenna returned to the living room while the detective bustled around his immaculate kitchen.

"Why did you do that?" she whispered to Finn.

"He's a lonely old man," he whispered back. "It won't hurt us to spend a little time with him, and it may pay off when we want him to give us information."

She sank into a green plaid armchair and felt it swallow her up, the springs sagging to the floor. She ignored Finn's laugh and helping hand as she struggled out of the chair.

When they were finally settled with their cups of tea and shortbread cookies, Jenna broached the subject of their visit. "Detective O'Grady, eight years ago you investigated the death of Angus McDougall."

"McDougall, McDougall," he said. He stared at the ceiling and seemed to search his cobwebbed memories. Finally, he pierced Jenna with a steel blue stare. "Ah, yes, you were convicted of your husband's murder, weren't you?"

Chapter Twenty-Five

Jenna tried to respond, but shock stilled her tongue. Her mouth felt like it had filled with dust.

"H-how..." She swallowed and tried again. "How did you...?"

"I recognized you when you walked in the door. You haven't changed much over these many years." He chuckled at her look of consternation. "Besides that, Sarge did a search on both of you. He called me just before you arrived. Sarge is a little uptight about my visits with convicted felons."

Jenna and Finn exchanged a look. "There have been others?" he asked.

The corner of the detective's mouth hitched up and he leaned back in his chair, arms folded across his chest. "Kind of a hobby, you might say."

Jenna scrunched her face. "Talking to criminals?"

"Aye. I miss the job, you see. I have a curious soul and I want, nay, I need, to know what makes Man do the horrific things he does. As me mam would say, Mickey, you'd want to unravel your socks if you thought the thread would lead you to an answer." His deep rumbling laughter filled the room. "They used to call me the Irish bulldog at the station house, because once I got my teeth into something I wouldn't let go."

"But you were satisfied with the McDougall case," said Finn, more a statement than a question.

His shaggy head wagged from side to side. "Satisfied is a relative term, lad."

Jenna's heart kicked up a notch. She leaned forward and begged him with her eyes for some sign that he believed in her innocence.

"My partner, Judy Farandino, God rest her soul, never felt easy about the whole case. We stared at the evidence until our eyes crossed. Of course, the DA was pressuring us to get this case tied up."

He nodded at Jenna. "It's a shame you couldn't defend yourself, lass."

She swallowed. Hope crowded her throat, but soon turned to ash when she remembered that this man hadn't stopped the misguided march of justice.

"Can you tell us what made Detective Farandino uneasy?" asked Finn. "Was there something that couldn't be explained away?"

O'Grady nodded and poured more tea into each cup, seeming to mull over the question. Finally, he sank back into his chair and held his teacup to his chin. They waited while he recalled the bits and pieces of the case he had woven together.

"The sister's testimony. She made him sound like a god, and I'm here to tell you, no man is that. The location of the gun."

"What about it?" asked Finn, leaning forward.

"It was lying just inside the apartment door. Odd, that after shooting her husband, she'd fling the gun down the hallway, dial 911, then sit in a rocking chair crooning a lullaby to her baby, her dead husband not five feet away."

Finn's eyes traveled to Jenna. She shook her head. "I can't remember."

"It doesn't mean it didn't happen like that. It just seemed inconsistent. Usually, when a wife shoots her husband and calls 911, she drops the weapon at the scene. Or hides it." He shrugged and spread his hands. "That's just the way things happen."

"What else?" asked Finn.

"The back door of the building had tape over the spring latch of the door lock. That's the part that moves in and out when you turn the doorknob from the inside. This evidence could agree with the Dutch woman's account of a person entering from the back door." He stopped talking at Jenna's quick intake of breath.

O'Grady scratched his head. His blue eyes held pity as if regretting the next blow. "No one else in the entire building saw or heard this alleged trespasser and we couldn't find any evidence of his or her presence at or near the crime scene. We couldn't verify it."

Jenna's hope melted under the heat of his doubt. This evidence would never exonerate her.

"You must understand that the situational evidence against you was overwhelming. Means, opportunity, motive. You had a gun in the house, you were in the apartment alone together, you had an abusive relationship,…" He ticked the evidence off on his fingers mimicking the prosecutor's closing remarks at Jenna's trial. Each point had felt like a nail in her coffin at the time, and nothing had changed. "Your fingerprints were all over the weapon and, other than the victim's, they were the only prints."

"But isn't there a test that would check to see if she actually shot the gun?" interrupted Finn.

"Yes, the paraffin test. It involves coating the hands with paraffin. After cooling, the casts are removed and treated with an acid solution used to detect nitrates and nitrites that originate from gunpowder. We did the test and it came back positive, but it's unreliable. The nitrates could just as easily have come from bleach. It would never hold up in court.

"Probably one of the most condemning and frustrating pieces of evidence, if you want to call it that, was that Jenna didn't deny it or give us anything else to work with."

"Wait a minute," said Finn, his face red with anger. "How could she defend herself if she couldn't remember anything? You can't convict someone for having amnesia."

Jenna smiled at him gratefully. "Actually, they can. They did." Her eyes challenged O'Grady to contradict her.

He didn't.

She raised her eyebrows in surprise when he nodded.

"Judy believed in your innocence from the start. She never gave up."

"What do you mean?"

"Just before she died, she called me, all excited. Said she had to talk to me. She'd found new evidence in the McDougall case and wanted to bring it over."

Jenna gasped.

The old detective shook his head. "Before you get your hopes up, I never spoke to her again."

"What? Why?" asked Finn, his voice rising in what Jenna assumed was frustration.

A spasm of grief contorted the old man's face. "Someone stabbed her. She died before I got to the hospital." He swiped at his eyes.

"I'm so sorry," said Jenna. She reached out to squeeze his hand, which he clasped gratefully.

"Judy…" He stopped, cleared his throat, and restarted. "Judy often relied on intuition." A sad smile tugged at the corner of his mouth. "I used to tease her about it, but it was right more often than not."

Finn turned to Jenna and his look brought tears to her eyes.

"And she felt that Jenna was innocent," he said softly.

"I wish I had met her," she said.

"You did. The uniformed officers took you down to the station house and Judy and I talked to you there."

Jenna shook her head and let her hair fall in front of her face trying to remember. It was all such a blur. Suddenly, she lifted her eyes to O'Grady.

"Did she have black curly hair?"

He chuckled. "And snapping black eyes."

"I do remember her. She was very kind."

"That's Judy. Her motto was that every aggressor was a victim in some way or another, so she treated them all the same. Biggest heart you'd ever see." His voice cracked on the last word.

"When Judy called, did she give any hints to what she'd found?" asked Finn.

"Not much." He smoothed his mustache. "She wanted to go over it with me in person. Let's see, she mentioned something about a…a…" He snapped his fingers. "A log."

"A log?" asked Finn, his voice laced with excitement. "What does a log have to do with this?"

"That she didn't say. As a matter of fact, she didn't say much. She was keeping the information pretty close to her chest."

"She must have kept a file on this," said Jenna. "Where is it?"

The old man sighed. "I asked the detectives in charge of her case that exact question. When they arrived on the scene, her purse was missing. They're treating it like a robbery gone bad."

Finn glanced at Jenna's compact purse. "Would she keep a file in a purse?"

O'Grady chuckled. "It wasn't an ordinary purse. More like a duffel bag. The kitchen sink could fit in that thing. She was hungry all the time, so she usually had it stuffed with food, make-up, diapers, and anything else she thought she might need."

Jenna looked at Finn, then back at the detective. The hair on her arms stood up. "So, if the killer knew she had a file on the case…" She left the thought dangling.

Finn sat up straight and stared at the other man. "Do you think her death was connected to this new evidence?"

Jenna shivered. Her mind rebelled at the thought of a killer who wanted information suppressed so badly he or she would kill a cop. This person wouldn't stop there.

The old man dropped his chin to his chest and his bottom teeth shot out of his mouth like a cash register drawer. After a moment, he flipped the denture back in and raised clouded eyes to Jenna.

"I haven't been able to convince the detectives in charge of her case of that. Yet."

"But you believe it?" asked Finn excitedly.

He nodded slowly and rested weary blue eyes on Jenna. "This person's killed twice now. You're the only one who can identify him. Or her."

Fear shot through Jenna like a bolt of lightning through her veins. It felt like a hand was squeezing her throat. "You think…?"

"I think you're safe until your memory returns. You're the only one who's seen the shooter. As long as that person believes you can't remember anything about that night, you'll be fine."

Finn swiveled to bolt Jenna to the spot with an intense green gaze. "Promise me that you won't tell anyone when your memory returns."

"Who would I…"

"Promise me."

She patted his arm and felt better for his protectiveness. "Okay, I promise."

"Jenna's life could be in danger," said Finn to the detective. "What are we going to do about it?"

The old man nodded several times and seemed to come to a decision. "We're going to find this killer."

Chapter Twenty-Six

Jenna sank exhausted into her bed. Detective O'Grady had assured them that he would contact Judy Farandino's husband about the missing file.

She crawled beneath the comforter and let her body relax for the first time since their visit with the old man. The apartment was her only safe haven from the killer who could have her as the next target. A shiver ran through her body. How would she keep Chase safe?

She rolled over and scrunched her pillow into shape. She knew sleep wouldn't come easily, but she laid her head down anyway.

Her gaze slid sideways to her night stand. The bottom drawer stood partially open. She sighed and reached over to slide it closed, but her hand stilled.

Something was in the drawer. She pulled it open, shrieked, and leaped out of bed.

Jenna, heart knocking wildly against her ribs, backed from the night stand and eyed it warily. It might as well have been a tarantula for all the fear it instilled in her heart. She shuddered at the thought of touching it, but if she left it there she'd never sleep in this room again.

The telephone on her night stand seemed to be on the other side of a roiling snake pit. She looked at the drawer, then back at the phone, and made a decision.

Turning on her heel, she hurried to the kitchen extension and dialed. Finn's number.

His deep voice wrapped around her like a warm blanket.

"Finn, can you come down here?" Her voice quavered.

"What's the matter?"

"I need you."

Fifteen seconds later, he stood on her threshold wearing a white t-shirt and a hastily donned pair of jeans, zipped but not buttoned.

"What happened?" he asked, his voice filled with anxiety. His eyes scoured the room as if searching out the cause of her agitated state.

She led him to her bedroom and refused to move farther than the doorway.

"There. That," she said, pointing a wavering finger at the night stand. "In the drawer."

Finn approached the night stand slowly, then reached into the drawer. "It's just a Ken doll, but wha…? Christ!" His eyes raised to Jenna. "Who did this?"

A hole had been drilled in Ken's neck and red nail polish blossomed from the wound.

She hunched a shoulder defensively. "I don't know, but it's obvious what it symbolizes."

"Angus. But, how could it have gotten there?"

Jenna shook her head and ran her fingers through her tangled curls. "I don't know. We were gone all day and we picked up Chase on our way home, so he wasn't here. No one should have been in the house." Her voice dropped on the last word as she tried to keep the hysteria out of it.

"Maybe it was put here a few days ago."

She made a dismissing motion with her hand. "No, I would have noticed the open drawer."

It was obvious Finn didn't want to ask the next question, but he finally blurted out, "Chase?"

"No. He was at Jason's all day. Besides that, he doesn't have any Ken dolls. He would never do this. I know my kid, Finn, and he would *never* do this."

"Do you think someone broke in?"

"What else?"

"Okay." He sighed. "I'll go check all of the doors and windows, see if any of them have been tampered with." He headed for the door. "In the meantime, you stay here."

"No," she yelled, fear taking a fresh hold on her throat. "No, wait! Don't go!"

He turned, startled. "What?"

Jenna bit her lip. "Can you check around the apartment before you go? Make sure no one's hiding here?" She felt incredibly timid asking, but the alternative of being left alone with an intruder hiding in her apartment brought fresh goose bumps to her arms.

Finn checked in every closet and large cupboard, under couches and chairs, behind doors and under Jenna's bed.

He had just stuck his head under Chase's bed when she heard her son's sleepy voice.

"Whatcha doin', Finn?" Chase was curled in the middle of his bed, his eyes barely open.

Finn's head smacked against the underside of the bed. He pulled himself out and kneeled beside the bed, rubbing the back of his head. "Just looking for dust bunnies, sport. Ow."

Chase chuckled. "Mom says this apartment is a dust bunny free zone."

"Really? I heard they're on the endangered species list, so I let them run free in my place."

"I like that." His voice was fading into slumber.

Finn pulled the sheet over the boy's shoulder. "Go to sleep, buddy. I'll see you in the morning."

He tiptoed from the room.

"Good night, sweetheart," murmured Jenna from the doorway, but Chase's breathing had already slowed into the steady rhythm of sleep.

She followed Finn into the living room.

"All clear."

She crossed her arms and pressed her lips together. If she could tamp down the fear, she might be able to keep the hysteria at bay. She felt so *invaded*. Someone had come into her home, touched her belongings, and snooped through her cupboards and drawers.

Finn rubbed her arms as if trying to increase the circulation. "You'll be fine now. There's no one here and they can't get in."

"They got in today," she cried. "What's going to stop them tonight?"

He pointed to the door. "You've got a dead bolt and a chain lock. Use them. If anyone can get through those two, plus the regular door lock, you'll definitely hear them coming.

"Program my number into your speed dial so you can get me quickly. We'll get the locks changed tomorrow."

The tension in her shoulders began to melt under the combination of logic and his kneading fingers.

He kissed her cheek. "I'll check on you in the morning."

As soon as he stepped across the threshold, Jenna locked the door, shot the dead bolt and slid the chain into its track. She hated the thought of barricading her and her son into their apartment, but it was the only hope for her to get some sleep tonight.

"Mo-om," said Chase the next morning. "I do *not* play with dolls." His tongue stuck between his teeth as he spread peanut butter in little swirls on his toast.

"That isn't what I asked you. I just want to know if you were in the house with anyone yesterday who might have brought one in."

"I was at Jason's house all day. We didn't come back here at all."

"Okay." She put more bread in the toaster.

"Why?"

"Oh, nothing. I found a doll in my closet. It must have been left here by the last tenant."

There was no possible way that doll had been here when she moved in, but she didn't want to scare her son. She reached for a plate out of the cupboard and tried to think who could have wanted to bring back that awful memory. Who knew about it?

She turned back to him. "Chase, do any of your friends know about me? That I was in jail?"

His chin dropped and he made little swirls in his peanut butter with the knife. "Eddie knows."

"He's the little one with the big brown eyes?"

He nodded.

Jenna watched him closely. "Did he say something?"

He shrugged one shoulder.

"Chase."

He dropped the knife and looked up at her with hurt eyes. "His Mom says he can't play with me anymore."

"Oh, honey." She pulled him to her and hugged him. "Why didn't you tell me?"

"It didn't matter." His voice was muffled because his face was pressed into her shirt.

She placed both hands along either side of his jaw and gently made him look up. "It does matter. What did she say?"

"She said she didn't want her son playing with the Devil's spawn. I don't even know what that means, but I knew it wasn't good. I hate her."

Jenna sighed. "You can't blame her, honey. She doesn't know what really happened. No one knows."

"Did you find out anything yesterday from the detective?"

She had told him where she and Finn were heading yesterday, and what they hoped to accomplish. Months ago, he had decided to believe in her innocence and his trust had been unflagging. She hugged him hard and let him go.

"Nothing yet, but Detective O'Grady's agreed to help us. I think he believes in my innocence." It gave her heart a tug to say that.

He hooted. "That's great, Mom. We'll catch the bad guy, you watch. Then, maybe Eddie's Mom will let him play with me again."

"I'm sure she will, honey. I'm sure she will."

"Mom...," said Chase, then he stopped.

"Mmmhmm?" She slathered peanut butter on her toast, worried about how her past would affect Chase. How it had already affected him.

Chase cleared his throat. "You never talk about my dad."

Jenna's head whipped up. She knew he'd ask about him some day, but she had hoped it wouldn't be for several years. Maybe then she'd know what to say. What if he asked about the murder? Wanted all of the grisly details? Should she tell him? Jenna's mind whirled as she tried to find an appropriate response.

"Did he love me?"

Jenna exhaled, unaware she had been holding her breath. "Of

course, he loved you." Did he? She'd never been sure. He had moments when Chase seemed like the brightest star shining in the winter sky. Then others, when pure hatred shone from Angus' eyes, as if his son represented lost freedom or lost hopes—as if Angus held Chase responsible for his unrealized dreams and his tie to Jenna.

Perhaps it was fear. Fear that his son would grow up with the same genetic flaw that plagued Angus and his own mother. Unleashed, raw, uncontrolled anger. Striking out with fists and words. One just as hurtful and poisonous as the other.

"Did he love you?"

That one stumped her. "I thought he did. At first." Or was it fascination with a woman young enough to be his daughter? Flattered by her attentions. "He was a complicated man. He had a tough childhood. His mother had some problems and she didn't always treat him well." That was an understatement. When Jenna and Angus first married, his sister had been thrilled. Irene had been desperate for a sister to confide in. Her stories of their abusive childhood had curdled Jenna's stomach. Later, she had surreptitiously found the scars from cigarette and rope burns on her husband's body. He had refused to discuss it and had been furious that Irene had told Jenna anything. From that point on, her relationship with her sister-in-law had deteriorated.

"What was he like?"

She wished she knew. "Let's see. He was very intelligent." She smiled. "He could recite whole scenes from Shakespearean plays and his voice could give you goosebumps, it was so rich and full. He should have been an actor."

"What else?" Chase's eyes brightened as if he could see an outline of the man for the first time.

"Sometimes he'd hold you in his arms and sing to you. You'd stop crying immediately and stare up into his face, as if wondering where that wonderful sound was coming from." She laughed. "You were the sweetest baby. And so chubby that it looked like you had elastics around your wrists."

Chase held his wrists up for her inspection.

"Where did all that baby fat go?" she murmured. The last time she'd seen him before they took her away, his plump arms had reached out to her. Fat tears had welled in his eyes and spilled over cotton-candy pink cheeks. Her heart twisted at the memory of leaving him in Irene's arms.

She turned to the sink and swiped at her eyes. "What are we going to do today? How about fishing? Or hiking? Do you want to have a picnic by the river?"

Chase draped an arm around her shoulders like a big brother. He looked up at her and smiled, as if trying to tell her he knew and understood her change of topic. "Sure, Mom, whatever you want."

Jenna hugged him hard and thanked fate or her lucky stars or whatever had blessed her with such a precious son.

Chapter Twenty-Seven

Karma picked up a velvety petal fallen from the single white rose and rolled it between thumb and forefinger. Dead flower smell. Like an old woman wearing stale perfume. Dead. Death.

White roses. That had been a brain child. Working up old memories continued to be the most effective procedure. The flowers must have scared her silly.

Karma's dry chuckle rang out around the room and ended abruptly as another thought collided with the first. The doll. That had been precipitous. Too soon. Timing is everything. Not clever at all. Her lack of response to previous ploys had forced Karma's hand. Jenna's fault. She should be frightened, leaning on her friends and family. Her spine of steel was unexpected, and absent before her prison stay. The Plan was based on the old Jenna and would need modification.

The leather-bound journal lay open on the desk. Karma's fingers trembled on the last page. The Plan wasn't achieving the desired results and the rages were progressing. Out of control. Lost moments. The seeds of unrealized dreams, fertilized by frustration, grew into the rages. Rages that obliterated time and space, creating gaps that hovered in Karma's memory. Black holes.

Was it time for drastic measures? Was this the moment? Was Karma ready? Yes. This weekend. Five days away. Finally a culmination to The Plan. Eight years was too long to wait. No! Karma's hands shook, rattling the paper. It's too soon. The Plan must be altered, not abandoned.

Karma ripped the page from the journal, balled it up and fired it into the corner of the candlelit room where Jenna's largest photo lay shredded.

Blind. She was blind to the forces around her. The love-hate. The jealousy. The need. Silly bitch!

The chair squeaked as Karma leaned back and visualized Jenna agitated to a frenzied pitch. Taut as a guitar string. Ready for plucking. That would be the optimum time to pounce. Soon.

Karma's hands cupped as if holding a tiny bird. *Her life in my hands.* The palms ground together.

The chuckle that filled the room held a hint of madness.

Chapter Twenty-Eight

Chase bounded into the office through the front door. "Home free," he yelled.

A breathless Jason followed three seconds later.

Jenna's first reaction was to scold Chase for running into their place of business, but when she looked at his flushed face and happy smile her heart flipped over. She wanted to throw her arms around him, hold him tight, and thank him for bringing such joy into her life. Instead, so as not to embarrass him, she smiled and ruffled his sweaty hair.

"What are you boys up to today?" she asked.

"Playing. Anything to eat, Mom?"

Jenna groaned loudly. "The bottomless pit strikes again."

Chase grinned. "I'm a growing boy, Mom." He leaned a hip against her desk and threaded her pen into the spiral binding of her notebook.

"You certainly are. If you can wait for a half hour, I'll come up and make you some lunch."

"Nah, we're hungry now."

"Yeah," piped up Jason, a red rooster tail sticking up from the back of his head. "We're starved."

Jenna rolled her eyes. An hour earlier they had both had peanut butter and jelly toast. She wondered aloud if they had hollow legs, but they just grinned. "We have apples." She raised her eyebrows as if that would make the fruit sound more enticing.

The boys looked at each other and shook their heads in unison. "Nah."

"Okay, then, have some carrot sticks and celery sticks, just to hold you over until lunch time."

"Oh, Mom," said Chase. "Can't we have some chocolate cake?"

"No, you may not. You can have some after you eat a healthy lunch."

They groaned and grumbled as they climbed the stairs to the apartment.

Chase stopped halfway up. "Hey, Finn."

Finn walked out of his office and stood at the bottom of the stairs. "Hey, buddy, what's up?"

"There's a note on the door to your apartment."

Jenna tensed, then forced herself to relax. This note was for Finn, not her, so it wouldn't be another threat. She expelled a breath she didn't know she had been holding.

"When were you up there?" asked Finn, hand on the curved base of the banister.

"We weren't. It's your outside door. It must have been there all night."

"What did it say?"

Chase shrugged. "I'm not allowed to go up there. Mom says it's your space."

The boys bounded up the stairs, hooting and laughing as they raced each other to the first-floor apartment door.

Finn scratched his head. "Who would leave a note on my outside door? Why not leave it on the front door, here."

Jenna shrugged and tried to unwind her pen from the spiral notebook. "Don't know. Why don't you go find out?"

He nodded, then climbed the stairs two at a time and disappeared from view on the first landing. A few minutes later, he returned, descending the stairs one step at a time.

"What the hell is this?" he muttered. He held a piece of paper by one corner between finger and thumb.

"What is it?" asked Jenna. The tension had returned.

He looked up, his green eyes intense. "Now, don't get upset."

"Okay, that did it, now my nerves are on full alert. What's wrong?" she asked, trying unsuccessfully to keep the edge out of her voice.

She reached for the note, but hesitated when Finn said, "It's on Angus' stationary."

She closed her eyes and groaned. "Who is doing this? Why? When is this lunatic going to leave us alone?"

"Not yet," he said grimly and handed her the note. "Careful, you don't want to mess up any fingerprints."

Jenna stared at the creamy notepaper and shuddered. Trying to make sense of it, she read the note out loud. "'Leave her alone, or you'll be sorry,'" it said in large childish letters.

Goosebumps pebbled her arms. She raised her eyes to Finn. "'Her' is me, isn't it."

He pulled a corner of his mouth in. "It looks like it."

"Oh, Finn, I don't want to involve you in this whole mess. If anything happened to you, I'd never forgive myself." She returned her gaze to the note and looked closer at the reddish brown letters. "What is this written in? It's not…"

"Blood," he finished for her.

"Ugh." She dropped the note onto her desk. "What kind of maniac would send a letter written in blood? Do you think it's human? Oh my God, what if…what if this freak has killed someone." She lowered her head into her hands and felt the band around her chest tighten.

"Slow down," said Finn. His large hand rubbed circles on her back. "You're getting way ahead of yourself. I'll call Detective O'Grady. Maybe he can get it checked for fingerprints and to see what kind of blood it is."

She dropped her hands into her lap and sighed. "I'll call him. I was going to do that anyway, to find out if he's contacted Judy Farandino's husband about the file she was working on."

Finn nodded and they both stared at the note.

"Maybe I'll invite him for dinner. He's probably lonely."

Finn smiled. "The eternal mother."

Jenna noticed something in his left hand. "What's that?"

"A jackknife. The note was skewered to my door with this."

A fresh icicle of fear slid down her back. "First me, and now you. What's next? Chase?" She clenched her jaw. "I will not let anyone threaten my son."

He touched her cheek in a gentle caress. "I won't let anything happen to Chase or you."

She squeezed his hand.

"Will you put these in a large envelope for me?" she asked, indicating the note and the knife. "I'll call Detective O'Grady."

Finn disappeared down the hall toward the storage closet while Jenna flipped through the Rolodex. She dialed the number and drummed her fingers on the desk through six rings. She was just about to hang up when a gruff voice answered.

"O'Grady here."

"Detective O'Grady, it's Jenna McDougall calling. You sound out of breath."

"Well, hello dear. I was outside tending my marigolds and didn't hear the phone. The ears aren't what they used to be." He chuckled, clearly unconcerned about the tricks time was playing on him. "What can I do for you? Did you remember something?"

"No, this is an unrelated matter, but I'm hoping you can help us out." She told him about the note and the knife. "We're wondering if you could check to see if it is blood, and also if there are any fingerprints."

Silence filled the line. "Jenna, is this an isolated event?"

She sighed. "No, there have been several warnings and weird things that have happened." She told him about the notes, the flowers, and even the Ken doll.

"What makes you think this is 'unrelated' to your husband's death?"

Jenna was stunned into silence by his question.

"Because…well, uh…because…" She stopped. "I don't know, it just never occurred to me. After all, that was eight years ago."

"And this person sends notes that sound like your husband, uses his notepaper, sends reminders of how he died, and you don't think they're related?"

"But, detective," started Jenna.

"Call me Mickey."

"Okay, Mickey, if this is all related, then it means that someone has followed me, or at least kept track of me, for eight years, and isn't finished with me yet. That's more terrifying than ever."

"I'm not trying to scare you, but it's better to know what you're up against. Ignorance is not bliss when you're dealing with an obsessive personality."

Jenna's hands shook and she pressed the phone to her ear as her imagination took over. "Maybe I was the target back then, but the shooter got interrupted. Now, he or she is coming to finish the job. Oh, my God, what about Chase?" Her voice had risen in panic.

"Calm down," said Angus in a stern voice. "Hysterics won't help. From what you've told me about the messages, it sounds like you're supposed to be scared, not dead. What did the police say?"

She didn't answer for a moment. "I haven't called them."

He muttered a curse. "For God's sake, Jenna, you're being stalked, and you haven't called the cops?"

Jenna rushed to defend herself. "I haven't exactly had the best of luck with them."

He snorted into the phone. "No reason not to call them now."

"I don't want them involved," said Jenna. "At least, not officially. Can you look into it? You said it's related to Angus' murder anyway."

He muttered something under his breath about being wrapped around her finger. "Oh, all right, but I'll have to see everything."

"No problem." Relief spread through her, like the first rush of caffeine from her morning coffee. "Can you come for dinner tomorrow night? You can meet my son."

He swallowed noisily. "I'd like that."

"Come early. I'll give you the file I've started and we can talk."

They firmed up their plans and Jenna headed upstairs to feed her starving son.

That evening, after kissing Chase good night, Jenna fell asleep on the sofa. Sleep had been more difficult to attain lately, and she accepted a loss of consciousness wherever and whenever it happened.

After what seemed like only seconds, her head lolled to the left and she jerked awake. The misty outline of a dream hovered on the periphery of her memory. She struggled to recall the essence of it, but like a layer of fog under the bright sun it dissipated as she turned her hot gaze toward it.

She stumbled to her bed and collapsed onto the soft comforter and waited for sweet slumber to return. She rolled over. She crawled under the covers. She punched her feather pillow and slammed her head into the resultant hollow. Sleep had deserted her.

Jenna groaned in frustration, threw back the covers and padded to the bathroom for a glass of water. She knew nothing would bring sleep except time. She'd tried using some yoga techniques she'd learned in prison, counting sheep, and making her mind a blank slate, but nothing worked.

She walked to the window. For once she felt safe from prying eyes, because her room was darker than the lit street. Even so, she stepped back slightly when she noticed a figure leaving Rhia's house wearing a black cape and hood.

With startling clarity, flashes of images from the night Angus died popped into her mind. One after another the pictures appeared as if a strobe light had been turned on in her head. She could see Rhia's visitor walking down the sidewalk, but at the same time a distant, past reality had taken over.

Jenna let the memories come, the sounds, the sights, and the bone-chilling fear. The dread that she had tamped down crept out of its dark hole and seized her again. She did not try to fight it.

She remembered a phone call from Angus and feeling frightened by his tone. She had hurried to put Chase to bed early, then waited nervously for her husband's return home.

A short time later, she heard him in the hall fumbling with his keys. At first, he railed at her about locking the door on him, but that rant turned into one against the Dean who had called him into his office in front of the whole staff for a little chat, as if he were a schoolboy in trouble. The indignity of it all sparked his rage and he had to take it out on someone. Jenna was available and, though she knew what was coming, she tried to calm him down, to talk rationally.

Angus wouldn't be calmed. He lashed out at his wife and sent her flying across the room with a vicious backhand. She refused to respond to his blows and just curled up into a ball, hoping he'd lose interest. Unfortunately, that seemed to enrage him further. He grabbed her arm and wrenched her to her feet, forcing her to backpedal from the living room to the bedroom screaming in her face the entire time. Chase cried out in the next room and Angus screeched at her to shut him up.

Veins bulged in his neck and his face turned a mottled red. She tried to pull her arm free of his bruising grasp, but he refused to let go. He shoved his face inches from hers and hissed, "Maybe I'll just have to shut him up myself."

He shoved her away and turned to the bedroom door. She could take the abuse herself, but there was no way Jenna would let him touch her son, the only bright light in her life. She rushed toward him, trying to hold him back, but with a cuff like a grizzly bear he knocked her back into the room. She ricocheted off the bed and hit the night stand, knocking it over with a loud crash. The drawer fell open and Angus' gun tumbled out to lay at Jenna's fingertips, as if it was a sign. With trembling hands, sobbing, she picked it up and followed him into the hall of their tiny apartment. She yelled at him to stop, but he just turned and laughed at her and reached for Chase's bedroom doorknob. She threatened him again, raised the gun to point at his chest, but he wouldn't stop. He taunted her one last time and started to describe what he'd do to their son. She couldn't stand it and screamed at him to stop, but when he opened the bedroom door, she couldn't pull the trigger.

Jenna shook her head and struggled to remember more, but the images stopped like a broken slide projector. She had pointed a gun at Angus, but she hadn't killed him. Had she? What happened next? She thumped the side of her head, trying to dislodge the next memory in the sequence, the one that would relieve her conscience or send her into a living hell.

Nothing happened. The images, like bits of stained glass, had aligned themselves, but an important piece was still missing. The most important piece.

Exhausted now, Jenna lay on her bed and let the tears slide down her face and neck until they finally lost themselves in her hair. She cried for a past that couldn't be changed, for the loss of Chase's father, and for the eight years she would never recover with her son.

Finally, emotionally drained and weary beyond anything she'd ever felt before, she allowed herself to fall into a fitful sleep.

Chapter Twenty-Nine

"You're finally starting to get a little color in your face. Not sleeping?" asked Mickey.

Jenna shrugged one shoulder, a habit she had inherited from Chase. "Just restless."

He nodded his shaggy head.

They watched Chase try to scare up a record number of grasshoppers on either side of the abandoned railroad bed where they were strolling. He ran into the colorful fields of wildflowers waving his arms and fanning the plants to raise the insects.

"Ah, and wouldn't it be nice to bottle that energy," said Mickey.

A feeling of contentment stole over Jenna. She hadn't felt like this since she'd walked the pastures with her father. Happy, relaxed, almost serene. They could walk for miles without ever saying a word, comfortable with silence and with each other.

As they sauntered along the path, Mickey rubbed plant leaves between his fingers and bent to inhale the scent of wildflowers. He ignored the bees taking their fill, willing to coexist peacefully with nature's messengers. Jenna floated through the afternoon while Mickey taught Chase the names of the wild plants.

She returned to earth with a bump when Mickey reminded her of the purpose of his visit.

"I called Judy's husband about the file."

Jenna's head jerked up and she searched his faded blue eyes for a clue to what he'd found.

"No answer. I learned from a neighbor that he packed up the kids and went to stay with his family in Italy to try to recover from his wife's death. He'll be back in a few weeks. I left a message, so he'll call me when he gets home."

"She was a nice lady."

He nodded. "The best."

"Mickey, I remember Judy quite well. Why don't I remember you? Weren't you there when I was questioned?"

He chuckled, a low rumbling in his chest. "Do you remember a clean-shaven, red-headed guy with a crew cut?"

"Yes, I do remember him. He was the 'bad' cop in their routine."

"That's me." He laughed out loud at her look of astonishment. "A few years ago, my hair turned white, almost overnight, and I haven't had a haircut since I retired."

"And you grew a mustache. Quite a disguise."

He looked at her intently. "You're a sharp cookie. I put away a lot of people."

"But you let me find you."

"I choose who finds me."

Chase sidled up beside them and stuck his hands in his jeans pockets. He looked up at Mickey with serious eyes and seemed to debate whether to speak. Finally, he blurted, "Are you going to find out who killed my father?"

Mickey's eyes darted to Jenna's, obviously startled by the question.

"We've talked about it," she said.

He looked back at the boy. "That's my aim, lad."

Chase nodded. "Are you staying for supper?"

"I am."

"Good," said Chase, and he ran ahead to throw stones off the wooden bridge that ran over a swiftly moving creek. The sound of the water tumbling over submerged rocks grew steadily louder as they approached the bridge.

"I'm so worried about him."

"He looks like a nice, well-adjusted lad to me."

Chase threw a stick into the water and dodged to the other side of the bridge to watch it float away.

"Not because of anything I've done."

"Don't underestimate yourself, lass."

"I didn't even have enough nerve to save him from an abusive father." She rubbed a hand over her face. Emotion crowded her throat. "Last night I remembered more about the night Angus died. I couldn't shoot him even though I knew he was going to hurt Chase. What kind of mother is that? I always thought I had a mother bear instinct. I'm such a coward."

Mickey stopped and took her hands in both of his. "Bravery has nothing to do with the ability to squeeze a trigger, Jenna," he said gently. "You should never mourn the fact that you failed to take another human life." He rubbed a tear from her face with a callused thumb, then threaded her arm through his. "Don't you worry about a thing, lass. Now, tell me everything you remembered."

As they strolled back toward the house, Jenna found herself confiding in this gentle man about things she hadn't been able to tell anyone else, including her suspicions, and dread, that the stalker was someone she knew.

By the time they reached her apartment she felt like she'd been given a gift, a feeling of tranquility that had been missing since the death of her parents. For the first time in months, she felt a renewed hope for the future.

During dinner, they chatted about other things, Chase's baseball camp, Finn's new business, and Jenna's fine cooking. Afterward, as prearranged, Jenna sent Chase to Rhia's for the evening.

Finn joined them as Jenna spread the stalker's notes and 'gifts' over the table in order of when they were received. She fidgeted while Mickey's eyes roved over the items. He didn't touch or say anything, just stared at each item as if it could tell him the secret of the sender's identity.

"White roses arrived with this," said Jenna, pointing to the small pink card. "Angus knew I hated white roses, because there were too many painful memories connected to them."

"'Remember who owns you,'" read Mickey. He raised his eyebrows questioningly at Jenna.

"Angus used to say that. He was extremely possessive. He hated it when I spoke to one of his colleagues or students in the supermarket." She wrapped a curly strand of auburn hair around her finger while she spoke. "Sometimes, he'd call from work and scream at me over the phone."

"Who knew he said that?"

"I didn't think anyone did, but I wouldn't be surprised if his sister, Irene, knew about it. They were very close. Maybe Everett. He was Angus' assistant."

"He didn't care who heard him," Finn inserted. "Any student walking by his office could have heard those words."

Mickey raised one bushy eyebrow.

Finn sighed. "Yes, I knew Professor McDougall. If that makes me a suspect, so be it. I'm not Jenna's stalker, but she needs more proof."

Jenna started to protest, but Finn placed his hand over hers.

"I'm not blaming you. The sooner we find this stalker the sooner we can get on with our lives." His green eyes held a promise that gave impetus to her resolve to find the stalker and clear Finn.

"Where'd the photos come from?" asked Mickey. He flipped through the glossy prints. Concern gouged a line between his eyes.

"Someone threw a rock through my window and Finn chased the person out of the bushes. He found the camera and had the film developed."

"Did you see the person, Jenna?"

"No," said Finn in a hard voice, "which, along with the fact that I'm not in any of the pictures, is why I'm still a suspect. I could have planted the camera and set the whole thing up to make it look like I'm not involved."

Mickey nodded and stared at Finn. "It's happened before."

Finn sighed and ran a hand through his thick hair. "I know, but it galls me. I want to find this creep as much as Jenna does. Maybe more."

Jenna tried to rub the tension out of his back, but the muscles stayed bunched in hard knots.

"Patience, lad. We'll find him. Or her." His finger touched the bloodied doll. "Obvious reference to your husband's murder."

"Doesn't this prove it's from the real murderer?" asked Finn. "Who else could recreate the murder victim? Jenna says he was shot in the neck, just like this doll."

Mickey shrugged. "Could be a good guess, or anyone who sat through the court case. They showed photos of the murder scene and it was open to the public. However, we can assume the person was close to Angus, and possibly Jenna, in some way. Access to his writing paper, knowledge of the way he spoke to Jenna and of the effect of the white roses. Anyone come to mind?"

"Irene, my sister-in-law."

"Or Everett Vandervries."

"Finn, Everett's been wonderful to me." To Mickey, she said, "Everett is the only reason I made it through those years in prison. He brought news and pictures of Chase every week. It kept me sane."

"So he has a lot invested in you," said Mickey.

Jenna shook her head in exasperation. "Not you, too."

He patted her hand. "Just don't count anyone out." He picked up one of the notes that Jenna had printed from her computer. "Karma," he said. He stroked his mustache and reread the note. "Karma, fate, kismet. It makes me think the stalker believes the outcome is destiny, not something that can be changed by mortal whim."

"The first e-mail message, the one I deleted, mentioned our 'destiny.' But what is the destined outcome?" asked Jenna.

She didn't expect an answer and none was given.

"I don't want to scare you, but the only thing I'm sure of is that time is running out. Look at what we have here. It started with notes and hang-ups and it's moved to knives and bloody warnings. I don't like it. The stalker's actions are escalating. We have to put a stop to it before something drastic happens."

Mickey's words filled Jenna with dread. One glance at Finn told her he wasn't too happy about them either. "What can we do?" she whispered.

"I'll get this stuff checked for fingerprints. The blood, too. In the meantime, be sensible about your safety. Don't go out after dark alone, keep your doors locked, you know the drill."

Jenna hated the thought of being a prisoner in her own home. She was sick of confinement, sick of playing by someone else's rules.

Finn must have noticed the stubborn set of her jaw. "It's only for a little while, Jenna, just until we catch this creep."

She stood and paced the room. She picked up a flowered pillow from the sofa and hugged it to her.

"What about Chase? Do I have to tie him down, too? Will he have to give up his freedom, just because some loony is out to make my life hell?" Anger seethed through her body. No one should be allowed to do this to her son. No one.

"Come sit down, lass," said Mickey. He patted the padded wooden chair beside him.

Reluctantly, she tossed the pillow onto the sofa, retraced her steps to the table and perched on the edge of her chair. He squeezed her hand.

"Chase will be fine, but you should explain to him what's going on. He needs to know that he shouldn't accept rides from anyone even if he knows them." He smiled. "I'll bet you've already drilled that into him anyway."

She smiled, a tiny curve to her lips. "Yes, and he knows he has to tell me wherever he's going." She pushed her curls away from her face and heaved a deep sigh. "Okay, I'll do it. I won't like it, but I'll do it."

"Atta girl. Okay, back to Angus' murder. I pulled out my notes and went over them again, but nothing leaped out at me. Let's go over M-O-M—means, opportunity, and motive. Who had all three that night?" He pulled a small, red notebook from his shirt pocket and jotted notes while they talked.

All eyes turned to Jenna as if she had an answer. She looked from Finn to Mickey and shrugged. "I guess anyone had the means, if you mean that as access to the gun."

Mickey nodded.

"I was holding it, so anyone who walked into the apartment could have grabbed it from me. The apartment door was unlocked because Angus had just arrived home. That would give an open opportunity to anyone who wished to enter. Motive is the tough one. I have no idea."

"Did he have any enemies?"

Finn snorted, then apologized. "Sorry. It's just that he wasn't well-liked by his students."

Jenna nodded. "He seemed to have constant clashes with the other faculty members, too."

"Any altercation seem especially nasty?"

"Not that I recall." She jumped to her feet. "Can I get you a coffee? I need to do something."

"That would be grand." Mickey flipped back a few pages in his notebook. "You mentioned the sister and the assistant. Did either of them have motive?"

Jenna shook her head and poured three coffees. "I don't think so. Irene depended on him, treated him like he could do no wrong. On the other hand, he was very volatile. If he turned on her, she could be so hurt that she might want to hurt him. Not likely, but I can't think of any other reason she'd want to kill him."

He made a few more scratches in his notebook. "What about the assistant?"

She thought a moment while she placed the coffee cups, creamer and sugar on the table. She inhaled the rich aroma of Brazilian coffee that filled the room. "They seemed to get along, certainly better than any other assistant Angus had. They usually only lasted about a month, but Everett hung in there for almost a year. I don't think Angus felt as threatened, academically speaking, by Everett as the others."

"Why was that?" Mickey reached for his coffee and sipped loudly.

"Everett wasn't as bright, or so Angus said, and he didn't seem to be a social climber, which is an important part of moving up the faculty ladder. I suppose that made Angus feel safer."

He flipped the notebook shut. "It seems to me we're not going to get anywhere until we figure out what Judy meant when she mentioned a 'log.' Have you thought about that?"

"I haven't the faintest…wait a minute." She snapped her fingers and turned to Finn. "Remember Wim's notebooks? They could be called daily logs, couldn't they?"

"I guess so. Do you think there's something in them that we missed?" She could hear excitement building in his voice.

"It's worth checking." She turned to Mickey. "Wim Vandermeersch is the woman on the first floor of my old building who sees everything that goes on in the building. And she writes it all down."

"The Dutch woman. Do you think she'll let you borrow them?" asked Mickey.

"I can ask."

He nodded.

"What's next?" asked Finn.

"We re-interview everyone on the original list. I'm sure that's what Judy would have done. She found something. So will we."

They divided up the list of interviewees and made plans to keep each other updated on their progress.

Mickey glanced at his watch and slipped the notebook into his pocket. He packed up the stalker's collection and filed them in a large accordion file from Jenna. As he turned toward the door, he pulled the photographs out for one last look. He shuffled the pictures, glancing at each one, but stopped halfway through the pile. One picture held his attention. He drew it closer and squinted at the bottom left corner.

He sniffed and stroked his mustache. "Does that look like a running shoe to you?"

Chapter Thirty

Jenna reached for the picture and peered at it. "Where?"

Mickey's stubby finger pointed to the bottom left corner of the print. "There. That green thing."

She looked again. A clearly defined size-eleven shoe with a gouge out of the toe stood near Jenna's elbow as she relaxed on a blanket of leaves at their picnic spot.

"Ohmigod. Ohmigod, Finn, it's your shoe!"

She squealed and hurled herself into Finn's arms.

He lurched backward under the onslaught of her joyous assault. "Whoa, wait a minute. Let me see that thing." He held her tight with one arm and reached for the picture. "You're right. That has to be my foot."

"Who else wears green sneakers to match his car?" said Jenna. She giggled into his neck.

He handed the photograph to Mickey and grinned.

"It's well-camouflaged against the leaves and grass, which is why we missed it," said Mickey. He clamped a hand on Finn's shoulder. "I guess this puts you in the clear, lad. Time for you two to celebrate. I'll have a closer look at all the pictures, see if I can find any other clues. I'll lock the front door on my way out."

He clomped down the stairs and out the door. When she heard the door snick into place after him, Jenna turned to Finn. "Oh, Finn, I'm so happy."

He picked her up and spun around the room whooping with joy. His lips found hers in a light kiss that quickly turned into something deeper and warmer.

Jenna felt so much relief at the knowledge of Finn's innocence, she was overwhelmed. She had no idea how much she'd been holding back, how much emotion she'd been denying all these months. Now, she let it all release. She was awash with a flood of feelings so awesome she was sure she'd stagger and slip to the floor if he wasn't holding her in his strong arms. She clung to him, luxuriating in the feel of his lips moving over her face and neck, devouring kisses that weakened her knees and sent sensations through her she never knew existed. A delicious tide started in the core of her being, built into a tidal wave, and spread out to tingle in her limbs. She wallowed in the combination of love and lust that left her body yearning for release in his arms.

With a start, Jenna pulled back. Love? Where had that thought come from?

Finn reached for her and pulled her back into his arms. "What's the matter?"

Jenna gazed into his green eyes. Love. Yes, that's what this feeling was. Not the idolization she had felt for Angus in the beginning, or the puppy-love she'd felt for her teenage boyfriend. This was the real thing. She smiled and lifted her face for his kiss. "Nothing's the matter. Nothing at all." She snuggled closer, feeling the need to climb inside his body. She couldn't get close enough.

Somehow, the ringing of the phone penetrated her fogged mind. Finn groaned and pulled her closer.

"Don't answer it," he murmured into her neck.

She relaxed against him, but the ringing persisted and she put her hands on his chest. "I have to get it. It might be Chase."

He sighed, but didn't release her. Instead, he pressed her body closer to his, leaving little doubt of his desire for her, and walked her backwards to the phone.

"Mom, can I stay overnight at Rhia's house?" asked Chase, excitement lacing his voice. "She's got a *kitten*. It's all black and fuzzy, and it *likes* me. Rhia says I can name it and it can sleep in my room tonight. It can't sleep on the bed, though, 'cause that's a rule. Can I, Mom? Can I stay here?"

Jenna's protective instincts immediately went on full alert. Let her baby stay at someone else's house all night? "I don't think so. You should probably come home now." Chase's groan echoed Finn's at her suggestion.

"Ah, Mom, I'm not a baby, and anyway Rhia will make sure nothing happens to me. Please? I really want to stay."

Jenna leaned her forehead against Finn's shoulder and inhaled his scent. "Let me talk to Rhia."

The other woman must have been standing close by, because Jenna heard her voice almost immediately. "Please let him stay. They're having so much fun together. You know I'll take good care of him. Besides, you need some time for yourself."

Jenna jerked her head up. This woman was a witch, but could she see through walls? Finn nibbled her neck and warm syrup ran through her veins. She cleared her throat. "I'll be over to pick him up in the morning."

"Come for coffee."

"Thanks, Rhia. See you in the morning."

Jenna let the phone drop back into its cradle. Her eyes met Finn's. Their bodies touched from knee to chest.

"Chase isn't coming home tonight."

A smile slowly spread across his face. "You mean we'll be alone for the rest of the night? That's too bad."

She nibbled on his lower lip. "Mmmmhmmm."

"This night just keeps getting better."

"I hope so."

He captured her mouth in a hungry kiss. Their hands clinging, caressing, fondling, he led her to the sofa.

Before he could draw her down, she whispered, "We'd be more comfortable in my bed."

He stilled. "Are you sure?" His green eyes deepened to the color of fresh evergreen boughs.

She nodded, never so sure of anything in her life as what she wanted to experience with this man. She led him to her bedroom.

She stopped in the center of the room, suddenly unsure and awkward, but when Finn's hand caressed her cheek she forgot her self-consciousness and reached for him.

His tongue left a moist trail from her ear to her neck. When his mouth found an erogenous zone just below her jaw line, Jenna felt a warmth blossoming through her belly. She stifled a groan of pleasure. She never knew her neck could be the origin of such delicious feelings. With Finn, she seemed to have several previously unknown spots that were hard-wired to the center of her being.

He slowly undressed her and laid her gently on the bed. She could feel him holding back, trying to leash his desire, but like a wild animal it broke free. His hands were everywhere, always kneading, caressing, producing sensations that sent tremors of passion through her body.

"You are so beautiful," he murmured while his mouth took possession of her body.

Her hunger matched his and they took each other in a frenzy and found rapture in each other's arms. With their fevered flesh pressed together, Jenna discovered a fulfillment she'd never known before.

The second time they made love slowly and with sweet tenderness, patiently exploring each other's body until they cried out for release.

Finally, they slept, only to awaken several times through the night and reach for each other in renewed ardor.

Hours later, sunlight streamed through the blinds in tiny yellow slits. Jenna allowed the wonderful dream to depart like a receding wave. She stretched her body like a cat and reached for Finn. It wasn't until her hand touched his cold pillow that she opened her eyes to the empty place beside her.

Had it been a dream after all? Impossible. Her imagination couldn't have conjured up a night like the one she had just spent with Finn. She blushed at the memory of her own wantonness, but, oh, he drove her wild with desire.

Refusing to allow any negative thoughts about his absence, she decided to get up and find him. She flung the sheet from her naked body.

"Now, that's a beautiful sight first thing in the morning," Finn said. He stood in the doorway holding a wooden tray.

She squealed in surprise and scrambled back under the covers.

Finn placed the tray on the small bedside table and leaned over to bestow a kiss that made her loosen the grip on the sheet clutched between her breasts. She wrapped her arms around his neck and pulled him back into bed with her.

Ten minutes later, they lay side by side, panting.

"You're insatiable, woman."

"Ex-cons are like that," she said and laughed. "We have a lot of time to make up for."

Her eyes moved to the side table. "I suppose our coffee's cold."

"Nope." He reached for a neon pink carafe from the tray. "It's insulated. I had a feeling you might be ravenous for my body this morning, so I took precautionary measures to save our breakfast."

"Me?" said Jenna, pretending outraged innocence in her best Scarlett O'Hara voice. "You're the one who started it. I was just lying here, innocent as can be, wondering how I would ever get over being ravaged last night, when you, you brute, overpowered me *again*. I do believe I'm going to swoon." She pressed the back of her hand to her forehead. Her speech would have been more effective if she hadn't giggled.

Finn grabbed her and tickled her until she cried uncle.

"Okay, okay, maybe I liked it a *bit*," she admitted. "Now, can I have breakfast?"

He poured them both an aromatic cup of coffee and handed her a bagel smothered in cream cheese and fresh, sliced strawberries.

"Mmmm, I've never had breakfast in bed." She watched him watch her lick the cream cheese from her lips and reveled in the power she could so easily wield over him. "I think I like it."

He leaned over to lick off the last traces of strawberry juice from her lips. "Me, too," he said huskily.

Later that morning, Jenna floated over to Rhia's house. The sun felt warm on her back and the sky was the most beautiful color of blue she'd ever seen. She followed the sound of Chase's excited voice to her neighbor's back yard and found Rhia sitting on a lawn chair watching Chase shooting a styrofoam airplane into the air. He chased after it as it glided across the yard. He retrieved the plane, then, catching sight of Jenna, he raced over for a quick hug.

"Look, Mom, Rhia gave me this plane. Isn't it cool? Watch how far it will go." With a mighty thrust from Chase, the plane soared into the air. He laughed and chased after it.

Jenna relaxed into a lawn chair beside her friend.

Rhia slanted her a look and smirked. "Am I going to have to tether you to the ground? You look like you're up in the clouds. I take it you had a, shall we say, satisfying evening?"

Jenna blushed. "It was lovely, thank you." She reached for Rhia's hand and squeezed it. "Thanks for looking after Chase. It sounds like he enjoyed himself. Where's the kitten?"

"In the house, sleeping. I don't think either one of them got much rest last night." She held up a red mug with a black cat on it. "Want some?"

"What is it?" asked Jenna.

"Witch's brew, of course."

Jenna smiled. "Sounds perfect, as long as caffeine is one of your secret ingredients."

"Of course." Rhia was out of her chair and back in minutes. She handed Jenna a steaming cup.

"Where is he now?" asked Rhia, her face half hidden by her huge coffee mug.

"Who?"

Rhia raised an eyebrow.

"Oh, Finn," Jenna mumbled into her mug. "He had to run a few errands. How do you know…about us?"

"I looked into my crystal ball, but don't worry, I didn't see any of the good stuff."

Rhia burst out laughing at Jenna's look of horror. "I'm kidding, I'm kidding. Actually, it's just deductive reasoning. Finn's living room light shines into my kitchen. I was up fairly late last night and he never turned it on. Ergo, fun night at the homestead." She patted Jenna's hand. "I want you to be happy, but what happened to holding back until you were sure who the stalker is?"

Jenna sat up straight. "Oh, I have wonderful news. It's not Finn." She explained about the photograph of Finn's size eleven green sneaker.

Rhia hugged her. "I'm so happy for you. Any more news from the detective?"

She nodded. "Mickey thinks it's all related. He says the stalker could be the same person who shot Angus."

"All those years ago?"

Jenna shrugged. "That's his theory."

Suddenly, a woman's screams rent the air. Both women surged out of their chairs, adrenaline pumping through Jenna like a shot of caffeine straight into her blood stream.

She felt the blood drain from her face. As if she was back in her old apartment with Angus, she could feel the fear in the scream, the knowledge of what was coming, and the helplessness it engendered.

A young blonde woman sprinted around the corner of Rhia's house and stopped dead in her tracks at the sight of Rhia and Jenna. Her screams stopped, too. A young man ran around the corner and skidded to a halt beside her.

"Are you okay?" Rhia asked the woman. She took a step toward the couple.

"Yes, I'm fine," said the blonde. "We were just fooling around." She turned to the man with coal black eyes. "Did you drop it?" she whispered.

He whipped his hand in front of her face and she screamed again.

"Oh, you, that's not a spider. I'm going to get you."

The man dodged out of reach and they ran off again. The young woman waved at Rhia as she raced after her boyfriend.

Rhia shook her head with a laugh. "That's Charlene, from next door, and her fiancé. They get a little silly sometimes, but they're in love." She turned to Jenna and stopped, frowning. "Here, sit down. You look as if you've had a terrible shock. What is it?"

Jenna melted into the lawn chair and stared into the reflections in her coffee. "I remember what happened," she said.

Chapter Thirty-One

"Hey, Mom, can—what's the matter?"

Jenna sat up and squinted at her son, his head haloed with golden sunlight. She wondered how her recollection would effect his life, and whether it would have a positive or a negative impact.

If she reached out to embrace him in a protective hug, he'd think she'd lost her mind, so she pushed her hair back and smiled up at him. "What's up?"

"Can I go to Joel's house to show him my airplane?" he asked with a grin, probably from the anticipatory thought of his friend's envy.

"No," she said. She couldn't bear the thought of him leaving her, even for a few hours, not while the memory of Angus' murder was clear in her mind. She raised her hand in a stop sign before he could protest. "How about you invite him over here and I'll make chili dogs for lunch."

Chase licked his upper lip. "With potato chips?"

Jenna sighed. "We might as well be totally unhealthy."

Chase beamed and raced for the door. "Can I use your phone, Rhia?" he called over his shoulder.

"Sure, sweet thing, but don't let Sir Midnight out."

"Sir Midnight?" asked Jenna.

"Chase knighted my kitten last night."

She nodded and chuckled. "He's been in a King Arthur phase lately. You're lucky he didn't call him Kaline. That's his favorite Detroit Tiger ever."

Rhia looked over her shoulder, then back at Jenna. "Do you want to talk about it?"

"I think I have to. I can't believe how the memories—memories that have been submerged for years—are suddenly there, right in front of my eyes in technicolor. It's like a thick, oak door has just been opened to display a whole part of my life I didn't know existed." She took a deep breath and expelled it before she started allowing the memories to tumble over her tongue.

"Chase and I were having a wonderful day. Kids are so funny at that age. You'd think I'd have had some inkling of what was to come, but no, I was safely ensconced in my pretend world where little boys and their moms live happily ever after." She snorted. "Stupid. I lived with Angus McDougall." She turned to Rhia. "We had fairy tale days, Chase and I, but I knew the ogre came home every evening. I knew it and I let my guard down."

"Jenna, you couldn't have prevented what happened. It wasn't your fault."

She sighed. "The rain had stopped earlier and it had left a bright yellow and blue day. I remember the colors of that evening so clearly. A peach glow on the wall from the setting sun, Chase's blue sleepers with navy trains on them, a black cape, and a blossoming red on Angus' white shirt." She shuddered.

Rhia placed a hand on Jenna's arm. "Start at the beginning."

Jenna stared at the grass between her feet. "Angus called. He was upset, as usual, but he seemed especially angry this time. Something about the Dean publicly embarrassing him." Jenna waved her hand. "There was always something; some imagined slight. After he called, I decided to feed Chase and put him down for the night. I didn't want him up when his father came home. I heard Angus fumbling with his keys in the hall and cursing me for locking the door. He walked in and didn't even close the door. I knew it was going to be a bad night. Our sunny day had just been shadowed by a thick, dark storm cloud."

Jenna felt a warning tap on her arm and she looked up to see Chase loping toward them.

"He's coming over right now, Mom. Do you want to see how far my airplane can fly?"

"Sure."

He trotted to his plane and hurled it across the yard. The plane accelerated through the air, settled into a float, caught an updraft, and gradually landed softly on its belly in the grass. He grinned at their applause and executed a deep bow, before sprinting after his plane.

"Did he go after you right away?" asked Rhia quietly.

"Not physically. He ranted on and on about the Dean calling him into his office in front of the whole staff for a little chat, as if he was a schoolboy in trouble. The indignity of it all sparked his rage and he had to take it out on someone. As usual, that was me. Then, he somehow got on the topic about me telling all of our personal secrets to his colleagues. I had met one of the professors in the grocery store the week before and she had asked about Chase. That's about as far as it went, but Angus, of course, blew it all out of proportion. It was okay for him to talk about our home life, but not me," she added with a grimace.

"Well, then, that explains his brutish behavior," said Rhia with a twist to her lips.

"I tried to explain what really happened, but he went after me, this time with his fists. He screeched that there was no excuse for my treason. Treason, as if he was a king or something."

"Definitely delusions of grandeur."

Jenna pushed her hair back from her face and inhaled deeply. "Sometimes he could seem so sane. Not that night. I couldn't defend myself. He was so much bigger than me and ranting like a mad man. I'll spare you the gory details, but eventually I curled up on the floor and refused to respond to his blows, hoping he'd lose interest." She sighed. "Unfortunately, he did. Chase was crying by then, and Angus decided the best way to hurt me was to 'shut him up for good.'"

"Oh, no," said Rhia.

"I was shocked. He'd never even spanked Chase before and suddenly he was threatening to hurt him? That's when I knew he'd really lost it."

"Hi, Mrs. McDougall."

Jenna turned to the small, tow-headed boy crossing the lawn.

"Hi, Joel. Do you know Rhia?"

"Yeah, she's a witch."

Jenna's mouth fell open, but Rhia laughed.

"That's right, and you better watch out, because I might put you in a little-boy stew." She cackled for effect.

He giggled nervously. "You're just teasing me," he said, trying for nonchalance. "Right, Mrs. McDougall? She's teasing, right? Chase says she's a good witch."

"Don't mind her, Joel." She lightly rapped Rhia's arm and said, "Be good."

"I remember now," said Joel. "If you do bad things it comes right back at you. Times three."

Rhia sighed theatrically. "A witch can't have any fun these days."

"Hey, Joel, come and see what I got," yelled Chase.

Joel galloped across the thick grass and began an animated conversation with Chase. Soon the smaller boy was launching the plane into the sky.

Jenna watched them play for a moment then continued her story. "I could take the abuse myself, but there was no way I would let him touch my son. Chase was the only bright light in my life at that point. I rushed toward Angus to stop him and he pushed me back into our bedroom. I ricocheted off the bed and hit the night stand, knocking it over. I was so scared. I could hear him pounding down the hall, hitting the walls with his fists. I pushed myself to my feet and realized that the night stand drawer had fallen open when I hit it and, as if it was a sign, Angus' gun had fallen out. I was shaking like a leaf, but I picked it up and followed him into the hall. I yelled at him to stop, but he just turned and laughed at me and reached for Chase's bedroom doorknob. I threatened him again, but he wouldn't stop. He taunted me one last time and started to describe what he'd do to our son. I couldn't stand it, but when he opened the bedroom door, I found I couldn't squeeze the trigger." Jenna covered her face with her hands. "Oh, God, I couldn't kill him, even though he was going to hurt Chase." Hot tears streamed from her eyes and seeped through her fingers.

Rhia's arms surrounded her and pulled her close.

After a few moments, Jenna pulled away and dried her face with a tissue Rhia had produced. With a twist to her lips, Jenna said, "Maybe

I have some magical powers, because it was as if I had called upon the dark side of my soul to deliver a physical entity who would come and do the job I was too cowardly to accomplish. It all happened so quickly. A gloved hand reached over my shoulder, pulled the gun from my hand, and an explosion went off near my ear. It deafened me for several seconds. I should have looked at the assailant, or savior, but I was fascinated by the red blossoming on Angus' collar as he slumped against the door jamb. He looked so confused, surprised. I finally tore my eyes away from him long enough to see the slim intruder running for the door, a tuft of brown hair hanging out of the hood, and a tiny flash of light reflected from something when he or she looked back."

"Glasses?"

"Maybe. Probably."

"Do you remember anything else about the shooter?"

"Medium height." Jenna strained her memory for more details. Finally, she shook her head. "That's about it."

"What happened next?"

"The rest is a blur. The next thing I remember is dialing 9-1-1. The police came and pretty much considered it an open and shut case. I didn't deny it. I couldn't, because I had blanked out the entire horrific scene. Then, due to an inept, court-appointed lawyer and a sister-in-law who lied to the court by telling them she'd heard me threaten to kill Angus many times, I was charged with murder and sentenced to twenty years in prison. I served eight years and was paroled."

Jenna slumped back in her chair, drained from her revelations.

"Oh, Jenna, to think of all the time that's been wasted!" cried Rhia. "It's so unfair." She pounded a fist on the arm of her lawn chair.

Jenna allowed the repercussions of the truth to seep into her mind. She turned to Rhia and allowed a slow smile to spread over her face. "I'm not a murderer, Rhia. I'm innocent."

Her friend flashed perfect teeth and nodded toward Jenna's back yard. "Looks like you have someone else to share this news with."

Jenna's heart did a little shimmy when she saw Finn walking toward her. She returned his smile and found she couldn't stop. When he reached her, he made a move as if to bend toward her, but he glanced at Chase and straightened. She squeezed his hand.

"Cut it out, you two. You're making me feel like a voyeur," grumbled Rhia. She tried to hide a grin behind a long elegant hand.

Finn laughed. "Sorry, I didn't mean to interrupt your girl-talk."

"Woman-talk," corrected Rhia.

Finn hooted. "In that case, I'll stay!" He turned to Jenna. "Mickey called about the blood."

Rhia gripped the arms of her chair. "Blood? You didn't tell me about any blood. At least, not any *recent* blood."

Jenna sighed. "It's just one more chapter in the ongoing saga of my stalker. Someone nailed a bloody note to Finn's door warning him to stay away from me."

Rhia raised an eyebrow at Finn. "You take direction well."

He was not amused. A muscle jumped in his jaw. "I'm not about to let some lunatic tell me what to do."

Jenna jiggled his hand. "Was it human?"

"No. Animal."

She exhaled noisily. "Thank goodness. Fingerprints?"

He shook his head. They hadn't really expected any, but she could hope.

"Jenna has some news for you, too," said Rhia.

Jenna clasped her hands under her chin, bursting to tell her news.

He stared at her. "You remembered?"

She dropped her hands and scowled. "You ruined the surprise."

"What? You really remembered? This is wonderful!" This time he didn't hesitate when he bent to kiss her.

"It *is* wonderful, because now I know I'm innocent."

"I already told you that."

"I know, and I appreciate your confidence in me, but it's nice to know for sure. The downside is that I still can't identify the murderer, and he or she is still out there *and* tracking me all these years. Now what? Is this lunatic going to try to finish the job? Am I the next target? Or is Chase? Why are we still being followed?"

Chapter Thirty-Two

Chase took a huge bite of his chili dog and seemed oblivious when an orange glob slithered down his chin. Jenna caught it with a napkin seconds before it hit his white tee shirt.

"Wanks, Gum," said Chase.

She smiled. "You're welcome."

Finn raised his glass of apple juice. "Here's to screaming meemies." His green eyes twinkled at Jenna.

Joel clinked his glass against the other glasses. "What's a screaming meemie?"

Chase swallowed. "Someone who screams. We had a screaming meemie today, didn't we, Mom. She was afraid of a spider," he added with scorn dripping from his voice.

"Have you called Mickey yet?" Finn asked Jenna.

"Was it a tarantula?" asked Joel.

"I'll call him later," said Jenna. "I thought I'd invite him to dinner." She tilted her head. "Want to come?"

"A tarantula!" yelled Chase.

Jenna and Finn jumped to their feet. "Where?" they asked in unison.

The boys burst into giggles. Chase fell off his chair and sat on the floor trying to catch his breath. "Oh, Mom, you should see your face. We were talking about the girl who screamed."

The boys looked at each other and tried to stifle fresh giggles.

Jenna's shoulders slumped. "Okay, you guys, just for scaring me half to death, you're on kitchen detail. Come on, Finn, we can talk in the living room."

The boys' laughter followed them from the room.

Finn dropped into an armchair. "I'd love to come, but I promised my sister I'd go computer-shopping with her tonight."

She made a face. "Do you want to drop in later?"

A smile slowly spread across his face and he wiggled his eyebrows. "I'd love to."

After Finn left, Jenna called Mickey, then spent the rest of the afternoon cleaning the apartment and preparing for dinner.

By five-thirty, when Mickey walked through the door, she had showered, changed, and with a light toss of raspberry vinaigrette on the salad, dinner was ready.

Chase ran into the kitchen ahead of Mickey. "Mom, look what Mickey brought me!" He held up a comic book and a Lego kit.

"Spiderman, your favorite. Mickey, you didn't need to do that."

With a flourish, the old man pulled a bouquet of fresh flowers from behind his back.

She kissed his beaming face. "You're too good to us, but we love it. Thank you."

He sniffed the air appreciatively. "Ham and scalloped potatoes?"

"You have a good nose, detective."

Jenna purposely kept the conversation light over dinner. She encouraged Chase to share his interest in knights and running, his silly jokes, and his love of baseball with Mickey. She didn't know how much to tell her son about her memories, so for now, she wouldn't tell him anything.

"When's your next game?" asked Mickey. "Maybe I'll come see you belt one."

"Cool!" Chase's eyes twinkled. "I'll hit a homer for you. Game days are Wednesdays. The rest of the week we practice."

Mickey nodded and scooped up the last of his ice cream. "I'll be there. Need some help cleaning up, Jenna?"

She stood and reached for his bowl. "That'd be great. Chase, you can clear the table, then take the night off."

"No dishes? Yahoo!" He scrambled out of his chair and reached for his plate.

Mickey and Chase cleared the table while Jenna filled the sink with hot sudsy water. Chase sidled up beside her and dropped a plate into the water, laughing when she jumped back from the tidal wave that ensued.

"Mom," he whispered. "Is this what it's like to have a grandfather?"

Hot tears pricked Jenna's eyes. Chase would have loved her own father. She pictured them taking long hikes, playing catch, and driving the tractor together. She nodded and hugged him, unable to get any words past the lump in her throat.

He grinned and wriggled out of her arms. "I'm going to put my new Lego set together."

He galloped away and nearly collided with Mickey on his way in.

"That boy's a bundle of energy," he said. He found a dish towel and waited, one hip against the counter.

They heard the clatter of plastic pieces hit the coffee table.

"Tell me what you remembered," he said in a low voice.

She told him everything about the night Angus was murdered, ending with her dialing 911.

"You must be relieved, lass."

Jenna shrugged. "I thought I would be, but…" She stared at the tiny bubbles bursting in the water.

"But what? What are you worried about?"

She rested the heels of her wet hands on the side of the sink and turned to Mickey. "Now I'm afraid the real killer will, or has, come back to try to kill Chase and me. I dread the thought that this maniac has not only been watching from the shadows all these years, but has returned to finish the job."

She shuddered. He placed an arm around her shoulders. "That's not going to happen, lass. Not on my watch. I've already got a few cruisers driving by your house, unofficially, of course. They'll notice if anyone's prowling around."

"Thank you. I'm just not going to feel Chase is safe until we find out who the real killer is."

He nodded.

"Next steps?" she asked, resuming her task.

"I've been trying to figure out what Judy must have done. She got closer to finding the killer than anyone, and she paid with her life.

That's proof she was onto something."

"Probably reviewed all of the evidence. I wonder if she found something everyone else had missed."

"Maybe, but Judy wasn't one for paper. I think she'd take the people approach. She would have gathered *new* clues, not just gone over the old ones. Have you talked to the old woman from your building yet?"

"I forgot!" Jenna slapped her forehead with a soapy hand. "Oops."

Mickey laughed and wiped her face with the dish towel.

"With everything else that's happened, I completely forgot about our plans to re-interview people. I'll go see her right away. What about you? Have you started talking to people?"

He nodded. "I've talked to some of his colleagues at the university. Strange bunch. They didn't like him much."

Jenna twisted her lips. She pulled the plug on the sink and watched the water swirl its way down. "Can't hold that against them."

She tugged the towel out of Mickey's hands. "All done. Let's go see what Chase is up to."

He placed a detaining hand on her shoulder. "His assistant has been noticeably absent during my visits. Any idea why?"

"Everett? He's shy, a loner, and he blames the police for sending me to jail. Why don't you leave him to me? I'll find out if Judy had been to see him."

They wandered into the living room. "Mom, Mickey, look what I made!" Chase jumped up to show them his Lego creation.

They showed proper appreciation for his talents, then sat down to relax and play Scrabble with Chase.

"I like to play beside Mom," he confided to Mickey. "She always sets me up for triple word score."

Jenna shrugged and grinned at Mickey's look of horror. "Not a competitive bone in my body," she said.

"Well, that makes one of us, lass." He selected his tiles and rubbed his hands together. "Who goes first?"

Jenna sighed forty-five minutes later when the doorbell rang. "Oh, no, we can't stop yet, I have a word worth thirty-nine points."

"Non-competitive, hmmm?"

She threw a pillow at Mickey and got up to get the door. His laughter followed her down the stairs.

She peeked through the screen on the door, then pulled it wide. "Everett, how nice to see you. What are you doing here?"

He stepped into the foyer and glanced left and right at the offices. "Just thought I'd drop in. I haven't seen my boy for a while."

"Come on up. We're just playing Scrabble. Mickey O'Grady's visiting."

He didn't seem surprised that she had a visitor, nor did he ask who Mickey was, so she turned to lead the way upstairs and into her apartment.

"Everett, this is Mickey O'Grady. Mickey, Everett Vandervries."

The air suddenly felt stifling. Mickey stood, but neither man offered his hand.

Jenna looked from one to the other, then down at her son. She clasped her hands at her midriff and wondered how she could stop the impending storm, or at least keep her son from witnessing it.

She needn't have worried.

"Chase, would you get me a Pepsi, please?" said Everett. "With ice."

The boy, seemingly oblivious to the tension flowing between the two men, jumped to his feet and sprinted into the kitchen.

Everett turned back to Mickey with narrowed eyes. "You're the cop who sent Jenna away for twenty years for a crime she didn't commit," he said in a low voice.

Mickey widened his stance, a pugilist preparing for battle. "We didn't know that at the time. Too many people were keeping secrets."

"You shouldn't be convicting people if you don't have enough evidence."

"We had enough evidence. It just pointed to the wrong person. Perhaps the real perpetrator set it up that way."

Jenna laughed nervously and reached for Everett's arm. "Everett thinks he has to take care of me, but really, Everett, I'm just fine. That's all behind us now. Oh, here's Chase with your drink."

She led him to an armchair and bade him sit down. "Come on, Mickey, sit, sit." She pointed to his chair. "Can I get you something to drink, Mickey? No?" She perched on the edge of the sofa. "Chase, why don't you show Mickey and Everett your new card trick." Jenna knew she was babbling, but she felt like she had to ease the uncomfortable void as the two men stared at each other through slitted eyes. She spent the next forty minutes filling the silence with talk of Chase's baseball, her work, and the vegetable garden she wanted to start in the back yard.

By the time Mickey rose to leave, the tension had created twin hammers in her temples.

"It's time for me to go," said Mickey. "Thanks for dinner, Jenna. It was delicious, as usual."

She stood with a sigh of relief. "I'll walk you downstairs."

"Bye, Mickey," said Chase. "Can you come back again some time?"

Everett muttered something under his breath and his fingers drummed an impatient tattoo on the arm of the chair.

Mickey's eyes flicked from Everett to the boy. "Yes, lad, I'll certainly be back," he said loudly.

Jenna led Mickey out of the apartment and down the stairs. "I'm sorry about Everett. He's very protective of me."

Mickey snorted. "Was he like this when your husband was alive?"

Jenna thought for a moment. "I don't think so. He was always very sweet, but he didn't need to protect me. After all," she added sarcastically, "I had a husband to do that."

He grimaced, then dropped a kiss on her forehead. "You be careful, lass, and don't let him stay too long."

She smiled. "Yes, Dad."

He laughed and wagged a finger at her. "Mind what I say, lass."

She closed the door behind him and leaned against it for a moment. She was lucky to have a friend like Mickey. Strange how life turns out.

She started up the stairs and jumped when she heard a voice from the landing.

"I don't like him," said Everett.

She put her hand to her chest and could feel her rapid heart beat. "Geez, Everett, don't do that. You scared me half to death. And it was painfully obvious you didn't like him." She stomped up the stairs toward him.

He stepped out of the shadows. "Stay away from him, Jenna, he's bad news."

"He's trying to help me find Angus' murderer," she said in a low voice, hand on the door knob.

"Jenna, he's the one who put you away in the first place. If you want to find Angus' murderer, let me help you. I'm the only one who's believed in your innocence right from the start."

"Actually, Ev, I'm hoping you *can* help me." She led the way into the apartment. "Chase, honey, it's time for bed. You can read for awhile, if you like, but Everett and I need to talk."

Chase hugged them both and scurried off with his new Spiderman comic book.

Jenna patted the sofa beside her. "Everett, you must have some speculations about who really shot Angus."

"Are you sure you want to travel that road? Why not bury it in an unfortunate past? Forget it, move on."

"I can't move on. I feel like there is unfinished business, as if the story's incomplete." She pushed a mass of curls back from her face. "I can't explain it, but I need to know your impressions from back then."

He reached for her hand. "I've thought about it quite a lot. As a matter of fact, I even tried to do a bit of amateur sleuthing back then." He shook his head and crossed his sneakered feet on the coffee table. He ran a tongue over his tiny teeth. "No talent for it, I guess. Dead ends."

"Did you have anyone in particular in mind?"

He ran his ponytail between his fingers. "You know Angus wasn't well-liked at the university, by either faculty or the student population. I looked through his records for anyone he had given a failing grade to in the six months before his death." He snorted. "There were several. His comments on below-par essays could be caustic and downright nasty."

"Did you mention your ideas to the detectives?"

He twisted his lips. "No. I didn't want them hassling the students. If it ever got back to the Dean that it was my idea, I'd never get promoted."

Jenna bit her tongue. There was no use reminding him that he hadn't been promoted anyway.

"I think I found a prime suspect, but I doubt if they'd be interested in my theory. Those cops are so cocksure of themselves," he added with a sneer.

"Who did you think it was?" she asked.

"A drama student who'd had a run in with Angus and had dropped out shortly after Angus' death."

Jenna made a mental note to ask Mickey if he could follow up on this lead. "Ev, has a woman detective been to see you in the past six months?"

Everett reached for both of her hands and turned slightly sideways so he could face her on the sofa.

"You know you wouldn't have to worry about any of this if you'd just give in to your feelings."

Jenna tilted her head, unsure of his meaning. "What do you mean?"

He moved slightly closer. "I've taken care of you and Chase the best I can. And I've loved doing it," he hastened to add. "But now, I think it's time to take our relationship to the next level."

Jenna's stomach clenched. She hated to hurt him. He'd been so good to Chase and her. "Oh, Everett."

"Look, we'd make a great couple. We share the same interests: classical literature, poetry, Chase. You love to feel safe and cozy and I love to provide that security. You know, Chase already thinks of me as a member of the family. I'm like an uncle to him."

Jenna gently pulled her hands from his grasp and rubbed a spot between her eyes. An uncle was nothing like a father. Why hadn't she seen this coming? More to the point, how could she let him down gently?

"We could move out of the city, get a farm like your father's, where Chase could run free."

The image of Everett on a farm holding a pitchfork brought a bubble of laughter to Jenna's throat. She swallowed it.

"Everett, stop."

"No, listen." He reached for her hand again and squeezed it. "Even your neighbors think we'd make a great couple."

Jenna sat up straight. "What are you talking about?"

"It's true. Florence, the old lady across the street."

"How do you know her?"

He shrugged. "I came looking for you one day and she was out sweeping her sidewalk. I asked if she'd seen you leave." He chuckled. "I'll tell you, Jenna, if you ever feel like you're being watched, you'll know who it is. Florence doesn't miss a trick."

A creepy feeling brought goose bumps to her arms. She glanced at the front window, a black rectangle in the wall, and wished she'd pulled the blind.

"That woman is watching me?"

"Don't worry, she's harmless," said Everett. "Just nosy. Anyway, she thinks you need someone just like me to look after you and Chase. I could protect you. You wouldn't ever have to think about this again. So, go and pretty yourself up, as if you need it, and we'll go out for a nice evening alone."

"Oh, Everett, you know I'm grateful for everything you've done for me, but we can't go out. Certainly not as a couple. Not ever."

"Of course, you don't want to leave Chase here alone." He chuckled. "I understand. That's okay, we'll just order in." He rose and reached for the phone book on the kitchen counter. "What do you feel like eating. Chinese, Thai, pizza?"

Jenna stood and put her hand on the phone book. "Everett, I'm not hungry." She sighed. "Come and sit down. We need to talk. Ev, I don't want to hurt you. I really don't, but I'll never feel that way about you." His jaw muscles bunched. "I love you like a brother, and you'll always be special to me. But that's as far as our relationship can ever go. I hope you understand."

He patted her hand and smiled. "Of course, Jenna. You've only been out a few months. I've rushed you and I didn't mean to do that. I know it's scary to start a new relationship, or even to change an existing one. You need some time to get used to the idea. No problem. I'm a patient man. I understand perfectly."

Jenna wanted to disagree with him, to tell him that she'd never change her mind, but the coward in her numbed her vocal cords and she remained silent.

She patted his hand. "Maybe you better go now. It's been a long day."

He smiled, showing his pink gums. "Of course. You've got a lot to think about," he said cheerily. At the door he reached over and kissed her cheek. "That's for luck and good thoughts. I'll lock the front door on my way out."

She nodded and closed the door. She walked to the front window and peered through the black night at the house across the street. No movement. No evidence of prying eyes. Jenna shivered and reached for the string to close the blind, but her hand stilled at a knock on the door. Exasperated, she stalked to the door, muttering under her breath. "Everett, go away. Quit pushing me."

She started talking before the door was half open. "You really have to leave—oh, come in."

"Boy, you're fickle." Finn chuckled and kissed her soundly, leaving her knees weak and her stomach fluttering. "Which is it? Should I go or should I stay?"

"Stay," she said breathlessly. "Definitely stay." She reached for his hand and pulled him in. "Sorry, I thought you were someone else."

"Who were you kicking out?"

Jenna started to answer, then shook her head and wrapped her arms around his neck. "It so doesn't matter. Kiss me again."

He gave in without a whimper and his kiss brought a moan deep in her chest. When he raised his head, he whispered, "I brought something to help us celebrate."

She giggled. "You mean there's more?"

He held up a bottle of Chardonnay. "Go get us some wine glasses." When Jenna returned seconds later, he had produced a candle and had it glowing on the window seat, turned off the overhead light, and opened the wine.

"Ambience," he said. His fingers caressed hers as he handed her a glass of white wine. He lifted his glass and touched it to hers. "To the return of old memories, to us, and to making new memories…together."

Her heart thudded against her ribs. Their eyes collided as she sipped her wine and let the crisp, oaky liquid run over her tongue.

He pulled her close, and with his lips whisper-soft on hers, he breathed, "Ready to make some memories?"

Chapter Thirty-Three

Karma stomped around the small room, ramming a fist into one wall, turning furiously, striding, kicking the opposite wall, exulting in the feeling of unleashed violence. The room, previously a shrine, showed the scars of Karma's deep emotional torment the past few months.

"Told that bitch detective too much. Should have kept the mouth shut and the lips sealed. Stupid. A break in strategy. Talked about Jenna, Angus. Let too much out. Stupid. Talked too much. Underestimated her."

Karma knew people talked too much when they were lying. The detective would know that, too.

An evil cackle filled the room. "She paid for it. Paid for snooping, for her pushy, hard-nosed pig attitude. Paid for it with a knife carving a lovely red ravine into her neck." Karma recalled the gush of blood, surprisingly warm over the hand that had severed her carotid artery with such swift glee. "Some trained expert. She didn't even see it coming. Didn't hear my approach. Just time enough to see a quick flash of terror in her eyes before she crumpled like a stuck pig. Hah! Yes, that's what she was—a stuck pig!"

Karma's mood changed with lightning speed. Hysterical laughter filled the room. God, life was funny.

Unfortunately, she died without relinquishing her findings. Karma still didn't know what discoveries she'd made, what information she'd surmised, what conclusions she'd come to.

Karma's mood sobered and an animal growl rumbled like thunder in the room. The file was still missing. Hidden, waiting like a time bomb to blow up and ruin the plan.

Maybe there was no file. No data to fear.

"Enough." With a hand slicing the air, Karma abolished thoughts of the female detective and strode to the open journal on the desk. There was much more interesting prey available to think about. Plans to carry out. Jenna-plans.

Chapter Thirty-Four

"Jenna, line one's for you," called Finn from his office.

"Who is it?" she asked absently. She shifted the mound of paper on her desk until she uncovered the phone. They were working on a huge proposal and her mind was filled with dates, locations, schedules, and training agendas. Her hand hovered above the phone.

"She won't say."

Jenna snatched her hand away as if burned. "Irene," she muttered.

"What?" Finn strolled over to lean against her desk.

She flicked a stray curl away from her forehead. "It's Irene. She's trying to scare me. She's been leaving cryptic messages on my answering machine. Something about me being in danger. She won't say more on the machine because she doesn't want Chase to be upset."

"What do you want me to tell her? She's still holding."

"I don't care. Tell her that I'm not here, or that I'm too busy to play her little game, or that I'm dead. Just get rid of her."

Finn picked up Jenna's phone and pressed a button. "I'm afraid Jenna's not available to come to the phone right now. If you'd like to leave a mes…" Finn looked at the receiver. "She hung up." He dropped the handset back into its cradle. "Are you sure there's nothing to this? She sounded a bit rattled."

"She's just trying to get to me. She blames me for ruining her life. She thinks I took away her brother, and then I took Chase away. She's got nothing left. Nothing left to lose." Jenna slammed a fist on the desk. "I refuse to let her affect me in any way."

She took a deep breath. "Enough of that. Do you have the screen capture for the spreadsheet manual yet?"

Finn smiled at the abrupt change of topic. "Just working on that. I'll email it to you."

"Mom, I'm ready." Chased bounded down the stairs and landed at the bottom with a thump. "It's just a practice today, you know."

"I know. I won't stay. I just want to go for a walk with my son, is that okay?" She ruffled his hair. "Where's your cap?"

He held up his bat to show her the glove and cap threaded on it.

They set out for the park, Chase alternately skipping, galloping, walking backwards and hopping. Jenna grinned at his boundless energy.

"Now, don't forget, Chase, I want you to stay here until I come and get you after practice. For no reason should you go with anyone else. No one, even if you know them." She held his face and forced him to look into her eyes. "Understand?"

"Sure, Mom, but I can walk home by myself. You don't need to pick me up."

She dropped her hands and he reached for his ball cap. He adjusted it low over his eyes and curved the brim like he'd seen the pros do.

"I'll need some fresh air by then. It'll do me good to go for a walk. You'll wait for me, right?"

"Sure. Bye." He ran off and was greeted with high fives by his teammates.

Jenna sighed and turned for home. She didn't want him jumping at shadows or afraid of every stranger he saw, but it was difficult to let him go. He'd be safe today, surrounded by his friends.

She immersed herself in work until the phone's persistent warble brought her head up. It was Finn's day to answer the phones, but a quick check told her he was on the other line. She picked up the phone.

"Good morning, TechnoTrain. May I help you?"

"Jenna, is that you?" The woman's voice quavered.

She sighed in exasperation. "Irene."

"I need to talk to you, and I can't do it over the phone. You and Chase could be in danger."

"Look, Irene, I'm really busy here. Why don't you just tell me what you want."

"We need to meet. Your phone could be tapped. Or maybe mine."

"I'm sure this is all very exciting for you, Irene. All the secrecy, the mystery. But I'm not playing that game. I want you to stop calling here. Stop calling and hanging up, stop leaving little messages from Angus, stop harassing me."

Irene gasped. "Angus is leaving you messages?"

"No, Irene, you are, and I'm on to you. You need to stop this right now, or I'll have the cops at your door."

"Jenna, I didn…"

"I don't want to hear your excuses. Just leave me alone!" She slammed the phone down and put her hands over her face. She jumped when a hand touched her neck.

"You okay?" asked Finn. His fingers massaged her shoulders, gently digging into the tight muscles and loosening them.

She relaxed against the back of her chair and let his kneading fingers work the tension from her neck. "That was Irene again."

"Figured."

"She won't bother me again. I hope."

"Let me screen the calls for a while. Maybe she'll lose interest."

She reached for his left hand and kissed it. Noticing his watch, she pulled it down so she could check the time. "I have to go pick up Chase for lunch. Want to come?"

"Nah. I have to finish this manual. My boss is a slave driver, you know." He laughed and avoided her playful slap. "Bring me back an English Toffee cappuccino, will you?"

Jenna grimaced. "I don't know how you can drink those things. They're so sweet."

"What do you think makes me such a sweet guy?"

Jenna laughed and stepped out into the bright sunshine. She debated about going back for her sunglasses, but decided against it. She didn't want to be late.

As she approached the ball park, her eyes scanned the field for her son. She looked at the tall, skinny redhead playing short stop. Not Chase. He must be having batting practice. She shielded her eyes to survey the boys sitting on the bench. Most of them wore Tigers caps, just like Chase's. Three had long hair, so she honed in on them as she wandered closer. One had a wide green streak running down the center of his ponytail, one had bleach blonde curls, and the other had straight black hair. Jenna's heart skipped a beat. Where was Chase?

She looked out into the field again, directly into the sun. She wished she had brought her sunglasses. Maybe Chase was playing a different position today. Of course, that had to be it.

She squinted against the glare and tried to pick out the fluid athletic movements of her son. She circled around toward the visitor's bench, so she'd have a better angle, but still couldn't pick him out. Her heart thudded painfully.

She spotted the coach and hurried up to him. "Ben, have you seen Chase?"

Ben Seabrook turned and smiled. "Hi, Jenna. We're almost finished for the morning. Give us a few more minutes." He turned back to yell encouragement to the batter.

She tugged at his shirt. "But where is he, Ben? Where's Chase?"

Ben's eyes stayed on the batter, but he pointed to the other bench. "He's waiting to bat. Run hard, Jamie. That's it. Good job." He clapped his hands loudly and the batter, Jamie, grinned proudly from first base.

She looked back at the home bench. No Chase. "Ben, he's not there."

Finally, he turned to give her his whole attention. Something in her face must have illustrated her worry, because he looked at the bench and yelled, "Joel, where's Chase?"

Joel looked down the bench to his left and right, then shrugged. "Don't know, Coach."

Jenna put her hands to her mouth and tears clouded her eyes. "Oh my God, oh my God. Something's happened to him." Fear clamped a band around her chest and made it almost impossible to breathe.

"Calm down, Jenna, he's got to be around here some place. He was here a few minutes ago." He waved his arms to the boys on the field. "Everybody in."

The sweaty boys jogged in and surrounded him. "Has anyone seen Chase?"

"Hey, Mom, what's up?"

Jenna whirled around and clutched Chase to her. "Where were you? I was frantic! Don't ever do that again, do you hear me, young man? I told you to stay at the park and not leave for any reason." The combination of worry and relief made her voice harsh.

"Geez, Mom, lighten up." He blushed when he saw the whole team looking at him. "I just went to the bathroom at the coffee shop across the street. The one here is broken. What's the big deal?"

Jenna closed her eyes. He had every right to be embarrassed and angry at her display in front of his friends. She made a decision. It was time she explained why it was so important for her to know where he was every second of the day.

"You're right. I overreacted. I'm sorry, honey."

"Everything okay, Jenna? Do I have to put a leash on this guy?" He put his hands on Chase's shoulders.

"No, Ben, he's just fine. I'm sorry for making a scene. I'll bring him back after lunch, okay?"

Ben slapped Chase's back. "See you later, mate." He strode off to send the other boys home, then turned. "Hey, Chase, I'm going to try you at pitching this afternoon."

"Cool."

They started for home. Luckily, Chase didn't spend much energy on sulking.

"Chase, you and I have to talk about some things. About your father and how he died. And why I acted like an idiot today."

He looked at her, a question mark in his lake-blue eyes.

"How about we go out for pizza tonight after practice. I'll explain everything then."

He slid a sly glance her way. "Can I get anchovies and olives on the pizza?"

She laughed. "You can ruin your pizza anyway you want. I'll get my own."

When they arrived home, Jenna listened to the answering machine tape. She had gotten into the habit of deleting any messages that began with more than three seconds of silence. Slow talkers were out of luck.

"Message erased," said the mechanized voice four times. Three others were from Irene, all saying the same thing: "I need to see you. Please call. It's for your own good."

Jenna deleted each of these, too, and wished she could eradicate the messages from her mind as easily.

"Message erased," she muttered and hurried into the kitchen to make Chase's lunch.

After practice, Chase showered while Jenna finished up her work for the day.

"Pizza time," he called as he slid down the banister and landed in a heap at the bottom. He sat on the floor laughing. "Mom, you have to try this. It's really fun!"

"That would be quite a sight for a customer walking in the door. I think I'll pass, but thanks for the thought." She reached a hand to pull him up. "Where to? Jaconi's or Pizza Partner's?"

"Aha, a trick question. Definitely Jaconi's, because Partner's doesn't have anchovies. Good try, Mom."

At Jaconi's, they ordered individual pizzas and sipped their Sprites at a cozy table covered with a red-checkered tablecloth. Tucked into a corner of the tiny restaurant, separated from the other diners by several yards of black and white tile flooring, Jenna told Chase how his father died, the stalker's poisonous antics, and the reason why they had to be extremely careful until Mickey had caught the perpetrator. She tried not to scare him, but she needed him to understand how serious their situation was.

"So I can't tell anyone?" asked Chase. "Not even Uncle Everett or Aunt Irene?"

"Especially not them. If you need to talk it over with someone, you can talk to Mickey, Rhia, Finn or me. That's it." Jenna reached for his hand. "Do you understand?"

He nodded and sat back as the waiter placed a pizza in front of each of them. When they were alone again, he leaned toward her and whispered, "I knew you didn't do it, Mom."

Jenna's throat tightened. This child of her heart could bring tears to her eyes with a single word. She watched him dig into his pizza with gusto and knew she was the luckiest woman alive.

They wandered home as the sky was turning from rose to magenta. The porch light beckoned them into the darkened house. Jenna unlocked the front door, then searched for her apartment key as they clomped up the stairs, laughing at Chase's story about Ben, his coach, showing up with a dogcatcher's net for afternoon practice.

She pushed the door open and screamed when something brushed against her ankle.

"What is it, Mom? What's the matter?"

She flicked a switch just inside the door. Light flooded the landing.

"Hey, it's Sir Midnight?" Chase stooped to pick up the tiny black puffball from the floor. "It's Rhia's kitten. What was he doing in there?"

Jenna backed out of the apartment. "Good question. Let's go get Finn. I don't like this."

They had only taken three steps up the stairs when Finn appeared in his doorway.

"What's the matter? I thought I heard a scream," he said, hurrying down to meet them.

"Look who was in our apartment," said Chase. He held the purring animal on his shoulder tucked into the hollow of his neck.

Finn's brows drew together. "You two stay here, I'll go check your apartment."

"No way," said Jenna. "We're going with you."

"Then stay close." He took a cautious step into their apartment, Jenna and Chase glued to his back.

They checked each room, but found locked windows and no evidence of intruders.

"Coast is clear." Back in the living room, Finn shrugged. "I've been home all evening and didn't hear anything. Maybe he slipped in when you were leaving."

Unconvinced, Jenna nodded for Chase's benefit. "Maybe that's it."

"If it makes you feel better, we can change your locks again."

She shook her head and tried to use logic to still the apprehension swirling through her mind. "It doesn't make sense that anyone could get in. We're the only ones with keys. I'm sure you're right." She smiled at her son and petted the silky animal. "Well, Chase, we better get this little guy home. Rhia's probably worrying about him."

She suppressed a shudder. Although she put on a confident face, Jenna couldn't shake the feeling that someone had been in her apartment and seemed to be able to get in at his or her whim.

Chapter Thirty-Five

Jenna stepped off the bus and walked the block and a half to Wim's apartment. A stroll through the old neighborhood held no sense of allure for her. No wave of happy memories washed over her as she passed the corner diner and hurried along the cracked sidewalk under a pewter sky.

She climbed the stairs into her old apartment building and wrinkled her nose at the smell of cooked cabbage that seemed to linger in every apartment building corridor. As she reached Wim's apartment, she raised her hand to knock, but slowly lowered it and turned around to face the door to the stairs. Immediately to the left was the elevator and at the end of the hall stood the heavy steel emergency exit door. She tried to picture an intruder stealing through the emergency door and creeping up the stairs, a gun at his side. Or had she walked boldly through the front door and taken the elevator to her brother's floor?

Jenna sighed and turned back to Wim's door, which was now opening wide.

"Jenna, my dear. Please come in." The old woman checked the hallway before closing the door firmly.

"Wim, thank you for agreeing to see me again."

"Pshaw. I'm only too happy to see you, but you must bring that precious child of yours one day. I'd love to see how he's turned out."

Jenna followed her into the congested room. "He's perfect." If possible, even more books lined the walls than her last visit.

"Ah, so he hasn't taken after his father. I'm relieved to hear it." She gestured to the tea service on the low coffee table, then sank into her chair by the window. "I've made us some Earl Grey. Would you pour?"

Jenna perched on the edge of the sofa and placed a wedge of lemon on each of the saucers before filling the delicate china teacups.

Wim accepted the cup and saucer with a murmured thanks. She sat ramrod straight, knees pressed together primly, and sipped her tea.

Jenna fiddled with her lemon, inhaled its fresh scent on a deep breath, then placed her cup and saucer on the lacy doily by her side.

"Wim, do you remember if a female detective came to see you a few months ago regarding the night Angus died?"

"Of course. A lovely Italian woman. Judy something, I think. Do you know she has eleven brothers? She wanted to see my journals."

"May I ask why you didn't mention her when Finn and I were here?"

The old woman placed her teacup on the table and leaned toward Jenna. "Oh, my dear, I thought it would upset you to know the police were still interested in your case. I knew you wanted to get on with your life and I was afraid you'd think they weren't going to allow you to do that. I hope you don't mind that I spoke to her."

Jenna patted her clasped hands. "No, of course not. Do you know what journals she looked at?"

Wim bent over and pulled a blue notebook from the bookcase by her feet. She placed it on her knees and leafed through it until she found the page she wanted.

"Here it is. Let's see, numbers R3678 and 3680," she murmured. "I've numbered them for organizational purposes." She pushed herself to her feet and hobbled to the bookcase on the far wall. After making her selections and skimming through the entries, she handed the books to Jenna and sank back into her chair.

"I had forgotten there was a second notation when you were here. It's probably nothing, but I didn't remember it until the next day, which is why it's in the other notebook."

Jenna scanned the first journal where Wim had recorded her impressions of the day of Angus' death. Nothing seemed to be different from the first time she and Finn had read it. She opened the second book.

Wim leaned forward and pointed to the first page. "See? Here. I remembered that the person with the cape was wearing running shoes. It seemed odd at the time. I mean, I never pictured Dracula in sneakers."

Jenna smiled. "Me neither, but it's perfect for someone planning on making a fast exit. Do you mind if I make copies of these? I promise I'll bring them back."

"That's just what the nice Italian lady said. And she did, too. Of course you can take them. I hope they help, my dear."

Jenna rose to leave soon after. She turned at the door as a sudden thought occurred to her. "Wim, do you ever refer to your journals as 'logs'?"

"No, I tend to call them my diaries or journals."

"Did Detective Farandino, the Italian lady?"

"Hmmmm, I don't think so. Is that important?"

"No, it's just a thought." She leaned over to kiss the older woman's cheek. "Thanks for your help, Wim. I'll get these back to you as soon as possible."

Jenna strode down the street and boarded the bus, clutching the notebooks to her chest. She slid into the seat and contemplated the open window, debating the levels of discomfort between the noxious smell of diesel wafting in the window, and the heat from the summer sun beating down on her through a closed window. She sighed and left the window open.

While the bus trundled along, stopping frequently on a milk run out of the city, Jenna leaned her head back and thought about Wim's notes. She didn't need to open the journals. Wim's words were etched in her mind. After all, they had provided Jenna with her first alternative for Angus' murder. Other suspicious characters had entered the building that evening, and she knew where the sneaker-footed Dracula had been heading. But, why? Who?

Jenna pulled the signal wire for the first stop in Mount Clemens. She stepped off the bus and walked across the street to the baseball park. She picked her way between the other parents on the bleachers and dropped down beside Mickey, patting his knee.

"Hey, Mickey, how's my boy doing?"

"He's a natural."

They cheered and clapped through the final inning, then waited for Chase at the fence.

"Did you see us win, Mom? We were awesome."

She hugged him and inhaled his puppy-dog smell. "I did and you were. Ready to go?"

Chase danced and skipped and galloped ahead while Jenna told Mickey about her visit to Wim.

"Nothing new?" he asked.

"Not really. Just the shoes. And Wim doesn't call her notebooks 'logs,' and neither did Judy, as far as she knew."

"Hmpf."

Chase leaped onto the porch with a clatter of cleats on wood.

"Chase, take your shoes—"

The screen door smacked shut behind him.

"—off," called Jenna.

She and Mickey entered the house at a more leisurely pace.

"Cool," said Chase. With one hand on Finn's shoulder and the other holding his shoes, he leaned toward the computer screen. "Mom, come see. Finn added an animated graphic to your presentation."

"Cool," she said, mimicking her son. "Hey, it's a revolving photo cube. How did you do that?"

Finn turned toward her with a grin. "I downloaded a neat little program from the Internet. I figured we could dazzle them with our technical expertise and maybe they'd overlook our lack of experience with this particular type of training."

He reached across his desk for a pink slip of paper skewered to a nail. "This is for you."

She could feel his eyes on her as she scanned the note.

"How about I take Chase and Mickey up to your apartment to start lunch while you return your call."

Jenna nodded absently. "That sounds great. Thanks."

She watched them climb the stairs, then looked back at the note. *Call Detective Cooper a.s.a.p.* Her heart kicked into high gear. What did the police want with her?

She reached for the phone on her desk, then stopped to take a deep, steadying breath. It had to be a mistake. Or a message for Mickey, from one of the officers he had watching her house.

Jenna picked up the receiver and punched in the numbers with trembling fingers.

"Detective Cooper, please," she said to the man who answered.

A click followed her request, then a deep baritone answered. "Cooper, here."

"Yes, Detective Cooper, this is Jenna McDougall. You called and left a message that I should call you."

"Yeah,…uh…" She heard paper rustling in the background. "McDougall, yeah, here we are. You know an Irene McDougall?"

"Yes."

"She a relative?"

"No, well, yes."

"Look, lady, the questions only get tougher from here on."

His tone pricked her anger. "Yes, she's my sister-in-law. What's this all about, detective?"

"She's been hit by a car and she's in the hospital. We found your name in her handbag as the person to contact in case of an emergency."

Jenna gasped. "Is she okay?" No matter what her differences with Irene, she had never wished her harm.

"Still alive, last I heard. Can you meet me at Detroit General ICU?"

"Yes, of course," she said. "It'll take me about forty-five minutes to get there."

"Fine." He hung up.

Jenna carefully replaced the receiver into its cradle. Why would Irene have listed her as a contact person? Surely she had someone she was closer to. A wave of pity brought stinging tears to her eyes. That poor woman was lying in a hospital and she had no one who cared. Her only close relatives, Angus and Chase, had been taken from her. Despite their past differences Jenna couldn't leave her there alone. She reached for her purse and hurried up the stairs.

When she reached her kitchen, she had to smile. Three males busily prepared lunch, all issuing orders at once.

Finn flipped the two cheese sandwiches on the grill and adjusted the heat. He turned and searched her eyes. She offered a reassuring smile, then sat on a kitchen chair and drew Chase onto her lap.

"What's up, Mom?" He wiped his hands on his shirt and left an oily streak of butter across his chest.

"I have some bad news about Aunt Irene." The men turned to listen, but she kept her eyes trained on her son. "She's been hit by a car and she's in the hospital."

"Is she going to be alright?"

She smoothed the hair back from his face. "I don't know yet," she said softly. "I'm going to the hospital right now. I'll be able to tell you more when I get back."

"Can I come, too? We should take her something. Do you think she'd like to read my new Spiderman comic book?"

Jenna pressed her face into his neck. "You're a sweet thing, but I think you should keep your comic book for now. Maybe we can send her some flowers. How's that?"

"Okay." He leaned into her.

"You can't come to the hospital with me this time, honey. They don't let kids in the Intensive Care Unit."

Finn moved toward them. "I'll take you," he said to her.

"No, Finn, you can't do that. Our presentation is tomorrow and we're not prepared yet. You have to get that finished and I won't be much help until later tonight. I'll catch a cab. Mickey, would you mind staying with Chase while I'm gone?"

Finn frowned. "I'd rather he was with you. I'll put Chase to work downstairs. You know how to use your mom's computer, don't you, sport?"

Chase jumped to his feet. "Sure. Can I, Mom? Can I go to work with Finn?"

She smiled. "As long as Mickey doesn't mind being my cabbie."

"Not at all, lass. Ready to go?"

Finn rescued two slightly charred grilled cheese sandwiches from the frying pan.

"Come on, Chase, help me out here. We'll wrap these up for your mom and Mickey."

Jenna hugged them both good-bye and followed Mickey out to the car. Traffic was light and Mickey's foot was heavy, so they made it to the hospital in thirty-five minutes.

On the sixth floor they stepped out of the elevator into the hushed atmosphere of the ICU. A cop flirted with a pretty nurse on the left, and a tiny waiting room, over-filled with castoff furniture, sat empty of visitors on the right.

Jenna stepped toward the red-headed officer. "Are you Detective Cooper?"

He laughed and shook his head. "Coop'll be here in a few minutes."

A matronly nurse stepped out of a back room behind the desk, a coffee cup in one hand and a clipboard in the other. "Are you here to see a patient?" she asked Jenna.

"Irene McDougall."

She glanced at the clipboard and nodded. "I'll take you in." She set the coffee on the desk and swatted the officer lightly on the arm. "Don't you dare drink my coffee. I'm coming back."

She led Jenna through the glass doors to the large open ward.

As Mickey made a move to follow, she stopped him with a stern look. "Only one at a time."

She slowed just inside the doors and placed a hand on Jenna's arm. "I want to warn you. She's not in good shape. She was in surgery for four hours. Fractured pelvis, cracked vertebrae in her lower back, and multiple internal injuries. You're only allowed to stay for five minutes."

Jenna surveyed the room and wondered which motionless body belonged to her sister-in-law. Machines whirred, chirped and beeped from every bed. She took a deep breath and almost gagged as the overwhelming taste of disinfectant and alcohol hit the back of her throat.

She swallowed. "Which one is she?" she whispered.

"This way," said the nurse, and steered her to a separate glass-walled room in the far left corner. They walked through the door and Jenna stared in horror at the body that lay in the bed. Tubes and wires ran from beneath the crisp sheet to the machines scattered around the bed. A respirator chuck-whirred, filling Irene's lungs with life-giving oxygen. She cringed at the mechanical rise and fall of her sister-in-law's chest.

"Go on now." The nurse nudged her forward. "Five minutes, no more." She slipped out of the room, leaving Jenna with a sudden fear of being alone with the fragile figure in the bed.

After a moment, Jenna stepped closer and traced her fingers lightly over Irene's bloodless hand.

"Irene," she whispered. "It's me, Jenna." The body didn't stir. "Chase sends his love." Not an eyelash flickered.

"I'm sorry I didn't return your phone calls. I thought…" Jenna gasped. "My God, Irene, this doesn't have anything to do with your warnings, does it? No, no, it couldn't." Jenna bit a thumbnail and pushed the terrifying thought away. "This was just an accident, right, Irene? I'll talk to the detective. He'll fill me in on what really happened." She patted Irene's hand, as if the unconscious woman was the one who needed reassurance.

The nurse's head appeared around the doorway. "Time's up. She needs her rest," she added apologetically.

Jenna nodded and squeezed Irene's hand. "I'll be back," she whispered.

She followed the nurse from the ICU and found Mickey sitting in the waiting room, his head bent close to a large man in a navy trench coat. The low rumble of their voices halted when the man looked up and spotted her. With surprising grace, he stood and approached her with an outstretched hand. The top of her head didn't reach his shoulder.

"Ms. McDougall, Gideon Cooper." Her hand was swallowed in his huge paw, then quickly released. He flashed his badge and dropped it back into an inside pocket, then pulled out a small black notepad and flipped it open. "I'd like to ask a few questions, if you don't mind."

Jenna nodded.

He licked his pencil and held it ready. "What is your relationship with the victim?"

"Her name is Irene."

He continued to stare.

She sighed. "Irene was my sister-in-law. I'm a widow."

"Yeah, I got that, but what was your *relationship* with her."

Jenna hesitated.

"Were you best buddies, sworn enemies, what?"

She shifted her stance. "We had our differences."

"Why, because you took away her nephew, or because you murdered her brother?"

"Back off, Cooper," growled Mickey. He shoved his face forward which put him at the height of the man's neck, an Irish Foxhound challenging a Great Dane.

She placed a hand on his arm, but kept her eyes trained on the tall detective. "It's okay, Mickey. Yes, she held me responsible for her brother's death."

Cooper snorted. "Have you spoken to her recently?"

"She phoned yesterday."

"What was that all about?"

"She said I was in danger, that I had to be careful."

"Did you feel threatened by her, Ms McDougall?"

"Threatened? Sometimes."

"What were you afraid she might do to you?"

"I was worried she might try to take my son away from me."

"That's a pretty serious charge. So, you'd want to stop her any way you could, right?"

Jenna lowered her eyebrows. "What are you getting at?"

He shrugged a massive shoulder. "Well, you did the brother. Maybe you wanted to get rid of the whole family?"

Jenna opened her mouth, but no sound came out. She felt like she had been sucker-punched in the solar plexus.

"That's it, Cooper. We're out of here," said Mickey.

"Look, Mick, I gotta ask the question. This wasn't any accident. She was hit in her own driveway. A neighbor saw a small dark car. No license plate."

A cold, familiar finger of dread traced its way down Jenna's spine.

"Jenna doesn't even have her driver's license, let alone own a car."

Detective Cooper shrugged. "That's what boyfriends are for."

Mickey cursed. "Let's go, Jenna. When you want to talk turkey, Cooper, let us know."

Detective Cooper pointed a finger at Jenna. "Don't you be taking any trips."

Mickey ushered her to the elevators and jabbed the button, mumbling about arrogant young bucks who didn't have the sense God gave them.

Jenna felt the blood drain from her face. Not again, not again, not again.

Mickey placed a hand under her elbow. "Don't faint on me, lass. He's just a lazy detective trying to find the easy way out. Come on, let's get you home."

They sat in Mickey's car in the hospital parking lot.

"Am I going to spend the rest of my life being blamed for things I haven't done?"

"Aw, lass, don't take it to heart. He was just doing his job."

Jenna nodded vigorously. "Yes, that's right. And so will every other detective who has a case to clear. I'll always be on someone's suspect list."

"Only until we can clear your name."

She groaned, then slapped a hand to her forehead. "Oh, I have to call Everett. He won't know about Irene. He'll be so upset. They're quite close, you know."

Mickey pulled his cell phone from the glove compartment and tossed it in her lap. "Use mine," he said.

He started the car and headed back to Mount Clemens.

She punched in the number for the university and marvelled that she could still remember it after eight years. Her call was efficiently patched through to the gum-snapping secretary of the English department. The last time Jenna had seen her, she had been wobbling down the hall on three-inch heels and wearing a very short red suede skirt with fringe. Her black lycra tank top fit her like a second skin.

"Hi, Brandi. It's Jenna McDougall."

"Jen-na, wow, they finally let you out of your cage. Way to go, girl. You know, Jenna, I never told you this, but I think you did this department a real service. Now, we just have one more head case to get rid of and we'll almost be considered sane."

Jenna had learned long ago to ignore most of what came out of the other woman's mouth. "Brandi, I'm looking for Everett Vandervries."

"Speaking of which," she muttered. "Didn't come in today, thank God."

"Is he sick?"

"Said he was. Who knows? Sounded like his usual sarcastic self to me, but who am I to say? I'm just the lowly secretary."

"Do you have his home phone number there?"

"Sure," she said on a sigh. "Just a sec." Vigorous gum-popping ensued while she looked.

"Here it is." She rattled off the number. "Make sure you tell him we all hope he's sick again tomorrow."

Her high-pitched cackle filled the air waves. Jenna pulled the phone away from her ear to avoid permanent damage to her ear drum. Mickey scowled.

"Thanks, Brandi." She hung up before the woman had a chance to respond.

Mickey glanced at Jenna. "She sounds like a doozie."

"Floozie, more like. No, that's not fair." She pushed her hair back from her face. "They're just so hard on Everett, and Brandi doesn't know when to keep her mouth shut."

She pressed more buttons and waited for Ev to answer. After ten rings she disconnected and dialled again. She covered the mouth piece and said, "I must have dialled the wrong number."

No one answered.

She hung up and handed the phone to Mickey. "I'll try him later. Maybe he's gone to the doctor's office."

Chapter Thirty-Six

Jenna waved at Mickey and turned to pull the mail out of the brass letter box by the front door. Bills, bills, junk mail, advertisements, and a padded, brown envelope addressed to Jenna. She flipped it over. No return address. She had just pressed her finger under the flap, when the door was flung open from inside.

"Mom, how's Aunt Irene?"

Jenna stepped through the door and hugged her son. "Not very good, honey. She's pretty sick."

"Does she have a cast? Patrick Korostecki had a purple one when he broke his arm."

She pictured the woman whose entire body could have been encased in plaster, and nodded.

"Do you think she'd let me sign it?"

"I'm sure she'd love that, but you can't go to the hospital just yet. She has to get a bit better before you can see her."

Chase sighed and pulled her toward the computer. "Come see what I was working on today."

She allowed herself to be dragged into her office. "Where's Finn?"

"Making us coffee."

She raised an eyebrow.

Finn sauntered in with two steaming coffee mugs and pecked Jenna on the cheek.

"Here you go, Sport." He handed one of the mugs to Chase. "Careful, it's hot."

She jammed her fists on her hips. "Finn, he can't have coffee!"

Chase giggled and sipped at his drink. "Mmmm, just the way I like it, Finn. Thanks."

Finn winked at Chase. "Now, about that mini-bike I'm going to buy you."

"What?" Jenna squealed.

Finn and Chase looked at each other and burst into peals of laughter.

She glared at Finn. "I don't see what's so funny," she spluttered. "What are you trying to do? Kill my son with poison and a mini-bike?"

"Want to try some, Mom?" He passed the mug under her nose. "It's pretty good."

She was breathing so hard it didn't take long for her to inhale the sweet scent of chocolate wafting from his cup.

"Hot chocolate," she said. "You two are a couple of teases."

They high-fived. "Boy power," they said in unison.

She shook her head. "I can tell I should never leave you two alone together."

"Actually, we got a lot accomplished this afternoon. Did Chase show you the introductory page he made for our proposal?"

Chase brought the file up on the computer. Jenna stood back, amazed at her son's talent.

"Where did you learn how to do that? That's quite impressive."

"Aunt Irene. She said I needed to snazz up my projects, so she taught me how to make title pages and stuff on the computer."

Fresh guilt swamped Jenna. Irene had obviously loved and cared for Chase during the past eight years. She had done a wonderful job raising him. Perhaps it had been cruel to sever their relationship so abruptly.

She chewed a thumbnail and smiled weakly at Chase. She would try to make it up to both of them.

"I guess it's my turn to get to work. Is there much left to do, Finn?" she asked.

He scratched his head. "Well, I ran into a little glitch, but with a couple more hours of work we could probably get it all tied up in a nice red bow."

"Chase, can you take the mail upstairs for me? And while you're there, you can shower and change out of your baseball uniform."

He got up to go. "Don't forget your hot chocolate."

She and Finn both waited until they heard her apartment door close.

"How is Irene?" asked Finn.

She collapsed into a chair. "Oh, Finn, it's worse than I thought. It wasn't an accident. And, they're making noises as if I'm a suspect." She reached up and caressed his cheek. "Worse yet, they're tarring you with the same brush by association. I'm so sorry to drag you into this."

"Don't be ridiculous. You didn't drag me into anything. You didn't do anything." He sounded angry. "Do you think this has anything to do with her phone calls?"

She sighed. "I don't know what to think. It's an awful big coincidence if it's not related. But if it *is* related, it means someone was trying to shut her up because she knew something and she was warning me about it." She shivered. "Oh, Finn, there are parts of this situation that remind me of when Angus died. It seems too familiar. I feel like I've come full circle. The interrogation by that awful detective, the accusations, his abrupt attitude, and his *assumption* that I'm somehow involved. I'm sick of feeling on the defensive all the time."

He stood behind her and kneaded the tight muscles in her shoulders. "Scared?"

She groaned, partially from his roaming fingers and partially from his question. "Scared, frustrated, nervous, angry, worried, you name it."

"Did the detective tell you much?"

Jenna shook her head. She sat up straight and reached for one of his hands as it slid from her shoulder. "Let's not talk about it. I need work to take my mind somewhere else. Please?"

He bent and rubbed his beard stubble against her cheek. "If that's the way you want it." He tugged her from her chair. "I've got the proposal saved on my computer. Come on, work time."

"Let me make a quick phone call, then I'll be right there."

She dialed Everett's number, then raised her eyes to follow Finn's athletic progress across the foyer. She watched his skin turn golden when he walked through a shaft of sunlight. Her mind snapped a picture of his bronzed image and, with a smile, entitled it "Greek Sun God."

With a shake of her head, she brought her attention back to the phone. After several unanswered rings, she sighed and replaced the receiver into its cradle. "Everett, where are you?" she muttered.

She hustled into Finn's office. They worked together for the next hour verifying schedules, prices, and instructional topics, and putting the finishing touches on their proposal.

Finally, he clicked on the print button and leaned back in his chair, stretching his arms over his head. "I can't believe we finished so quickly. I would have been here until midnight."

"Teamwork."

He reached over and pulled her into his lap. "We do make a great team, don't we?"

She nuzzled his neck. "Mmmhmm."

He moaned. "In more ways than one." His hands explored her waist and moved upward.

"Mom," called Chase from the top of the stairs.

"Ah, the other member of our team is heard from."

Jenna leaned into Finn and chuckled. She peeled herself away and walked to the stairway.

"You bellowed, my liege?"

Chase grinned. "Are we having supper soon? I'm starved."

She looked at Finn. "What do you think, Finn, should we feed this little varmint?"

"We could feed him to the dogs."

"Fi-inn," sang Chase, making the name two syllables.

Jenna laughed. "We'll be right up, honey." She drew Finn to his feet and gave him one last lingering kiss. With her mouth just a breath away from his, she whispered, "Tough luck, buster."

She danced away from his playful slap, giggling at the look of astonishment on his face. She stopped with her hand on the newel post. "Are you going to join us for supper?"

He pointed to the printer, still spewing paper. "I'll put this together and be right up, but don't think you've gotten away with anything, little girl. I'll teach you to tease me."

She smiled, flipped her hair at him, and ran lightly up the stairs. The smile wavered as a thought of Angus crossed her mind. Finn's threats were made in jest, but Angus' had been serious and always followed by physical, emotional, and mental punishment. She pushed the thought away. That part of her life was in the past and she was determined that it would never hurt her again.

Her mood sobered further as she opened the apartment door and remembered what she had to do. She stepped over Chase, sprawled in front of the TV, and reached for the phone.

"Who you calling, Mom?" he asked. His eyes never left the screen where the super hero rappelled down the side of the skyscraper on a silken web.

"I have to tell Everett about Aunt Irene." She dialed his number and breathed a sigh of relief when he answered.

"Everett, I've been trying to reach you all day. Where have you been?"

"Jenna? What's wrong? You sound upset. How can I help?"

"It's Irene. She's been in an accident."

Silence. She knew this must be very difficult for him and pictured him covering his eyes with a hand.

"They're not sure if she's going to make it," she said quietly, so Chase wouldn't hear.

"She's alive?"

"Yes, barely. She's in a coma. Everett, they think someone tried to kill her."

"Who would want to hurt Irene? Unless it has some connection to you. After all, you're the one who's been receiving threats. You and Chase must be very upset, and scared, too. You could be next."

Jenna shivered.

"I'll come out and stay with you tonight. At least until they find out who's behind this."

"That's kind of you, Everett. You're always there for us, but there's no need this time. We're fine, and besides, Finn is here if we need protection."

There was the barest hesitation, before he asked, "He's not...not staying in your apartment, is he?"

"No, but he's just upstairs. I suppose he could stay here. Do you think that's necessary?"

"No, oh, no," he said quickly. "Just lock all your doors and keep your windows closed tight. You should be fine. Uh, Jenna, do they have a description of the car that hit her?"

Her hand tightened on the phone. "How did you know it was a car accident?"

"You must have said."

"No, I don't think so. I just said accident."

"I guess I just assumed. I've been listening to the news too much lately. Everyone seems to have summer fever and they're driving like maniacs."

Jenna relaxed. She'd be accusing him of hurting Irene next. *Get a grip, girl.* "Yes, there have been a lot of accidents lately. If you want to see her, she's at Detroit General."

They said their goodbyes and she replaced the phone gently thinking how lucky she was to have a friend like Everett who never asked or expected anything of her. He was a rare man.

She wandered into the kitchen and began pulling salad ingredients from the crisper. When she placed them on the counter, she noticed the mail tucked under the phone. She smiled. Chase had to be the tidiest kid she'd ever met. Another legacy of Irene's care and guidance.

With damp hands, she reached for the brown envelope. The rest looked boring, but this had some potential. Receiving mail had been one of the few high points in prison and some of that excitement stayed with her each time she flipped open the little brass lid of their mailbox to reveal letters and parcels addressed to her. She started to tear the envelope open, but stopped and crinkled her nose at the faint smell. Almost fruity. She pressed it to her nose, but couldn't place the scent? A familiar aftershave, perhaps? Definitely not something Angus would have worn, or Finn, either. She shrugged and ripped it open.

She reached into the decapitated envelope and pulled out a cassette tape. She flipped it over, but there was no label. She ignored the tightening in her stomach. She refused to live her life in fear.

"Chase, can you get your tape player for me?" she called.

She heard him scurry to his bedroom and open his closet door. Moments later he appeared with the machine under his arm and placed it on the table.

He reached for the cassette tape in her hand. "What's this?" he asked as he slid it into the slot and pressed PLAY.

"Don't know. It came in the mail."

The strains of a country song filled the room at an eardrum-splitting decibel.

She shook her head. "How can you listen to music that loud?"

He shrugged and adjusted the volume.

After a few seconds, Chase rolled his eyes. "Not you, too."

"What do you mean?"

"Joel's mom loves that song. It's called *Chained Souls*."

Jenna curled her lip. "I'm not thrilled about the title."

He hummed along at first, then joined in with the chorus. " *'In spite of everything I've done for you, this is how you do it to me, do it to me, do it to me, this is how you treat me,'* " he sang.

Jenna couldn't explain the reason for her sudden uneasiness, but she felt it just the same. Perhaps it was the faintly sinister quality to the song. She glanced at the thick brown envelope.

"Chase, please turn it off."

" *'...you're still learning, I'm still giving lessons.'* Look, Mom, Joel's mom taught us how to line-dance to it." He stared at his feet as they moved through the complicated steps.

She backed away from the tape player. "Chase, turn it off."

He continued to sing and dance, lost in concentration.

"Chase, *please*, turn it off!"

Finally, he looked up at her and must have seen something in her face. He hastily pressed the OFF button. The music ceased, but the deep bass still thrummed in Jenna's ears.

She grabbed for the envelope, peered inside, then ripped it open. A small turquoise note fluttered to the floor. Jenna stooped, but before she could reach it, she saw the signature: *Karma*.

Chapter Thirty-Seven

The following day, still shaky from her last encounter with Karma, Jenna walked Chase to his baseball camp, then went on to the gourmet market on the edge of town.

The long walk would do her good, clear her head of the lingering thoughts of Karma that seemed to cling to her mind like flies in a web.

Strong south winds tugged her hair out of its clips. Curled strands flew wildly about her head, tossed anew by each great gust. She stared at the cotton ball clouds scudding across the sky, changing shape, then reforming into mare's tails. Jenna felt a change in the air and shivered though the day was warm.

Right now she needed the circus atmosphere of Wojo's Market. As she approached the building she saw the colorful trademark awning, which looked like fruit raining from the sky in the midst of a huge W. Piles of fruit filled the wooden trays that reached out onto the sidewalk.

Mr. Wojokowski bustled to meet her, although he could have stayed inside the open-air building and greeted her from behind his stall.

He reached for her hand and placed a kiwi in it. Some people shook hands; Wojo handed out fruit.

"How are you today?" he bellowed.

From inside the store, four men chorused "How are you today?"

Mr. Wojokowski turned his back on them. "Don't mind them."

"Don't mind them," they yelled.

Jenna laughed. This was a routine they had perfected to amuse their customers. It worked. She always felt better after a visit to Wojo's. He leaned in close and whispered, "What can I do for you?"

The quartet yelled, "What can I do for you?"

The old man stomped off, waving his hands in the air and muttering something about getting no respect.

A tall red-headed man, one of the foursome, appeared at her side. "What are you looking for today, Ms McDougall?"

She smiled at the youngest Wojokowski son. "Your best oranges, please, Jeff."

He plucked an orange from the pile of fruit and tossed it in the air, like a pitcher waiting to throw the first ball. "One? Two?" He picked another orange and juggled the two. "Three? Four?" Two more oranges flew into the melee. "Five? Six?"

Once, Jenna had let him continue until he had a dozen tangerines whizzing through the air in a bright orange ring. Finally, he had dropped them one by one into her wicker Wojo's bag designed for carrying the produce home.

"Just four today."

He replaced two orange orbs perfectly on top of the pile of fruit without missing a beat, then placed the remaining four, one at a time, in her bag.

She shook her head. "I don't know how you do that."

He shrugged and sauntered away, then turned back and grinned. "Just luck," he said with a wink.

Jenna was still smiling when she turned back to the bulging trays of multi-colored fruit. She selected another kiwi and put it, along with the one Wojo had given her, in her bag.

She reached out a steadying hand when a young woman in mauve platform shoes stumbled against the counter and nearly dislodged a pyramid of apples.

"Oh, these shoes," the woman cried. "I'll never get used to them."

The woman looked up and Jenna realized it wasn't a young woman at all. She must have been closer to fifty. Jenna's memory flashed an image of a woman dressed in elegant clothes, not a hair out of place, and forty pounds heavier.

"Muriel?" she asked.

The woman peered into Jenna's face. "Oh, Jenna, it's so nice to see you. You're out, then."

"Muriel, you're so thin."

The woman ran a hand over her spandex-covered hips and pushed out her chest. "I work out four times a week and watch every calorie that passes my lips."

"You look great." Actually, her face looked like a deflated balloon stuck on top of a Barbie doll body. A few extra pounds might smooth out some of those wrinkles. Jenna shrugged mentally. Muriel seemed to expect the compliment and Jenna couldn't think of a good reason to ruin her day.

"How's Professor Billingsley?"

Muriel grimaced. "Oh, Bob, he's the same. You know, making the rest of us pay for not living up to his expectations."

From the makeover, Jenna guessed that Muriel had finally heard the rumors slithering around the university about her husband and his young, female students.

Muriel moved in closer. "Have you heard the latest? Bob is absolutely *thrilled*."

Jenna shook her head. The university community was always rife with juicy gossip, but she had never had a taste for it.

"Ding dong, the worm is dead!" Muriel crowed.

"Pardon?"

"Surely you remember our resident creep. You *must*. He worked for Angus for a time."

"Everett?" She put a hand to her chest, suddenly short of breath. "Everett is dead?"

"Not literally, but as far as the university is concerned, he's a goner."

"He was fired? He'll be devastated. What happened?"

The woman snorted. "What *didn't* happen? He wouldn't follow directions, he missed days, he lied. He wouldn't even *read* the papers he was supposed to mark." She waved a well-manicured hand in the air. "That man has a severe hang-up about authority. You wouldn't believe the vocabulary he used with the tenured professors. This has been coming for a long time. Personally, I think they've been *more* than fair with that little creep." She shivered theatrically. "He just makes my skin crawl. Why, he told me to stick my big nose in someone else's business when I tried to give him some fashion tips."

Jenna glanced at Muriel's mauve shoes. "Imagine." Her sarcasm was lost on the other woman.

Muriel used a twenty-year-old's gesture to push back the mass of bleached tangles on her head which masqueraded as the 'casual look.' "Ex-actly. Good riddance to strange rubbish, I say."

"Well, Muriel, it's been…interesting talking to you. I better finish my shopping or I'll never get home."

As she turned to leave, Muriel placed her hand on Jenna's arm. "We really *must* get together to talk about your prison experiences. I'm absolutely *fascinated* by that whole 'underbelly of society' element."

Jenna offered a weak smile and headed toward the turnips, which, she was sure, had bigger brains than Muriel. Yes, if she wanted the whole world to know about her life for the past eight years, she would talk to the queen of gossip. *Not in a million years, Muriel.*

Her mood, temporarily lightened by the antics of the Wojokowski family, had taken a serious downturn.

She hurried home holding the wicker bag tight to her side away from the tugging wind.

She would call Everett, offer him support. Maybe just a shoulder to cry on or someone to listen to his side of the story. She had never felt they'd treated him fairly at the university.

She felt sad for Everett, but something else, too. Hurt, that was it, and bewildered. Why hadn't Everett told her himself? Weren't they friends? Good friends? Didn't they lean on each other in times of trouble? She certainly had, many times, over the years. It hurt to think that he didn't feel the same about their relationship.

Jenna dragged herself up the stairs to her apartment and headed for the telephone. Someone else answered his extension at the university and confirmed with a snicker that he had departed 'for browner pastures.'

She dialed his home phone number. After two rings, it was picked up. "Everett?" she said, before he could answer.

"The number you have dialed is not in service. Please check the number and dial again. This is a recording."

She sighed and let the receiver slide down her neck before cradling it. She'd have to go see him. But how? She didn't drive and the buses to Detroit had already left earlier this morning. She glanced around her apartment as if looking for a clue. Finn was out delivering their presentation to, hopefully, interested ears. Mickey would have to drive too far. Besides, neither man would be thrilled about her visiting Everett.

She nibbled on her thumbnail and glanced out the back window when she saw movement in the yard below. She leaned closer to the glass, then blinked and stared.

"What the...?"

Rhia was leaning over a huge black cauldron stirring its contents with a large wooden stick. She wiped her forehead with the back of her hand, then resumed stirring.

Jenna flew down the stairs and jogged around the house toward her neighbor.

"Need any eye of newt?" she asked.

Rhia looked up, but continued stirring.

"You're going to have the whole neighborhood talking, you know. What are you doing?"

Rhia let go of the stick, but it continued to rotate as if enchanted. "My mom sent me a beautiful new cape, but it's *pink*." She said the word as if she was describing a particularly gruesome creature.

Jenna raised her eyebrows. "And?"

Rhia cast her a scornful look. "I don't do pink. I'm dying it black."

"Rhia, you have to think outside the box," she teased. "What's wrong with a pink witch? Didn't Glenda, the Good Witch of the East, wear pink?"

Rhia sighed. "I'm no Glenda." She pushed back her hair and resumed stirring. "Did you want something?"

"Why aren't you at work?"

"I had to take my car into the shop today, so I took a vacation day."

Jenna's shoulders slumped. "Darn, I was hoping you could take me into Detroit today."

"I can do that if you don't mind riding in a rent-a-heap. This garage advertises free loaner cars, but you should see the junker they stuck me with. A canary yellow station wagon with wooden panels."

Jenna laughed. "You're making that up."

"I'm not!" she cried. "Do you still want a ride?"

"Yes. I have to talk to Everett and his phone's out of order."

"Aren't you supposed to be steering clear of him?" asked Rhia.

"He's on Finn's suspect list, and Mickey's, but not mine. Not really. Everett would never do anything to hurt me."

Rhia grunted as she hefted the sodden garment out of the pot. "Okay, give me ten minutes and I'll meet you in the banana boat."

"Great." She turned to go, then turned back. "Oh, and would you mind if we picked up Chase? I don't want him to come home to an empty house."

Fifteen minutes later they were barreling down the highway on their way to the city in what Jenna's father would have called 'a bucket of bolts.' It shimmied and shivered each time Rhia tried to coax it up to the speed limit. Eventually, she allowed it to putter along in its comfort zone.

Rhia waved gaily at the angry honks from impatient motorists who wheeled around them.

Chase, secured in the back seat, seemed to think this was hysterical. "Did you see that guy's face when you waved?" He burst into fresh peals of laughter. When his giggles petered out he leaned forward as far as his seat belt would allow. "Rhia, what happened to your car?"

She grimaced. "Just a little fender bender."

"Someone hit you?" asked Jenna, concerned for her friend.

"It was silly, really. The guy in front of me stopped and I didn't. I'm fine, he's fine, we're all fine. Except my car. My grill looks like a gorilla stepped on it."

"My aunt was in an accident, too," said Chase.

An image of Rhia's dark green Saab flashed in Jenna's mind and, as if he was sitting in the back seat, she heard Detective Cooper's voice: *A neighbor saw a small, dark car.* She tensed. Could Rhia...? *No, no, no!* She pushed her fingers through her hair, scraping her scalp. She was getting paranoid. Every little coincidence seemed magnified until she suspected good friends of despicable acts. She sighed and smiled weakly when Rhia glanced her way.

Jenna spent the remainder of the drive staring out the window, silently apologizing to her friends for ever doubting them.

An hour later, Rhia pulled toward the curb in front of a crumbling gray building. Peels of paint flaked from every window frame. Somehow, the fresh yellow paint on the front door only served to highlight a sense of hopelessness in the area.

Rhia glared at the building. "Lock the doors! Jenna, you're not going in there alone."

"I'll be fine," Jenna said, rummaging in her purse. "Like vampires, the people in this neighborhood are only a threat at night." She handed Chase a five dollar bill and turned back to Rhia. "There's a nicer neighborhood only three blocks away with the best ice cream you've ever tasted. It's on this street, back the way we came, and it's called 'Just Desserts.' You can't miss it. By the time you get some ice cream and come back, I'll probably be ready to go."

"Yum. Can I get pineapple bubblegum with chocolate chips?" asked Chase.

"Only if you want a bellyache," said Rhia.

Jenna slid out of the car and inched her way around a man sleeping at the base of the cement steps, a wet spot slowly spreading out around him. She caught a whiff of urine and nail polish remover as she hurried up the stairs.

The light near Everett's apartment door flickered and sputtered out as Jenna rapped loudly for the third time. "Everett, it's Jenna, open up! I know you're in there." She pressed her ear against the door and stumbled when it was yanked open.

She squinted into the darkened room, then stepped backward when Everett slipped through the opening and pulled the door shut behind him.

"You shouldn't be here. This isn't a place for you," he said, his chin jutting out belligerently.

Jenna stared, shocked at his appearance. His hair, usually tied back neatly, hung in long greasy strands. Dark shadows were smudged beneath his eyes. She reached out to touch his arm, but pulled back when he wheeled away to pace the narrow hallway in angry strides.

"I suppose you heard. Those blood-sucking vipers just can't wait to spread their venom." He slammed a palm into the wall.

Jenna jumped at the explosion of sound. "I was worried about you. What happened?"

"What happened?" He laughed bitterly, baring his small teeth. "Those Stepford Wives at the university decided I didn't fit their mold. They convinced the dean that I couldn't be trusted, that I wasn't pulling my weight, that I was *harmful* to the staff morale." He snorted. "They're all programmed, mere automatons. They can't think for themselves anymore. They were looking for someone to persecute and I'm the one in the cross-hairs this time."

He slumped against the wall. Silence echoed loudly after his outburst.

"Everett, I'm so sorry. What will you do?"

"I don't need them," he muttered almost to himself.

After a moment, he pushed away from the wall and faced Jenna. He squared his shoulders and raised his chin. "It doesn't matter, anyway. I've got other plans. Big plans. This is just the nudge, huh, the kick, I needed to put them into motion."

Chapter Thirty-Eight

Karma's mind scurried with bits of information that would help him launch The Plan. Phone calls, shopping, packing, getting the car readied. The list went on and on.

He slumped into his chair.

The procedure must be exact, precise. If Jenna wouldn't comply, he'd have to use force.

Perhaps she liked force. After all, she'd stayed married to Angus all those years. Perhaps Karma had made a mistake by thinking he was saving her. Perhaps she didn't want to be saved.

He drew his journal forward.

If she wouldn't be with him in life, he would arrange it so they would always be together in death.

Feeling poetic, he picked up a pen and tried to put his feelings for Jenna into words. The ink scribbled across the page, racing, recording his thoughts as they rushed into his mind.

Love is a long narrow road
We've traveled together.
We've weathered the ruts,
The bends, the winds of change.

Our destiny draws near,
Dear Jenna.
Like Romeo and Juliet,
We shall sip from death's nectar.

Our dreams, our hopes,

Our souls entwin'd,
As we leave our corporeal
Images behind.

Our spirits will rise
To Heaven's Gate.
Joy, everlasting,
Will be our fate.

Karma bit the end of the pen and grimaced as he reread his amateurish efforts. He shrugged and determined to return to clean it up after his delivery.

He laid the pen in the seam of the leather journal, stood, and pressed his lips to the life-sized photograph of Jenna, her hair haloed with angelic light.

"I've tried to be patient, my angel, to wait for you to overcome your shyness, your reticence to give your heart to the truly deserving. Your time runs short. Prepare to meet your destiny…with me."

"Together," he whispered, lifting a plastic vial from the desk, "until the end of time."

Karma wrapped a black cape around his narrow shoulders and pulled the red silk-lined hood over his head. He tucked his hair out of view, slid an ivory-handled Bowie knife down the side of his black boot and reached for Jenna's apartment key hanging from a satin hair ribbon on the cork board.

It was time. Time to show her who had all the power…and who would soon be using it.

Chapter Thirty-Nine

"Ready to go?" Finn stood in the open doorway to her apartment, a huge grin on his face, a Hawaiian shirt tucked neatly into khaki pants.

Jenna stared at the brightly-colored shirt.

"What?" he asked looking down at his chest. "I have to be 'one' with the carnival." He placed his fingers on his temple, closed his eyes, and said, "Ummmmmmm."

Chase giggled. "Mom, I want to be 'one' with the carnival, too."

She rolled her eyes and glared at Finn. "See what you've started? Come on, you guys, let's get out of here. Chase, he can be 'one' with the carnival and you and I will be 'two' with it."

Finn patted Chase's shoulder. "Don't worry, buddy. We'll get you outfitted once we get you there."

Jenna locked the door and turned to follow them.

"Do you know what tomorrow is, Finn?" asked Chase eagerly.

"Hallowe'en?"

Chase snorted. "No."

"Christmas?"

"Nope. You know, don't you?"

Jenna smiled. She was as excited about Chase's birthday as he was. It would be their first birthday together for eight years and she wanted to make it extra special.

As her foot touched the first step, she heard the ring of the telephone and hesitated.

"Leave it," called Finn from the bottom step. "The whole point of this excursion is to get you away from everything. Just forget about Irene and Everett for one night, put your worries aside, and *don't answer the phone.*"

She wavered, then turned back to her apartment and unlocked the door. She could hear her own voice on the answering machine, but snatched up the phone when a gravelly Irish voice called her name.

"Jenna, lass, are you there?"

"Mickey, hi, I'm here."

"Are you screening calls on this line, too?"

"No, we were just going out and I heard the phone ring. What's up? Any news?"

"We're finally going to get a break, I think. Judy Farandino's husband just called. He's back from Italy and he says he's going to go through Judy's stuff tomorrow. If he finds anything that looks like a case file or notes, he'll give me a call."

"That's wonderful. I'll keep my fingers crossed, and my toes, and my eyes, and…"

"Me, too. This could be it, lass. We could finally have access to the information that Judy dug up. She was the best at making connections the rest of us missed." As usual when he spoke about his dead partner, his voice sounded gruff. "I'll talk to you tomorrow."

Jenna dropped the phone back into place and hurried outside, making sure she locked the door behind her.

The carnival was in the center of town, just a few blocks away, so they decided to walk.

Chase tried to stroll along the sidewalk with them, but his excitement soon won out and he galloped ahead.

"Can we eat something at the carnival?" he called over his shoulder.

"No," said Jenna. "You need vegetables."

"Ah, Mom."

"You like vegetables."

"I like candy apples, cotton candy, caramel corn, cheese puffs, french fries, hot dogs, hamburgers…" He gave a little jump at each item as if the mere thought of all that sugar and grease was enough to make him giddy.

"Well, there you go," said Finn. "We'll stop at The Bus Stop for hamburgers and salad."

"Hold the lettuce," said Chase.

"Deal."

Chase ran ahead and pulled the lever to open the two narrow bus doors to The Bus Stop grill.

"I suppose you're waiting for a tip, now," said Finn, walking through the door.

Chase's eyes lit up. "Sure."

"Okay, here's a tip. Never hold the door open for a cheapskate."

They both howled with laughter.

"That's a good one, Finn."

Jenna rolled her eyes and shook her head. *Male humor.*

She found a bright yellow booth with high-backed vinyl bus seats near the front window and sat down.

Finn slid in across from her. Expecting Chase to sit beside her, she was surprised to see him slide in beside Finn. His eyes followed the older man and he mimicked a flick of the paper menu.

A waitress, clad in a bus driver's uniform, appeared at their table.

"A beer for my buddy and me," said Finn, jerking his thumb in Chase's direction.

Chase's eyes grew round and he looked at his mother.

"Make that three," said Jenna.

While they waited for their drinks to arrive, Jenna and Finn chatted quietly, but Chase seemed distracted. He cast furtive glances toward the waitress behind the counter.

Within minutes, she was back and plunked three frothing mugs in front of them.

Finn clinked his glass to Chase's. "Gezundheit."

The boy grinned. "That's what you say when someone sneezes!"

"Oh, yeah. Cheers!" Finn took a hearty swallow of his drink, but kept his eyes on Chase who sipped tentatively.

A suspicious look crossed the boy's face. He took a bigger gulp, then narrowed his eyes at Finn. "Hey, this is root beer."

"Of course. You wouldn't like the other stuff."

Finn placed his elbows on the table and crossed his arms. "We need a plan for the carnival. What should we see first?"

Chase eyed him, then placed his elbows on the table and crossed his arms.

Jenna listened absently as they planned out a strategy together. She hid a smile behind her hand as Chase copied Finn's moves. It was obvious Chase was getting to an age when he needed a man in his life. She smiled. He could choose a lot worse role model than Finn. Her eyes strayed to the green-eyed man across from her. He was poking Chase in the ribs and teasing him about something. They laughed together, Chase lapping up the attention. She hoped Finn would be around long enough to make a difference in her son's life. And hers.

After a hastily eaten meal and several prompts from Chase, they finally set out for the carnival. The excited voices of children swirled around them as they clamored past through the gate.

Jenna felt uneasy the moment she entered the carnival grounds. A prickly feeling on the back of her neck told her she was being watched. Her eyes roamed over the crowds of people.

No one seemed even remotely interested in them.

She tried to shrug off the feeling and followed Chase and Finn. Chase circled each ride, assessing what he called 'squeal appeal.'

"That one," he said, pointing to a long-legged contraption with seaweed green cars.

Finn reached into his pocket for the tickets he had purchased at the front gate, but Chase refused to take them.

"All of us have to go," he said stubbornly.

"On the Octopus?" said Finn. "That thing just shakes you up and spits you out."

"How about a nice exciting ride on the Ferris Wheel?" said Jenna hopefully.

"Nuh-uh." He waved a finger at them. "You guys said you'd come on the rides with me. This is the one I want. Come on." He led them, groaning, through the gate, directed the scruffy, cigar-sucking ticket taker to Finn, and hurried to get in line for the next available car.

Chase was giggling before the ride even started, but Jenna kept a white-knuckled grip on the safety bar. She hadn't been on a carnival ride for fifteen years and if she dared to move her feet she'd kick Finn for telling Chase they'd accompany him. As Finn's luck would have it, she was pinned between Chase and the cracked green vinyl on the wall of the car, and couldn't reach him.

The ride started slowly, but quickly picked up speed. She screamed each time the machine reached out a tentacle toward the crowd and whooshed over their heads. It seemed to go on for hours. When it finally slowed, then stopped, she was sure her eyes were spinning around in her head. Chase and Finn grabbed her hands and led her staggering onto solid ground.

"Okay," she said, once she caught her breath and could see straight, "here's the rule. I go on the Ferris Wheel, the Teacup, and the Carousel. Finn goes on all the rest."

Chase and Finn cackled at her lack of enthusiasm, but they agreed to watch the carnies while she recovered.

As they sauntered down the midway, avoiding sticky hands and eager, rushing children, the carnival workers called out to them, explaining the ease and simplicity of their games, and holding aloft powder blue teddy bears and eight foot purple pythons.

Chase seemed particularly fascinated with a ring toss game, his gaze repeatedly coming back to it. He nudged Jenna in the ribs.

"Mom, do we know that guy?"

Jenna looked around, but didn't see anyone she recognized.

"The guy behind the counter, Mom. With the ponytail. He keeps staring at us."

She stepped closer to get a better look. Around thirty, the man had long blonde hair and a slim build that fit snugly into black jeans and a white tee shirt. A gold hoop sprouted from his upper lip.

She was shaking her head when he turned and looked directly at her. And she knew.

His eyes were so pale she had wondered if he was blind the first time they met. She stepped toward him and his face relaxed in a grin.

"Jenna, I knew it was you."

He still had the crooked front tooth that had given him a reckless look, but the hair and the lip ring were definitely new.

She pulled Chase forward. "Morgan, this is my son, Chase."

He stuck his hand out, clasped the boy's hand, and shook it once.

"Finn, Morgan. Morgan, Finn." The men eyed each other warily, but shook hands.

"Morgan and I took a university English class together," she explained.

"Renaissance Literature. I remember it well," he said with a wink and a laugh.

She tapped Chase on the shoulder. "That was your dad's class."

Morgan's mouth hung open. "You married old man McDougall?"

Her smile froze. She nodded and prayed he wouldn't ask about Angus.

As if reading her mind, Finn jumped in. "Anybody ready for a candy apple?"

Jenna sent him a grateful smile.

"Yeah, baby," said Chase in his best Austin Powers voice.

"We better let you get back to work, Morgan. I'm so glad I bumped into you."

Morgan nodded and waved, a puzzled look on his face.

As she was walking away, Jenna still felt like she was being watched, but now realized it must have been Morgan's eyes that followed her. She shrugged off the creepy feeling and followed Chase and Finn to the candy concession.

For the next hour, they wandered through the fair grounds nibbling on candy apples, cotton candy and caramel corn. She was sure they'd all have bellyaches by the time they got home, but she hated to ruin the look of enjoyment on her son's face.

Just as they were about to leave, Chase insisted on one more ride. As a concession to his mother, he agreed on the Ferris Wheel. They climbed aboard and slowly made their way to the top, stopping intermittently to let other thrill seekers board the ride. The car swayed gently at each stop. When they reached the top of the graceful arc, Jenna drew in her breath at the bird's-eye view of the carnival grounds and the town around it. If she squinted and used a bit of imagination, she could see the peak of their house.

Bringing her eyes back to the crowds far below, she gasped.

Chase laughed at her apparent fear of heights, but it wasn't the ride that had tightened her belly in fear. She had seen something that chilled her blood and made the hair stand up on her arms. A person—a man, she was sure—in a black cape and sunglasses stared at them intently from several feet away from the base of the huge wheel. The setting sun cast flames against his lenses, as if the fires of Hell burned in his soul.

She turned to see if Finn had noticed, but his eyes were on a helicopter roaring overhead.

"Look," she said and pointed to where the man had stood only seconds before.

The spot was empty.

She searched the crowd for a glimpse of the cape, but the ride had started revolving and she lost her vantage point overlooking the grounds. Each time their car rose, she scanned the area for her stalker, but to no avail. He had vanished into the sea of revelers.

When the ride deposited them back onto the ground, Jenna rushed forward through the crowd, searching, scanning. Finally, she spotted a caped man amidst a ring of people. She pushed through the spectators and grabbed his arm.

"Why are you...?" She stopped, flustered.

The man turned and stared at her hand. His mouth frowned behind a black goatee and a Snidely Whiplash mustache.

"Kindly remove your hand from our person," he said in a snooty English accent. He tapped her hand with his baton. Like magic, the baton turned into a bouquet of flowers and the circle of spectators burst into applause.

"Oh, I'm sorry," she murmured, embarrassment heating her face. This was not the man she had seen from the top of the Ferris Wheel.

She bumped into several people as she backed away, squirming through the pressing bodies. As the crowd released her, Chase and Finn jogged up to her.

"Mom, why did you run away? Jeez, I thought you were going to puke or something."

She hugged him close and laughed shakily. "I'm sorry, honey. I...I thought I spotted someone I knew. Are we ready to go?" she asked, trying for a light tone. She wanted to get away from there, from *him*, whoever he was, as quickly as possible.

"Do we have to?" moaned Chase.

She checked her watch. "It's almost bedtime already and I don't want you overtired and grumpy on your birthday."

His face brightened. He grabbed both of their hands and they walked out looking like a real family.

Unfortunately, Jenna couldn't enjoy the moment. Every few seconds she checked over her shoulder for glimpses of her pursuer. She finally relaxed a half block from home.

At least one positive thing had come out of the encounter tonight—she was fairly certain the caped person was a man. His overall shape and the size of his shoes left little doubt about that.

The familiarity of their home was a welcome sight.

Chase, wired from the excitement, the rides, and the overload of sugar, danced across the wooden porch. Finn unlocked the front door, pushed it open and followed them in and up the stairs, after relocking it behind him.

At the top of the steps, Jenna reached for her apartment key, but her hand stopped. She stared at the door. Her heart thudded against her ribs.

"Hey, Mom, what's that?" Chase darted around her.

"Don't touch..." Too late. He had pulled the ribbon off the door knob and held a familiar-looking key in the palm of his hand.

"How did this get here?" he asked, bouncing the key in his hand.

"Good question," said Finn in a dangerously low voice.

"It looks just like yours, Mom, and don't you have a hair ribbon like this?"

He seemed oblivious to the strange mixture of terror and anger that roiled through her and begged to be released in one long scream.

The key was identical to the one in her hand. She took it from Chase and slid it into the door lock. With a flick of her wrist, the tumblers fell into place.

She turned her eyes to Finn. "It works," she said dully.

"Try the other one," he said, nodding at the deadbolt lock. The bolt slid back into its pocket with a clunk.

She leaned her forehead against the door. "How could this happen? I'm so careful about the keys." She felt like kicking the door, but she didn't want to frighten Chase.

His eyes swiveled between her and Finn.

"We just got the locks changed when we moved in, so it's someone who's had access in the last few weeks," said Finn.

"But, *who*?" she moaned, as if he could give her an answer.

"Where do you keep your keys?" he asked. "In your purse?"

"No." She shook her head. "I keep them on a hook by the door. That way I can run downstairs if I need to, lock the door behind me, and come right back up. I've gotten quite paranoid about them, which is why this comes as such a shock."

"Alright, let's think. Who's been in the house the last few weeks?"

She looked at Chase. "Mickey, Everett, Rhia…"

"Joel and Shane," added Chase.

"And you, of course," she said to Finn. "Wait, wait, wait! I remember putting a key in Chase's backpack in case he came home when I wasn't here. Maybe someone took that key when he was at baseball practice."

She pushed open the door and ran toward Chase's room, ignoring Finn's shout. She was unzipping the bottom pocket of the canvas bag when Finn and Chase ran into the room.

"Dammit, Jenna, he could still have been in here."

Belatedly, she looked around. "I never thought of that." She reached her fingers to the bottom of the pocket. Her shoulders slumped and she held up a small brass key with a fluorescent green shoelace tied to it.

"It's still here. That's a dead end."

"Not necessarily," said Finn. "The thief could have taken it, made a copy, and returned it, for all we know. Do you remember seeing anyone near your backpack during practice, Chase?"

The boy shrugged. "I just drop it and go play."

Finn nodded. "I'm going to take a look around. Why don't you pack a few things. You can stay with me tonight."

"No," she said fiercely. "I won't let some creep drive us out of our home." She wrapped an arm around Chase and pulled him close.

"We'll be just fine. I have a chain lock. We'll hear if anyone tries to get in."

Chase squeezed her. "We could put a chair under the doorknob. That's what they do in the movies."

Finn sighed. "Okay, but scream bloody murder if you hear anything. We'll get your locks changed in the morning…again."

Chapter Forty

"I'm worried about Everett." Jenna scraped the last of the double chocolate cake batter into the pan. She slapped Finn's hand as it strayed too close to the bowl.

"Ouch. Vandervries is a big boy. I'm sure he'll handle it."

"What if he decides to strike back at the other professors? They're the ones who drove him out, you know. I've never seen him so bitter." She handed the bowl and spatula to Finn and bent to slide the cake pan into the oven.

He leaned against the counter and licked the spatula. "Mmmm. What's he going to do? Trash their offices? Slash their tires? If he's that psycho, or should I say 'juvenile,' there's nothing you can do to stop him. He probably just needs some time to get over it."

"Hmph. I don't think he'll ever get over this. After all, the university is his life, not to mention his livelihood."

Finn pushed away from the counter and wagged his head back and forth. "In my opinion," he started forcefully, but was interrupted by the warble of the phone. He snorted. "Saved by the bell."

Jenna pushed her hands under the warm tap water and rubbed at the chocolate batter on her knuckles. "Can you get that, please?"

He reached for the phone. "Hello? Oh, hi, Mickey…yeah, she's here…that's great…yeah…give me the address…okay, we'll meet you there in thirty minutes. Bye."

She waved her arms and shook her head, but he had already hung up.

"I'm not going anywhere," she told him. "I still have tons to do to get ready for Chase's birthday celebration."

"Jenna, this is really important." He placed his hands on her shoulders. "Judy Farandino's husband just called Mickey. He thinks he's found something."

"Files?"

"No, it's a black, leather-bound book, but it looks like it contains information from Judy's last investigation. This could be *it*!"

"Nothing is more important than my son's first birthday with me after eight years apart. Call Mickey back and tell him I'll meet him tomorrow. We've waited this long; one more day won't hurt."

"I can't. He was calling from his car on his way to Farandino's and I don't know his cell number. Do you?"

She sighed. "No. You'll have to go by yourself."

"He wants you there."

Jenna placed her fists on her hips. "I'm not going, Finn."

"What if there's something that only you recognize as important? Something that only makes sense to you?"

"Then, I'll see it tomorrow."

He made a face. "I don't want to leave you by yourself. The locks haven't been changed yet. Somebody could get in."

"I'll keep the chain locks on."

"And don't go out."

"I won't. I have too much to do before Joel's mom brings Chase home at noon." She glanced at her watch and groaned. "Only two hours. Go, go." She herded him toward the door.

"Okay, but I'll call you when I get there." He kissed her forehead. "Lock the door behind me," he called over his shoulder and took the stairs two at a time.

She locked the door and returned to the kitchen, busily cleaning up the mess. She washed the dishes, wiped the counters, blew up twelve balloons and, after the timer buzzed, pulled the cake out of the oven to cool. The room filled with the sweet aroma of warm chocolate.

She had decided to use blue and red icing, Spiderman colors, with black string licorice crisscrossing the top like a web. Chase would love it.

Icing sugar, blue and red food coloring, licorice, candles. Jenna gasped. *Where were the candles?* She had purchased a brand new box last week, but now she counted only seven. Who would take her candles? She would have to ask Chase when he got home and warn him about the dangers of playing with fire.

She stared at the box and chewed on the inside of her cheek. Chase couldn't have a birthday cake with only seven candles on his *twelfth birthday*.

She nibbled on her thumbnail. She had to go to the store, but she'd promised Finn she would stay inside. Of course, in the case of an emergency, he'd understand, and this was an emergency. Nothing could mar this birthday. She'd just slip out and be back in less than fifteen minutes.

Jenna grabbed her purse and dashed out the door and down the stairs. She hesitated before stepping off the porch, looked up and down the street, then braced herself and strode out onto the sidewalk.

By the time she had walked two of the three blocks to the small grocery store, she was feeling silly for checking over her shoulder and scrutinizing every passerby with suspicion.

Instead, her eyes strayed to the dark clouds hanging low over the city. She hurried her step. The automatic doors, a recent improvement, slid open and she walked directly to the shelf that held the birthday candles. As she strode to the cashier, she picked up a bag of milk, powdered chocolate, relish and a few other necessities. Twenty minutes later she struggled through the door with three brown paper bags full of groceries. The owners of the family-run store wanted to maintain an old fashioned atmosphere, but right now, with a storm brewing, she would have preferred the modern convenience of plastic bags.

Jenna hitched the heaviest bag onto her hip and crushed the other two to her chest, cursing herself for buying more than she could carry comfortably. She would have made it, though, if the skies hadn't opened up and spattered fat raindrops on her head and paper bags. She moved as fast as she could, lugging the soggy bags, but only one block closer to home the bag of milk broke through the bottom of the grocery bag and started to slide down her leg.

"Get in."

She hadn't heard the car drive up or the door swing open, but she recognized the voice. She stooped to look into the car.

"Oh, thank goodness. You're a life saver."

"I'll always look after you, Jenna," he said as he helped her place the grocery bags in the back seat.

A thunderous crack of lightning made them both jump and they climbed quickly into the muggy car. The fruity scent of his aftershave brought a faint trace of a memory, but it was gone before she could grab onto its misty edges. The windows fogged and he turned the defroster on high and pulled away from the curb.

"Are you all ready for Chase's birthday?"

The storm was picking up and the wipers flapped madly at the driving rain. Jenna could barely see where they were going.

"Just about. I was short a few candles, and a few other things," she said, chuckling and thumbing toward the bags in the back seat.

"Candles like these?" He pulled something out of his shirt pocket and held it up.

"Where did you get that? And why would you have candles in your pocket? Those are exactly the kind I was looking for."

"I had a feeling they might slip your mind, so I was coming to drop them off at your house."

"I wish you had come a half hour ago. You would have saved me a trip to the store."

She squinted through the blurry window. "Oh, I think you missed our house."

He glanced around, but didn't slow the car. "Actually, there's something I want to show you."

She darted a quick look at her watch. "Oh, I'd love to, but I really don't have time. I still have to ice the cake and Chase will be home in about a half hour."

He patted her knee. "This won't take a minute."

A surge of anger left her feeling guilty. She didn't *want* to go sightseeing right now, but he had been kind enough to save her from the storm, so she guessed she owed him a few minutes of her time. She sighed and fidgeted with the strap of her purse.

A sign to the I-94 appeared through the rain and he steered the car toward the ramp and turned toward Detroit.

"I really have to get home. Can't you show me whatever it is another time?"

He stared through the windshield, unblinking, his jaw muscles bunched.

"Come on, can't this wait?" she asked hopefully.

Slowly, his head turned until he was looking into her face. His eyes seemed to burn with an inner fire and the first sliver of fear slid through Jenna. Goosebumps rose on her arms and her skin felt clammy.

"I've given you more than enough time, Jenna."

Chapter Forty-One

"More than enough time?" she echoed. "Time for what?"

His eyes skittered away from hers and he tapped his fingers on the steering wheel as if listening to a song only he could hear.

Jenna stared at Everett, waiting for an answer, but none came. She crossed her arms over her chest and stared angrily out the side window past the winding, silvery streaks of rainwater.

When they turned onto I-75 South her stomach tightened. She grabbed his arm. "Where are you taking me? Chase will be home any minute. He'll be worried. I have to go home! Why are you doing this?"

"I left a note for Sawyer to look after Chase for a while."

"A while? What does that mean?" When he still didn't answer, she yelled, "Everett, I demand an explanation!"

His breath hissed through his teeth. "I really don't think you're in a position to demand anything." He inhaled and blew the air noisily through his thin lips. "However, I believe it's time.

"Do you remember the first time we met, Jenna?"

"What does that have to do with anything?"

"It was in Angus' office at the university. He was reaming me out about some minor flaw in my lecture on Renaissance theater. That was nothing new. He was never satisfied. But this time, you walked in and defended me." He said the last words as if they awed him still. "No one had ever done that for me before. I took so much abuse as a child from my mother and her boyfriends that I just came to accept it. To *expect* it, really. Angus' words were like the sound of a mosquito in a tent—annoying, but not life-threatening—but, you jumped right in and swatted that pesky mosquito. For me.

"That's when I knew." His head bobbed up and down. "That's when

I knew we were cosmically joined and that Angus was in the way of our ever realizing our full potential as a couple." His speech had become impassioned, like a preacher's sermon and flecks of spit flew out of his mouth and hit the dashboard.

Jenna pressed her back against the car seat. What did he mean, 'Angus was in the way'?

"You never had a true connection to Angus. How could you, he never had a soul. You'd never really felt love, had you? Well, I hadn't either—until then. Your love blossomed through me like life-giving blood. I hated that Angus abused you and took you for granted. I could give you so much more. I knew then that he had to be eliminated. I knew you needed to be freed, saved, from his domination. It's our karma that we be together."

Jenna's spine snapped to attention. *Karma? My God, was Everett the stalker? Was he Angus' killer? How could that be?* A million questions buzzed through her head, but she clamped her jaws tight.

She wanted out of the car, away from this delusional man she had thought she knew. She glanced out the window. They were traveling well over the speed limit and the asphalt flashed by in a slick gray blur. If she jumped now, she'd be killed or badly injured.

"I often waited outside your apartment building, and sometimes just outside your apartment door, to assure myself you were okay. The night of the shooting I followed Angus into your building. I went through the back door, though—I had taped the lock so I could get in anytime I wanted. He was in a foul mood and I knew he'd try to take it out on you. I heard you screaming. I couldn't take it anymore. I let myself into the apartment. I'd copied Angus' keys in case of this eventuality, but I didn't need them, because the bastard was in such a hurry to hurt you that he didn't even close the door properly behind him. I got such a kick when I saw you holding a gun on him, but he was taunting you and I knew you wouldn't shoot him. I rushed in, grabbed the gun, and finished the job myself."

"You were wearing a cape," she said through stiff lips, unable and unwilling to digest the more abhorrent details of his confession.

He chuckled. "Ingenious, don't you think? I stole it from the Drama Department. That was my disguise in case Angus ever found me in the building. I knew he'd fire me in a heart beat. He always underestimated me. Just like everyone else." His eyes softened when he looked at her. "Except you."

"You shot Angus?" she said more to herself than to him. Eight years of missing Chase, of recoiling from the idea that she was a murderer, of living in a cage with killers, child abusers, and drug addicts. Eight years of her life lost forever. Rage gnawed a hole in her chest and spewed out of her mouth. "You shot my husband, then watched them send me to prison for a murder *you* committed?"

Everett stuttered in his haste to explain. "Y-y-you don't understand, Jenna," he said pleadingly. "I didn't think you'd be convicted. I really didn't, because they'd find other prints on the gun and you would tell them the truth. I thought if worse came to worse you could always plead self-defense. I hadn't counted on you offering no defense at all. How could I know you'd get amnesia? Then, Irene lying in court, saying you had threatened Angus, and the ineptitude of your lawyer. He didn't even mention the unexplained set of prints during the trial."

He tried to pet her arm, but she cringed against the door.

"I didn't mean for you to be blamed for Angus' death," he cried, pleading with his eyes on Jenna. The car veered into the left lane and cut off a monstrous transport truck. The truck driver laid on his horn and shook a fist at Everett who yanked the car back into the center lane.

He kept his eyes on the road as he continued in a low voice. "I was stunned when you were convicted. I sat in the courtroom every day of your trial and watched in horror as you were railroaded. There was nothing I could do."

"You mean like stand up and take responsibility for your actions?" she asked bitterly.

He went on as if he hadn't heard her. "I tried to make your separation from Chase less painful. I brought you pictures and news of him every week. You were so grateful. Remember?"

"How could I forget? You went to play with him every week, too. You watched him grow, and celebrated his birthdays with him, and took him to baseball games and did all the things a parent would have done with him."

"That's right," he said, obviously delighted she was catching on. "I was like a father to him. That's how I knew, if you gave me a chance, we could be a happy family together, you, Chase, and me."

Jenna inhaled deeply through her nose and exhaled through her mouth, pushing her lips out the way the yoga instructor in prison had taught her. "Everett," she said carefully, "you know I've always liked you."

He beamed at her. "Of course I do."

"But basically, you have made me serve *your* time in jail, terrorized me, kidnapped me, you're taking me God-knows-where, and you expect me to fall into your arms? Have you lost your mind? For goodness sake, Everett, do you hear yourself? Do you comprehend what you're asking? You're a murderer!"

His face whitened. "I did it for you! Everything was for you. Look, I admit you may need some time to come around to the idea, but I'm confident you'll eventually love me as much as I love you."

Jenna's hysterical laughter filled the car. "You just don't get it. *I will never love you!* I hate you for what you've done, for what you've taken from me." She reached for the door handle, desperate to escape any way she could.

"No," he yelled. He clasped her wrist in a vice-like grip, fumbling in his pocket, steering with his knee. She tried to pull away, but he squeezed harder. They swerved into the other lanes of traffic, car horns blaring in their wake. With the speed of a striking rattler he pulled handcuffs from his pocket and slapped one ring around her wrist and the other around his own. "I didn't want to do it this way, Jenna, but you're forcing my hand. You just need a little time, that's all. That's why I'm taking you away on this trip. You'll have time to think about us without any distractions."

She knew he was referring to Finn by the way he growled the last few words.

Through the murky soup of rain a large blue sign loomed. Jenna squinted at it, then pressed her free hand to the dashboard.

"Oh my God, Everett, you just crossed into Ohio! Turn around, I'll be violating parole if I cross state lines. Please, Everett!"

Chapter Forty-Two

Jenna brooded as she stared out into the gloomy day, the rain stippling the asphalt, runnels of water coursing down the window. One arm lay across her waist and the other lay, tethered to Everett, on the seat between them. She clenched her hands into fists. She had ignored her intuition when it came to Everett, because she thought she knew him so well. She had always thought he was a little odd, but perfectly harmless. Now she and her son were paying for that miscalculation.

She fought back tears as she thought about Chase coming home to an empty house on his birthday. Life hadn't treated her son fairly and she had wanted to make up for that by giving him the best she could offer. She peered through the windshield and felt as bleak as the day. How was she going to get out of this?

By now, they'd crossed into Kentucky. Jenna's empty stomach roiled with acid, but the thought of food made her nauseous. How had she let this happen? Although she was loathe to speak to him, she needed more information.

She cleared her throat. "Are you Karma?"

He smirked, apparently pleased at her interest.

"How did you get into my house? And how did you know my email address?" she asked.

"Elementary, my dear Jenna."

She hated that he was enjoying this.

"I took the key out of Chase' backpack while he was busily running bases, had it copied, and put it back. That took a little bit of fancy foot work. The email, on the other hand, was child's play." He sniggered. "I simply called the local Internet Service Provider, said I was Sawyer and that I couldn't remember the email addresses I had signed up for. They were only too happy to assist me."

"And Detective Farandino?"

His eyes flicked her way and back to the road. He chewed on his lower lip. "Who?"

"You know, Judy Farandino, the Italian detective who was on to you. What did she find out, Everett? Did she know you killed Angus? Did you confess something to her? Did she outsmart you, Everett?"

"Shut up!" he said in a low furious voice.

"What did she know that would warrant you killing a mother of three little boys?"

"She knew that I loved you. Okay? Satisfied? It's your fault she's dead. She caught me at a low moment, when I wasn't sure of your love. She seemed so sympathetic, so sensitive. I thought she *understood*, but all she really wanted was to trap me. I told her you needed to be protected and she called me your savior. Yes, *she* said that. How could I deny it? We talked about having to save people from themselves, from bad situations, bad relationships, that sometimes the lines between right and wrong got hopelessly blurred. Then, after I had bared my soul to her, she stared at my shoes, asked if I wore sneakers a lot, nodded as if that explained everything." He was breathing fast and he rubbed his forehead.

"Wim's journal," murmured Jenna.

"What?"

She shook her head. "Nothing."

"It wasn't until she was gone that I realized she'd been playing with me, leading me, giving me enough rope to hang myself. I couldn't let her get away with that. She was going to ruin everything. All my plans."

"So you killed her."

He shrugged. "The second one's not so hard."

Jenna's blood turned to ice at the callousness of his words. Where would he stop? She shuddered at the answer.

Ten silent moments later, the rain eased into a light mist and Everett turned the car toward the exit leading to a rest area. Jenna clenched the door handle. They pulled into a wide parking lot surrounded by tall majestic oaks and swaying willows.

At the far end of the lot, away from the other parked vehicles, he slid the car into reverse and maneuvered between two large trees. "We can eat and rest for a while here. We've got a long drive ahead of us."

Jenna's lip trembled. She thought of Chase waiting at home for her. "Where are we going?"

He turned toward her and placed a hand on her forearm. Jenna flinched, but he didn't seem to notice.

"For a little vacation," he said. "Somewhere for us to spend some quality time together, where you can re-evaluate our relationship without any outsiders around to confuse you, where you can remember all of the good times we've had."

Good times? She couldn't recall any good times with him that he could construe as anything other than casual friendship.

A deep sense of fear settled into her bones. He had lost touch with reality. She would have to be very careful not to provoke an insane rage or she could end up like Judy Farandino.

Jenna nodded and she forced a smile to her lips.

Everett seemed to relax as he smiled back at her and pulled his keys from the ignition with his left hand. He fumbled with them for a moment, then unlocked his bracelet of the handcuffs.

Jenna's heart leaped. As she sought to think of a plan of escape, he re-locked it over the steering wheel with a decisive click. Her spirits plummeted.

Still grinning, he reached for a blue insulated bag in the back seat. Along the side of the bag, in bold black letters was printed 'Billingsley.' He saw her look and sniggered. "Professor Bob went and misplaced his favorite lunch bag. Stupid man. How about some lunch? I brought your favorite—salmon sandwiches." He produced the plastic wrapped sandwich with a flourish.

Jenna's stomach flipped at the pungent smell of fish that permeated the car. She swallowed. "Um, I have to go to the washroom, Ev. Could you please unhook me? I'll be right back."

He looked at her pityingly and wagged his head from side to side. "Now Jenna, do you really think I'm stupid enough to let you go alone? I'll take you."

"You can't go into the ladies room."

He snickered. "Of course I can, I have my magic disguise with me." He got out of the car, slammed the door, and rummaged in the trunk. A moment later, Jenna turned to look out the side window and screamed.

She was face to face with her stalker in the black hooded cape.

Everett howled with laughter.

Jenna closed her eyes and breathed deeply.

He opened her door and leaned in close. She felt a hard object pressed against her ribs and she knew it was a gun. "Here are the keys to unlock the cuffs. If you try anything, anything at all, I will shoot you and you'll never see Chase again. Do we understand each other?"

She cringed back from the gun, but nodded. With trembling fingers, she unlocked the handcuffs and rubbed her wrist where the steel bracelets had creased her flesh.

He took back the keys, drew her toward him, and whispered in her ear, "Now, we're going to walk closely together all the way to the washrooms. Same routine. If you speak to anyone, look at anyone, make eye contact, acknowledge them in any way, or attract any attention to either one of us, I'll shoot you and them. Are we clear? You don't want to be the cause of *another* death, do you, Jenna?"

She shook her head, fighting the urge to scream and run. She had no doubt he would shoot her and anyone in his way. However, once they reached the building, she was determined to raise an alarm.

Several people sent Everett strange looks as they hurried back to their cars, but no one spoke. Just another kook out on our roads, they probably thought.

By the time they reached the door, Jenna had formed a plan. She would pull open the door swiftly, taking him off guard and hopefully hitting him with it. Then, she'd dart inside and run through to the doors on the opposite side of the building screaming her head off.

Her heart thumped painfully against her ribs. She raised her hand to the door handle. Her muscles tensed, but before she could clasp the handle, the door pushed toward her and a giggling Shirley Temple clone skipped out.

"Sorry," she said with a lisp to Jenna. She turned wide blue eyes to

Everett. "Are you a magician?"

He pushed Jenna through the door and steered her toward the washroom on the left.

Frustration and disappointment swept through her body and left her weak, but seconds later she straightened her spine and resolved to find another method of escape.

She entered the stall he indicated and locked it. Thankfully, he didn't insist on coming in with her, but stood guard outside her door.

This was her chance. She could climb over the stalls, but he'd probably spot her in the mirrors that covered the wall above the sinks. She looked under the left side of the cubicle, the side closest to the door. No feet for three stalls. She crouched and started to crawl under. She was halfway through when the ladies room door opened and closed. Six short chubby legs and two long slender ones walked by. Jenna stilled. One child was walking toward her.

A small cherub with twinkling green eyes stared at Jenna, his face upside down as he peered under the door. He grinned. "Mommy, there's a—"

"Marcus, get over here right now. You're covered in Popsicle juice and Daddy won't let you back in the van if we don't get you cleaned up." The other children giggled.

The face disappeared.

"Will he let Jacob and Lauren in the van?"

"Nope, not unless they're clean, too." The water ran.

Jenna ducked back into her own stall and covered her face with her hands. She couldn't put three tiny lives in danger just to save her own.

She heard a tap on the cubicle door. She flushed the toilet, wiped the dust from her tee shirt and unlocked the door. Everett stepped aside to allow her to pass, but he stayed very close. A tall, slim woman was busily wiping the faces and hands of her three children. Triplets, who looked about the age of Chase when she had left him to go to prison. Jenna's heart hurt. Another baby slept in a pouch on the woman's back.

Jenna quickly washed her hands and hurried out of the washroom before the child could say anything, Everett like a shadow against her back.

When they returned to the car, he locked her to the steering wheel and offered a sandwich and some raw vegetables. Despair still heavy in her chest, she could only nibble on carrot sticks and sip from the bottle of warm water he handed to her. She couldn't stomach anything else.

After filling himself on sandwiches and Twinkies, Everett yawned and patted his belly. "Time for a little nap. I'll take the back, you can have the front."

She watched him climb into the backseat. "Why are you napping now? It's still daylight."

He bundled the cape under his head. "We still have a way to go and I want to travel at night. You should get some sleep, too."

As if she could think of sleeping. She sat, her mind reeling, and listened to his breathing as it slowed and deepened. If she could attract some attention, she could get someone to call the police, but she had to do it without making a sound. The problem was that most of the other vehicles had parked near the building while they were at the end of the lot.

The rain had stopped, but heavy rhythmic drops falling from the trees onto the roof of the car reminded Jenna of a scary story she had heard long ago while sitting around a bonfire with her teenage friends. The drops had been the blood of a man hanging from a tree above a car. She shuddered and tried to suppress the images of blood dripping from his lifeless fingertips and running down the car windows.

She leaned forward and waved her arms as a dark green van rolled toward the exit. Her heart leaped when it stopped with a jerk and reversed until it was almost directly in front of Everett's car, but still about fifty feet away on the opposite side of the lot. The side door slid open and a young teenage boy jumped out and ran for the washroom.

Jenna checked over her shoulder. Everett was snoring lightly and seemed to be sleeping peacefully. She rummaged in her purse and pulled out a cylinder of lipstick. She wished it was fire engine red, but pink was the best she could do.

With quick strokes she printed in tall backward letters on the windshield, "HELP! CALL 911!" Then, she waited.

The boy jogged back toward the van bobbing his head to a beat that only he could hear. He seemed to be in a world of his own until he glanced to his right directly at her. Jenna waved and pointed to her sign. Hope blossomed in her chest.

He squinted at the car, then took a step toward her, but his head whipped around to the van when an angry voice yelled, loud enough for Jenna to hear, "Brent, get in here, we're leaving."

The boy leaped into the van and it peeled away.

She tried to suppress a sob as she watched the back of the van disappear around the curve toward the highway, but she must have made a noise.

She jumped when she heard an enraged bellow from the backseat.

Chapter Forty-Three

Jenna wheeled around to see Everett's bulging eyes as he stared at what she'd done. The veins in his neck looked like engorged dew worms.

"No, no, no, no, *no!*" he screamed. He clamored over the back of the seat and rubbed at the lipstick with his hand. An oily pink smear blurred their vision of the parking lot.

"What were you thinking? I can't believe you'd do that to me, to us," he ranted, turning to her and squeezing her elbow with bruising fingers. "It's obvious that your mind is closed. You don't think you could ever love me. Do you? *Do you?*"

Jenna pressed her back against the door, trying to put as much distance between them as possible, but the handcuffs held her captive.

He calmed suddenly and stared through the rose-tinted windshield. "If you really don't think you can love me maybe I should end it here."

A wave of relief washed over her. He was going to end this madness, let her go back to her son. She started to nod.

"Yes," he continued, "I should kill us both, then we'd be bonded together forever…in death."

She gasped. "No. Everett, you can't do that."

He turned eyes filled with madness toward her. How could she have ever thought he was harmless?

"Yes, I can, Jenna." He pulled the gun from his waistband and pressed it against her temple. "I can do anything I like. Haven't I already proven that to you? How much will it take to convince you that I'm not some impotent little boy you can toy with? I have power. I *am* power!"

Jenna froze, afraid the slightest movement would provide him with a reason to squeeze the trigger. "I'm sorry about the lipstick," she whispered. "I was just scared, and I miss Chase."

"I told you," he yelled, jamming the barrel of the gun harder against her head. "I told you we would get him, in time. When I say it's time."

She could feel her life with Chase sifting through her fingers like a fistful of sand. Tears stung her eyes. "Please, Everett."

Suddenly, he backed off. He slid the gun under the seat and reached for the cape. He scrubbed at the windshield with short, angry strokes and managed to clear a small area just big enough to see through. He slammed the car into gear. The car jerked forward. Although Jenna was still handcuffed to the steering wheel, he turned the wheel sharply and smiled grimly when she cried out in pain.

They flew by the other cars on the highway, Everett fluctuating between ranting and silent brooding. "How will I ever trust you again if you keep pulling pranks like that? You can't trust anyone these days. Society has lost its sense of honor. Where are the morals, the scruples, the principles? Lost, lost."

Jenna held onto the door handle hoping they didn't crash before he quelled his rage. The clock on the dash read ten o'clock. She should be tucking Chase into bed right now, kissing him goodnight. The thought brought a lump to her throat.

"Everett," she said in her calmest voice. "I've already lost eight years, three months and twenty-seven days of Chase's life. I can't afford to lose anymore time. In a few years he'll be grown up and gone. I can't lose a day."

"Even Irene tried to betray me," he muttered, as if he hadn't heard her say a word.

Jenna jerked, a puppet with a deranged puppeteer. "Irene?"

"She heard too much. Saw too much. Little pieces, really, but she put it all together. She was always good at puzzles. So," he said dreamily, "I had to stop her."

"What did you do, Everett?" she asked cautiously.

He looked at her swiftly, then back at the road. "You know. You saw her. She was going to tell you about my plans. She would have ruined everything."

"Irene was trying to help me?" That was a new concept.

"You never did understand her, Jenna. She only ever wanted what was best for Chase."

His previous words finally sunk into her brain. "You didn't...the accident?"

"Oh, yes, I did, and it was no accident."

She stared at him, shock and fear shoving a fist against her ribs. "My God," she whispered.

He chuckled. "No, He didn't help at all. I did it all by myself. Meticulous planning, once again, but simple enough once the plan was in place. I knew her schedule inside and out. Luckily, she was a woman who liked routine. Up at six, out to the car at seven-thirty, at work by eight. It was a simple matter of getting her to walk in front of my rental car. 'Gee, Irene, jump in the passenger seat and I'll take you for a little spin in my new car.' She fell for it, literally. Left quite a mess."

Jenna stared out the window at the dark highway. She couldn't think about what he was saying or she'd scream and never be able to stop. She caught quick glimpses of eyes low to the ground near the edge of the road reflecting off the headlights before the animal scurried away. Probably opossum. *My God, Irene.* Maybe raccoon. *How could he do that to you? He's mad, deranged. And I'm in the car with him.* She pressed trembling fingers to her mouth, stifling a sob. She had to think. *Think.*

"Put your foot on the seat."

His voice interrupted her thoughts. "What?"

"Do it!"

She did what he asked.

"Put your wrist close to my keys. Don't try anything, or I'll run us right off the road. We'll die together." He unlocked the handcuff from around the steering wheel and, before she could move, clasped it around her ankle, the other end still around her wrist. "Since I can't trust you, this will ensure you don't run away."

He slowed the car as he turned off the highway onto a dirt road that wound its way up a mountain, climbing, turning. Everett jerked the wheel left and right as he drove through one hairpin turn after another.

The erratic movements brought the bile rising to the back of Jenna's throat, but she didn't speak. She knew her discomfort would only please him.

Finally, they swung to the right onto a poorly lit driveway. A small gray sign pointed the way to the registration building of the Back Country Mountain Resort.

Everett pulled to a stop beside the log building, removed the shackle from her ankle and clipped it to the steering wheel.

Jenna groaned as she stretched her leg. She massaged her thigh trying to relieve a muscle cramp from holding her leg to her chest for the last forty-five minutes of their journey.

When Everett turned off the headlights, darkness fell on them like a blanket. He glanced at his watch and frowned at the dark building. "I told them we'd be here by one. It's only midnight, so someone should be here."

As he spoke, a light went on in a front room. He slammed the car door and the darkness swallowed him whole until she saw him climb the front stairs. She stared out the side window. Pitch black. So dark a blindfold could have been covering her eyes. So black someone could be staring at her from three feet away and she wouldn't know. Jenna shivered. She locked the car door and kept her eyes on the small square of golden light from the office window.

A bubble of relief ran through her body when Everett emerged from the building.

"Better the devil you know than the devil you don't," her mother had always said. Jenna never understood that saying until now. Despite the madness of Everett's actions, she still thought she could reason with him. She wasn't so sure about a mad mountain man.

He scanned the map of the heavily wooded resort, transferred the handcuff from the steering wheel to his own wrist, and drove around the back of the building to a narrow service road that eventually led to a cabin built into the side of the mountain. Jenna didn't see any other cabins along the stretch of road and the registration office was about four miles back. She wished she was a jogger.

Everett dragged her into the cabin and down the stairs to a bedroom at the back. He went directly to the patio doors and flipped a switch. A pool of light spilled onto the ground outside the window. Because the land sloped sharply downward, this room was actually at ground level and led to a tiny patio beneath a green and white striped awning. Beyond the patio the land looked like it dropped off into a deep ravine. Everett checked and relocked the patio doors.

"See that, Jenna?" He nodded toward the ravine, the darkness, and the thick black trees that stood like sentinels outside her room. "No where for you to go. If you didn't break your neck falling over a cliff, you'd wander around lost forever. Remember that."

She nodded, already making plans for her escape. As soon as he left her alone, she'd break the window and run like hell. Fear suddenly gripped her throat like an unseen hand. She looked around the room. Maybe she'd take a club just in case she encountered that mad mountain man. The base of the bedside lamp would do nicely.

He tugged the curtains closed and flicked off the outside light.

"Beddy-bye time," he said and moved around the bed toward the door.

So eager to put her plan in motion, she almost pushed him out the door.

"One last thing," he said and handcuffed her to the bedrail.

"No," she gasped, almost a sob, her plans dissolving like vapor.

"Yes, Jenna," he said like a patient father. "You have to earn my trust." He closed the door behind him.

She crumpled onto the bed, sobs wracking her frame. He would keep her prisoner forever and she would never see Chase again. Her poor, sweet son would grow up an orphan. A fist squeezed her heart. She thought of Chase, of Finn, of her friend Rhia, picturing their faces in her mind. She'd never see them again. Her new life was being stolen by a delusional mad man. A man she thought she knew. How could she have been so blind?

Jenna's head throbbed and her eyes burned as she curled into a fetal position on the bed. She didn't think she could sleep, but exhaustion finally took over. The tears dried on her cheeks, her eyes drooped, and she allowed herself to sink into a welcome oblivion.

Dark dreams played behind her eyes, like storm clouds scudding across the sky. The trees turned into men, tall and menacing, guarding her castle. Marching, marching. A drum pounded.

Suddenly, she jerked awake. Someone was tugging at the handcuffs, trying to get them unlocked, cursing softly.

Sweet relief surged through her. "Finn?" she whispered.

Chapter Forty-Four

"Shut up," hissed Everett, "or I'll shoot him the second I see him." Jenna's spirits plummeted.

"He's caused enough trouble by bringing the police here. He'll pay for that."

He grabbed her wrist and she staggered after him up the stairs. On the main floor, she could hear the loud drumming on the door.

"Vandervries, we know you're in there. Police. Open up. We have you surrounded."

Everett clenched her wrist tighter and towed her up a narrow set of stairs that led to a small alcove. He barricaded the door with a chair. As he pulled her out onto a widow's walk she heard the front door splinter.

"Jenna, where are you?"

At the sound of Finn's voice tears stung her eyes. "Finn, we're up here, on the catwalk."

Everett snarled like a wounded animal. With a vicious swipe, his arm lashed out. The back of his hand hit her hard across the face. As she stumbled back from the blow, head swimming, the low balustrade hit the back of her thighs. Arms flailing, she screamed and flipped over the railing. She could feel herself falling, falling, dreading the thought of what lay below. At impact, the air left her lungs in a single whoosh. She laid still for a moment, gathering the air into her depleted lungs, afraid to move, afraid to find out she couldn't move.

Slowly, she realized she hadn't hit the ground. She was lying on the green and white awning outside her room. She sat up and started to slide down the gentle slope of the tarpaulin until she dropped to the ground. After a quick assessment to assure herself that nothing was broken, she took off in a dead run.

"Jenna!" Everett screamed.

Jenna scrambled over the blanket of dead leaves and twigs through the ravine and down into the inky blackness of the woods. She ran with her hands in front of her, bouncing off trees, blinded by the dark.

A single gunshot reverberated through the hills. She felt fear so profound it replaced every other feeling in her body. Branches slashed at her arms and face. Through the roar in her ears, she heard someone calling her. A man's voice. Everett must have jumped from the balcony. Surprising, since he had a distaste for heights. Not exactly a fear, but close enough.

She chanced a quick glance over her shoulder. The faint glow of a flashlight bounced through the woods, coming her way. Probably following the trampled and broken underbrush from her mad rush over rocks and trunks, around trees, and through bushes. Her progress was impeded by the lack of light and her fear of running headlong into a tree or over a cliff. Her pursuer had an edge.

Jenna's breath rasped in her throat, the smell of rotting undergrowth strong in her nose. She tripped on an exposed root and went down hard on her kneecap.

Her pursuer was crashing through the woods, closer, closer. She had to keep moving, keep running. She got to her feet and hobbled a few paces, the pain in her knee excruciating, but she didn't stop. The pain was soon obscured by fear and panic. She ran.

Jenna broke from the woods, a stitch in her side that felt like a knife, and stumbled onto a road directly into the path of an oncoming car. Her senses were bombarded. Blinded by the lights, her ears and nose were filled with the squealing of tires and burning rubber. She turned to run again, but strong hands grabbed her arms.

"Jenna-girl, it's Mickey, you're safe!" Arms surrounded her in a fierce hug as she gasped for breath. Relief drained the strength from her legs and he led her to the side of the road where she sank to her knees in the wet grass.

"Jenna." The voice from the woods. She stiffened, then scrambled to her feet when she saw the bobbing flashlight emerge from the dense foliage. She turned to flee, but Mickey held her.

"It's Finn, girl. Everett's dead."

"Dead?" she croaked.

"Shot himself before we could take him."

Then Finn was there, crushing her to his chest. "Jenna, thank God you're okay."

She buried her face in his chest, clinging, holding on to life, to love.

"Chase?" she asked through her tears.

"He's fine. He's with Rhia."

Chapter Forty-Five

"How did you find me?" asked Jenna. She was snuggled as close to Finn as their plastic chairs would allow. They were waiting in the Louisville airport for Finn's brother, Richard, to pre-flight his Cessna 172. Mickey was following the pilot around like a puppy dog.

"There was a note, ostensibly from you, telling me to look after Chase for a few days until you returned for him. Right away that sounded fishy to me. I knew you'd never leave Chase, especially on his birthday, but, just in case, I checked to see if you'd taken any clothes. The cake was still out, of course, and it didn't look like any of your clothes were missing. I called the police immediately. They said, because you were an adult, they couldn't do anything until you'd been missing for forty-eight hours. By then I was ready to rip my hair out with worry and frustration."

"Was Chase home?"

"He had been, but Joel's mother said she'd take him home with her until you came home. I didn't tell him you were missing. He just thinks you had to go out for a while and got delayed. Rhia said she'd pick him up around nine to stay at her house with Sir Midnight. He thought that was a great idea for a birthday surprise."

Jenna chuckled. "What a kid. So, after you struck out with the police, what did you do next?"

"I called Mickey. We were already suspicious about Vandervries. Judy's notes returned to him time and again. It was pretty apparent that she thought he was involved in the shooting.

"So Mickey and I went to pay him a little visit, but he didn't answer the door. We convinced the super to let us in. After all, Vandervries was missing and he could have been dead in the apartment. Imagine the stink. That was enough. He unlocked the door and waited for us to run out gagging."

"What did you find?" she asked.

Finn took a deep breath and blew it out. "A shrine to you."

Jenna sat up straight and stared at him. "What?"

"It's true. The place was covered with Jenna memorabilia. A collage of photographs and your missing stuff covered a large dining room table. A scarf, a fluorescent green shoelace, a tiny picture frame of Chase as a baby, photos of Chase, hair ribbons, you name it. The worst part was a huge yin-yang wall poster with your picture on one half and Everett's on the other. Made me sick."

"So that confirmed your suspicions, but how did you know where to find us?" Jenna was impatient for the details.

"He kept a diary and we found some travel brochures stuck between the pages of the book. A check of his last entries and a quick phone call to the Back Country resort verified his reservations for tonight—well, last night. Mickey made a phone call to the police down here and I called my brother, Richard, who happens to be on leave right now. He agreed to fly us down and the police, as a courtesy to Mickey, agreed to wait for us."

"I heard you calling me. I'm surprised the cops let you in the cabin."

Finn sucked in his lips and tried to suppress a grin. "Well, they didn't exactly. Actually, they got a little peeved when I ran in ahead of them." He spread his hands as he tried to explain. "I was going out of my mind. I had to get you away from that lunatic."

She reached up to kiss his cheek. "Thank you. You have no idea how your voice gave me new hope."

She leaned her head against his chest listening to the steady rhythm of his heart.

"He killed Judy," she murmured.

Finn nodded. "Mickey figured as much."

"And he tried to kill Irene."

He raised his eyebrows. "That's a new one. Why would he do that?"

"Because she was trying to warn me about him. Somehow, she

figured out enough of his plan to know that he meant trouble." Jenna shrugged. "Maybe she realized he was the one who shot Angus."

"Hey bro, ready to go?" Richard stood before them with Mickey just a step behind.

"You're a poet and you didn't know it," said Finn standing.

"My feet are Longfellows."

They laughed together.

"That's one of Mom's favorite sayings," Finn explained.

Mickey reached for Jenna's arm as they walked out to the waiting Cessna. "The police want you to go to Vandervries's apartment tomorrow morning to identify the items that belong to you. They want to make sure he wasn't stalking anyone else, too."

Jenna groaned. "Do I have to?"

"You can wait until later in the day if you want to have Chase's birthday party in the morning."

She shook her head. "No. I want this over with so we can put it behind us. I never want to think about this ugly episode again."

The next morning, while Chase was enjoying buttermilk pancakes with raspberry syrup at Rhia's, Jenna and Finn met the police at Everett's apartment.

They led her into the spare bedroom where her pictures stared back at her from the walnut paneled walls. Partially-melted candles dotted every surface. A recessed windowsill, a cork board, and a table held myriad trinkets, papers, postcards, and items that could only mean anything to her. Her hand shook as it touched a pair of pearl earrings, a last gift from her mother. She nodded to the officer who inventoried each item and placed it carefully in a plastic bag.

In the center of the table lay a leather-bound diary open to the previous day. She read Everett's last words and tried to make sense of it. *How did a person's mind get so distorted? How did he come to this?*

She flipped back a few months. Compassion and sorrow squeezed her heart for her tormented friend. Pity for what he was and what he had become. What secret anguish had lain in his past? She would never know.

April 18
Bad day, dark day.

These days I spend every moment of my existence regretting my past (the action and the inaction) and planning to change the future. I crawl away like the reptile I am from the defining moments of my past, put them behind me like bad dreams. My pale underbelly scrapes over the stones and twigs of my cowardly life. My plans will annihilate the shameful past and gild my future. Guilt will no longer dog my steps. Like a dog, she paced the boundaries of her cage.

Now she's out on parole. I've been watching her. She doesn't see me. She's too busy smiling at the sky and feeding the sparrows. She'll see me soon enough. Oh, yes, then she'll notice me.

Jenna gently closed the diary and left the room.

Chapter Forty-Six

"This is the best birthday ever, Mom." Chase scooped more Triple Temptation ice cream into his mouth.

"For me, too, sweetheart." She ran a hand down his cheek, so happy to be home, to be safe, to be together.

His eyes shone. "I can't wait to go flying with Uncle Richard. Joel's gonna be so jealous." He laughed gleefully.

Finn rolled the dice and moved his game piece eight places.

"Marvin Gardens is mine! You owe me a hundred dollars," hooted Chase.

Finn counted out the money. "You're a shark."

Chase stacked his money carefully, then looked up at Jenna and Finn. "This feels like we're a real family," he said.

Finn looked at Jenna, then back to Chase. "We could be."

Her heart did a back flip.

"Really? We could?" asked Chase.

Jenna echoed that thought silently.

"Sure. We'd make a great team," said Finn. He leaned over the game board toward Chase. "Of course, your mother would have to agree. We couldn't do it without her. Do you think if we let her win this prize she'd agree?" He handed a blue velvet ring box to the boy.

Jenna gasped.

Chase opened the box and beamed. He looked at her hopefully. "It's really pretty, Mom. Do you agree? Do you?"

Jenna let visions of the future roll out in front of her like a red carpet. Images of family picnics in the cool shade of a huge willow, working side by side with the man of her dreams, her son wrestling and giggling with Finn. A slow smile spread across her face. "I do."

Printed in the United States
61687LVS00003B/82-96